OLD LOVE AND NEW DANGER

Cecily had been an inexperienced chit of a girl when she was informed by her guardian how unsuitable a suitor Mr. Dennis Drummond was. Nonetheless, he had almost swept her off her feet—until the Viscount Trowbridge virtually yanked her out of Drummond's arms to take her for his own.

But now things were very different.

She was no longer an innocent country miss but a young lady who had learned all too soon the ways of the world—and society.

She was no longer a starry-eyed bride but a wife who saw every reason to seek vengeance on her husband.

Once Dennis Drummond had been on the very threshold of success with Cecily. Now when he appeared again, he had a most excellent chance to cross it. . . .

KISSING COUSINS

KISSING COUSINS

 by

Diana Campbell

A SIGNET BOOK

NEW AMERICAN LIBRARY

NAL BOOKS ARE AVAILABLE AT QUANTITY DISCOUNTS
WHEN USED TO PROMOTE PRODUCTS OR SERVICES.
FOR INFORMATION PLEASE WRITE TO PREMIUM MARKETING DIVISION.
NEW AMERICAN LIBRARY. 1633 BROADWAY.
NEW YORK. NEW YORK 10019.

SIGNET, SIGNET CLASSIC, MENTOR, PLUME, MERIDIAN AND NAL BOOKS
are published by New American Library,
1633 Broadway, New York, New York 10019

First Printing, May, 1986

1   2   3   4   5   6   7   8   9

PRINTED IN THE UNITED STATES OF AMERICA

1

"Uncle Frederick." Cecily cleared her throat. "I should like to begin by reminding you that I shall be one and twenty years of age the day after tomorrow."

Cecily squared her shoulders and examined her reflection in the cheval glass, hoping to find a handsome, mature woman who would command Sir Frederick Osborne's immediate respect. Instead, she beheld the familiar image of a short, slight figure clad in an ancient, shapeless muslin dress, and her shoulders sagged. She had somehow fancied that the exalted age of twenty-one would wreak a remarkable transformation in her appearance, but she could not perceive the slightest hint of change.

She had not expected miracles, of course. She had not, for example, expected to grow taller; she had long since accepted the fact that she would never exceed five feet and just under two inches in height. And—though she had continued to entertain distant hopes to the contrary—she hadn't actually *expected* that she would suddenly assume the voluptuous proportions of the models in the costume plates in *Ackermann's Repository*. No, she had come to accept her boyish figure as well and had even learned to take some comfort in Aunt Esther's observation that she was unlikely ever to be fat and *certainly* would not sag in later life.

That left her facial features and her coloring, and, upon consideration, Cecily was hard pressed to cite the specific modifications she had anticipated. She would much have preferred her auburn hair to be blond and her brown eyes a compelling lavender blue, but she realized that these characteristics were not subject to alteration. At one time, she had fervently wished that her dark complexion were delicately fair, splashed with just a hint of peach—or perhaps rose—at the cheekbones. However, when she voiced this wish to Aunt Esther, the latter pointed out that a redhead with fair skin would undoubtedly have freckles, and Cecily decided at once that her dusky complexion was infinitely more desirable than a host of horrid little brown spots scattered about her face. Though one could not tell from the drawings, she was quite sure that the models for *Ackermann's* fashion plates *never* had freckles.

Freckles or no, the models did generally have perfect little heart-shaped faces, and in this respect, Cecily suffered from a singular deficiency. Her face was *almost* heart-shaped, she thought optimistically: her forehead was broad, her cheekbones high, and her cheeks were rather hollow. But below the cheeks, where the models' faces tapered to delicate, pointed chins, Cecily's turned square— the prominent jawbones and rather broad chin seeming almost to form a straight line. As if this indignity were not enough, Cecily's short, upturned nose bore no resemblance whatever to the elegant aquiline noses in *Ackermann's*, and—in contrast to the models' tiny pink lips— her wide mouth appeared to occupy fully half her face. Fortunately, she had excellent teeth, and since the models were invariably shown with their dainty lips closed, she spitefully chose to believe that many of them did not.

At any rate, Cecily had not supposed that her twenty-first birthday would change the shape of her face either, and she eventually concluded that she had merely hoped to look . . . *older*. Yes, she had hoped that when she confronted Uncle Frederick, he would recognize her as an adult and acquiesce to her decision with relatively little argument. And there was no reason to despair, she assured herself. She would wear her best gown to dinner, and perhaps—seated at the table—she would not appear so small. She drew herself up again and once more cleared her throat.

"As I shall soon be one and twenty," she continued, "I am sure you will be delighted to learn that Dennis Drummond has offered for my hand."

The brown eyes in the mirror flickered and fell, and Cecily sighed; she could not successfully lie even to herself. The first deception in her statement was that Dennis had offered for her hand. He had *implied* his eagerness to wed her on numerous occasions—most recently and memorably last Sunday afternoon, when he had stolen several enthusiastic kisses in the privacy of the stable behind his father's inn. At some juncture, Dennis had murmured that he really didn't feel it necessary to "wait until we are married," whereupon Cecily had slapped his hand away from the front of her spencer and insisted most firmly that it *was*. While she was prepared to concede that Dennis's remark did not constitute a formal proposal, she did view it as evidence of his ultimate, honorable intentions.

Which was precisely why Cecily had elected to take matters into her own hands; poor Dennis was in no position to introduce the subject of marriage in any but the most oblique terms. Indeed, this was the second—and much the graver—component of her lie: far from being "delighted," Sir Frederick would be *horrified* to learn that she desired to wed Dennis Drummond.

"You wish to marry the son of an *innkeeper?*" She could almost hear his objection; it would emerge in a tone just below a roar. "You? Cecily Osborne? The daughter of a baronet?" Uncle Frederick had succeeded to his title upon the death of Cecily's father, his elder brother.

There were two possible responses to this violent outburst, Cecily thought, frowning into the cheval glass. The first was to point out that Henry Drummond, Dennis's father, was probably the wealthiest man in the community, not excluding Sir Frederick himself, for he owned dozens of properties in addition to the thriving King and Dragon inn and served as the local banker as well. However, she suspected that this rejoinder would serve to prompt a second tirade, one dealing with Ill-Gotten Gains or some similar topic, and she judged it best to put Uncle Frederick on the defensive. She must remind him that he had kept her sequestered in the country while other girls of her age were being introduced into London society and making allegedly splendid matches. If she adopted just the right approach, employed just the right words, Sir Frederick would come to see—he must come to see—that Dennis was the only man she could conceivably wed.

"I daresay there are other young men you might deem more suitable," she said, injecting a note of humility into her voice. "But, as you no doubt recollect, I have not had the opportunity to meet them. You have postponed my come-out every year since I turned eighteen." She thought she should lower her eyes for dramatic emphasis, but she discovered it impossible to look away from the mirror and evaluate the effect at the same time, and she emitted a small, sorrowful sigh instead.

At this juncture, Cecily calculated, Uncle Frederick would indignantly reiterate the circumstances which had delayed her debut. He had been *eager* to send her to town for a Season, he would sputter, but he had been thwarted year after year by Aunt Esther's absurd demands. Specifically, or so Sir Frederick claimed, his estranged wife insisted she would need "several thousand pounds" if she was to bring her niece properly out. Lady Osborne's letters to Cecily told an entirely different story, of course. Aunt Esther wrote that she had advised *him* (she never referred to her estranged husband by name) of her requirement for "a few new gowns," and *he*—in his usual unreasonable and penurious fashion—had refused to accede to this very modest request.

Cecily heaved another sigh, this one quite genuine. Uncle Frederick and Aunt Esther were the only family she had ever known: her mother had died when Cecily was but two days old; her father had drowned in the small lake behind Osborne Hall a scant fifteen months later; and the new Sir Frederick and Lady Osborne—not blessed with children of their own—had taken their orphaned niece into their home. For virtually the whole of her life, Cecily had viewed them as her parents; and despite their incessant bickering, she'd been stunned by their announcement that they had determined to separate. As Sir Frederick could not possibly leave Osborne Hall—the family seat for countless generations past—they had further determined that Aunt Esther would repair permanently to their London townhouse.

After Cecily's initial shock subsided, she began to fear that she would be asked to choose between them, to decide whether to accompany Aunt Esther to London or remain in

Derbyshire with Uncle Frederick. However, the latter speedily resolved this issue by declaring that Cecily would naturally stay with him: she was, after all, his blood niece, and he owed it to his dear departed brother to protect her from the nefarious influence of a woman so obviously deficient in character as Lady Osborne. He was sure he need not add, Uncle Frederick added, that there was also the question of Cecily's financial support. If he entrusted the requisite funds to Aunt Esther, she would no doubt fritter them away on one bauble or another, and Cecily would be left to starve. This—starvation—was a fate Sir Frederick would wish on no one. No one but Lady Osborne, he amended; were it not for the legal consequences, he would let *her* leave without a groat.

On this happy note, Aunt Esther had, in fact, left for London; and over the ensuing four years, Cecily had missed her terribly. Which was not to say that she resented Uncle Frederick's stand because she was certain she would have missed him equally had the situation been reversed. No, the thing she could scarcely bear was that she was hopelessly trapped between them. Sir Frederick's day was not complete unless he could devise some reason to criticize his absent wife; barring all else, he might grumble about the color of the tablecloth, which Lady Osborne had selected decades before. Cecily would tender a noncommittal mutter of response and wearily await Aunt Esther's next letter, which would be fairly smoking with the fury of *her* latest grievances. Cecily fervently wished there was a means of muttering on paper, but as there was not, she had mastered the art of composing long, sympathetic replies that said nothing. She had long since abandoned any notion of puzzling out who was "right" and who "wrong" in their perennial disputes, for she recognized that there was ample fault on both sides and wild exaggeration of the opposite party's every flaw.

But she was digressing, Cecily chided herself. Much as she regretted her aunt and uncle's separation, she was powerless to effect a reconciliation between them; she could only turn their estrangement to her own advantage. She gazed at the face in the cheval glass, pretending it was Sir Frederick's, and tried to predict what he would be saying at this point in the conversation. She suspected he would still be enumerating Lady Osborne's myriad transgressions, and she essayed a polite cough of interruption.

"I realize that Aunt Esther has been excessively uncooperative in the matter of my come-out," she said. She deplored the necessity to deliver still another falsehood, but she judged this the perfect way of talking Uncle Frederick round. "And—though you are, of course, far too noble to complain—I can well surmise how weary you must be of attempting to bring her to reason. Indeed, I was thinking of you as much as myself when I decided to marry Dennis. My future can be settled without a debut, and you will be spared the burden of further correspondence with Aunt Esther."

Yes—Cecily nodded at her reflection—yes, this was by far the best approach. She reviewed her planned remarks from the beginning and made one modification. She would not state that Dennis had offered for her hand; she would say from the outset that she had "decided" to wed him. Sir Frederick would naturally *assume* there had been an offer, but Cecily would not technically have lied about it.

The clock in the corridor struck five, and Cecily instinctively stiffened, for dinner was normally served at four. She then recollected that Uncle Frederick had postponed today's dinner till six, and she turned away from the cheval glass and proceeded toward the wardrobe. As she passed the front window, she heard the sounds of a carriage, and she glanced idly out, expecting to see Sir Frederick's curricle in the drive. But the vehicle, which was just rolling past her window, was a great, gleaming traveling carriage drawn by four horses, and Cecily stumbled to an astonished halt to watch its progress.

The neighboring gentry had ceased to call after Aunt Esther's departure—a circumstance Cecily ascribed more to discomfiture than to actual disapproval of the Osbornes' marital bumblebath. And in any event, this could not be a neighbor; one did not employ a traveling coach for a journey of but a few miles. Cecily entertained a brief hope that it might be Lady Osborne herself, but since Aunt Esther's last letter had been more scathing than most, she counted this prodigious unlikely. She was tempted to open the window and lean out in order to obtain a better view, but she feared such obvious curiosity would be discourteous in the extreme. She consequently stepped to the far right edge of the window, from which vantage point she could observe the center of the drive with minimal risk of being observed in turn.

The carriage halted directly opposite the front entrance, and the coachman climbed down from the box; but before he could reach the carriage door, it flew open, the steps were shoved out, and a man descended to the drive. His head was positioned in such a way that Cecily could not discern his features, but as he strode toward the front stairs, his hair was caught in a shaft of sunlight, and she sucked in her breath. Cousin Stephen! Logic dictated that it could not be he: there was no reason for Viscount Trowbridge to appear at Osborne Hall, every reason he should not. But the hair—that thick chestnut hair shot all through with gold—could belong to no one else.

Stephen moved out of Cecily's limited range of vision, and she left the window, crossed to the bed, and sank upon the counterpane. Her heart was drumming most peculiarly against her ribs, and she sternly reminded herself that she was no longer a schoolgirl suffering a schoolgirl's violent *tendre* for her handsome, dashing cousin. She could well remember the precise moment she had conceived this *tendre:* she had been a cockleheaded child of eleven, Stephen a grown man of five and twenty; and he had come to Osborne Hall for the New Year's holiday. He had cut a most dashing figure indeed in those days, for he had been a captain in the army; and in Cecily's adoring eyes, his uniform rendered him considerably more impressive than a king in full ceremonial regalia.

A year or so after Stephen's New Year's visit, his elder brother died, and Stephen resigned his commission to become Viscount Trowbridge. Some months later, he returned to Derbyshire for a week of hunting, and Cecily observed at once that he had changed. She initially fancied she was merely disappointed in his appearance, but, in truth, he looked quite as well in his civilian attire as he had in his uniform. At length, she concluded that Stephen seemed dreadfully subdued, restrained almost to the point of dullness, not at all the gay, rather mischievous fellow who had smuggled half a glass of champagne to her bed-chamber and joined her in a toast to the New Year. However, in view of her still-burning *tendre*, she charita-bly elected to regard the change as a temporary one, attributable to the recent death of his brother and his subsequent assumption of the crushing responsibilities of a viscountcy. She was confident that the next time she en-countered the new Lord Trowbridge, he would be his former, charming self.

But he had not been. Cecily had seen him only once more, nearly five years ago, and, if anything, he had grown more severe since their previous meeting. Indeed, as his visit drew to a close, she was sadly forced to own that his behavior had become a trifle priggish. The flames of her *tendre* flickered and died, and by the time Sir Frederick and Lady Osborne parted, Cecily had nearly put Stephen out of her mind. In fact, she had so far forgotten him that many weeks passed before it occurred to her that, now Aunt Esther was gone, Stephen would not come to Derbyshire again.

Which introduced the perplexing question of why, against all reason, he *had* come. Stephen was Lady Osborne's nephew, the son of her elder sister; and though he and Uncle Frederick had always got on exceedingly well, blood did run thicker than water. Stephen would naturally be inclined to take Aunt Esther's part in the marital feud, and since he spent a goodly portion of each year in London, she had had ample opportunity to reinforce this prejudice. After four years of exposure to her venomous accusations, Stephen must surely be persuaded that Sir Frederick Os-borne was a depraved monster quite unfit to associate with respectable human beings.

Cecily shook her head, then felt a jolt of terror in her midsection. Perhaps Stephen had come to deliver bad news. Maybe Aunt Esther was gravely ill. Or worse. Maybe she had . . . had . . . But Cecily could not bring herself even to think the word, and she shook her head again. A letter sent via the royal mail could travel from London to Derbyshire far faster than a man in a coach. Furthermore, now she thought on it, she believed Uncle Frederick had anticipated Stephen's arrival; why else would he have delayed dinner?

The hallway clock struck a quarter past the hour, and Cecily leaped up and hurried to the wardrobe. She would learn the reason for Stephen's visit soon enough. Perhaps he, like Cecily herself, had recognized the absurdity of Aunt Esther's allegations and elected to make his private peace with Sir Frederick. Perhaps, in short, his journey to Osborne Hall was nothing more than a social call.

Cecily opened the wardrobe doors and withdrew her new gown, a primrose muslin trimmed with white lace at the neck, the sleeves, and around the bottom of the skirt. "New" was a relative term, of course—the dress was two years old rather than four or five—but Cecily did not attach much importance to its chronological age. Bitter experience had led her to suspect that Miss Lane, the mantua-maker in Buxton, could execute only one basic dress pattern: that of the style *au courant* in approximately 1810. Consequently, though Miss Lane had promised to dupli-cate the costume plate Cecily clipped from *Ackermann's Repository*, the finished gown had a high, square neck, entirely unlike the narrow, plunging, V-shaped corsage in the drawing; straight sleeves to the elbow instead of short, puffed sleeves; and a hemline which ended much nearer the shin than the ankle. As if to heap insult on injury, Cecily could detect no similarity whatever between Miss Lane's modest little lace trimmings and the magnificent flounces in the costume plate, but—after four fittings and four impassioned arguments—she was prepared to concede defeat.

Since it was now 1817, Cecily reckoned that her "new" gown was at least half a dozen years out of date. But it was, in fact, the best she had, and she carried it to the bed, laid it on the counterpane, and smoothed out the wrinkles in the skirt. It was probably fortunate, she reflected wryly, that her come-out had never come, for her wardrobe could not have survived the first day of a London Season.

Cecily walked toward the dressing table, but something in her recent thoughts caught her up, and she stopped at the edge of the Axminster carpet. The Season; that was it. The Season started in early May, and this was the last day of April—a very odd time for Viscount Trowbridge to pay a social call in Derbyshire. Unless he had become so incorrigibly prudish that he no longer permitted himself a single moment of amusement—

The corridor clock chimed twice, as if to warn that there was no more time for speculation, and Cecily scurried on across the room. She sat in the chair before the dressing table, and when she glimpsed her reflection in the mirror above, she remembered the speech she had so painstakingly rehearsed. To no avail, it now appeared, because she certainly couldn't broach such a delicate subject in Stephen's presence.

No, she would have to wait until Viscount Trowbridge returned to London, and she could only hope he planned an exceedingly brief stay. She had no desire to waste the glorious dawn of her maturity on her priggish, middle-aged cousin.

"Cecily!" Evidently Uncle Frederick had been watching the corridor, for he leaped from his chair at the head of the table just as she reached the dining-room archway. "Come in, my dear! I have arranged the most wonderful surprise!"

Cecily stepped obediently through the entry, composing an appropriate exclamation of astonishment, and Stephen rose from his own chair on the far side of the table. During the preceding half hour, she had resigned herself to the probability that he would look immensely older, and the reality struck her quite speechless. Middle-aged or no, he was still a splendid figure of a man; and she could only stare at him, her tongue seemingly riveted to the roof of her mouth.

As a child, she had fancied him extremely tall, but she had subsequently come to realize that he could not much exceed six feet; and she now surmised that his excessively broad shoulders, his narrow waist and hips, his long, slender legs created an illusion of height. An illusion cleverly enhanced by his tailor, she further conjectured, for Stephen's fashionable moss-green frock coat and snugly-fitted rust pantaloons made him appear taller and leaner than he had in his youth.

"Cecily?" Stephen said dubiously.

Her eyes flew to his face. Her initial impression was that he had altogether escaped the ravages of time, but, upon closer inspection, she perceived a web of tiny lines radiating from the corner of either eye. Apart from these, his features were exactly as she remembered: high, wide-set cheekbones, spare jaws, a longish nose. And, dominating the rest, disproportionately large eyes in a remarkable shade of pale green.

"Cecily?" he said again.

His voice was tinged with amazement, and he was regarding her in a most disconcerting manner—his pale eyes traveling slowly, relentlessly, from the top of her head to the toes of her worn satin slippers. His bold scrutiny brought an inexplicable flood of warmth to Cecily's cheeks but, fortunately, seemed to thaw her tongue as well.

"Stephen!" It was hardly the sophisticated exclamation she had planned; her tone was so shrill as to offend even her own ears. "I . . . I am pleasantly surprised indeed."

"Not half so surprised as I." His eyes had returned to her face, and Cecily thought they seemed a trifle darker. "You have quite grown up, little cousin."

"Well, of course she has grown up!" Sir Frederick said heartily.

Cecily started. She had entirely forgotten her uncle's presence, and she deduced—from the sudden spin of his head—that Stephen had as well.

"Yes," Sir Frederick continued fondly, "my dear niece has grown up, and . . . But let us eat. We can chat during dinner."

He nodded to Hedges, the butler, and the latter scurried forward to assist Cecily into her chair, which was situated directly across the table from Stephen's. As soon as she was seated, Stephen resumed his place, and she observed an additional sign of his advancing years: threads of silver hair woven here and there among the chestnut and the blond. But his gray hair—like his facial lines—rendered him more attractive rather than less, and her heart began to race in the same odd, irregular way it had that afternoon. She wouldn't be half so nervous, she thought irritably, if he would stop *watching* her. At length, it occurred to her that she could resolve this problem by ceasing to watch him, and she peered with keen interest into the depths of her soup bowl.

"Excellent mulligatawny, would you not agree?" Uncle Frederick punctuated his remark with an appreciative belch. "When Esther left, I discovered the household in a shocking state of disarray, and it has required considerable effort to put matters aright. My very first action was to discharge and replace the cook, and I trust you can taste the difference for yourself."

In point of fact, Mrs. Sparks—the cook at Osborne Hall from time immemorial—had resigned her post a week after Aunt Esther's departure, declaring between sobs that she could not work for a man who insisted on a strict accounting of every farthing spent on every last green bean. However, the second half of Sir Frederick's statement was perfectly accurate: one could indeed detect the fine touch of Mrs. Gillman, the new cook, in everything she prepared, for it all tasted more or less like water. But Cecily perceived no advantage in arguing the relative merits of Mrs. Sparks and Mrs. Gillman, and she forced herself to look back up at Stephen.

"How . . . how *is* Aunt Esther?" she asked.

A simple question, and she wondered what it was about him that reduced her to a skittish, stammering adolescent. Memory probably, the memory of that silly girlhood *tendre*. Or perhaps it was his eyes, which were now exploring her face—roving from her chin to the curls on her forehead, from her left ear to her right. She distantly noted that his eyes, like his hair, were generously flecked with gold; and she speculated that in certain lights, they might appear almost as yellow as green.

"Stephen has advised me that Esther is well," Uncle Frederick snapped.

Cecily had forgotten him again, and she peered at the head of the table just as he signaled Hedges to remove the soup bowls and bring the entrée.

"But why should she *not* be well?" Sir Frederick added bitterly. A rhetorical—albeit dramatic—question. "In view of the vast sums of money I supply her, I can only suppose she lives in a splendor considerably surpassing that of the Princess of Wales." Another, and rather more famous, estranged wife. "If Esther expends even half what she claims to require for food, she must be seating half of London at her table every evening. Indeed, I hope that is the case, for if she is consuming all the food herself, she must have grown most enormously fat."

Uncle Frederick concluded this commentary with a frenzied attack on his meat, and Cecily bit back a smile. Sir Frederick was on exceedingly perilous ground when he undertook to criticize the girth of others, for Cecily calculated he had gained nearly two stone in Lady Osborne's absence. The bulk of the evidence—so to speak—was presently hidden, the rotund belly and chubby thighs out of sight below the top of the table. However, his burgeoning double chin was clearly visible above the folds of his neckcloth, and his face had grown unmistakably round. Though, Cecily conceded, Uncle Frederick's unruly hair no doubt made his face appear much plumper than it was. He had always had an abundance of wild, sprouting curls, and now they were graying, they had faded from auburn to . . . to . . . Well, to say the truth, his hair was almost *orange*, and Cecily believed his appearance would be much improved when his uncontrollable curls turned altogether white.

"Superb veal, would you not concur?" Sir Frederick dabbed a wayward drop of gravy from his chin.

Was it veal? Cecily wondered. This was the only exciting aspect of Mrs. Gillman's cuisine: the new cook employed heavy, tasteless sauces to such an extent that it was often impossible to identify the specific substance beneath. Cecily would have wagered her last groat that tonight's offering was chicken, but she was forced to own that it could be veal. Or pork. There was even a remote chance it was beef.

She stole a glance across the table and detected a quiver at the corners of Stephen's mouth. But it died at once, and he sawed politely at his meat, which—whatever it was—was monstrous tough. He would not smile, she recollected. That had been the first symptom of his priggishness: he had virtually ceased to smile. Nevertheless, after all the years, she vividly remembered the sudden flash of his teeth, the sparkle of his gold-green eyes . . .

"However," Uncle Frederick said, "I am prepared to let bygones be bygones. As I indicated earlier, Stephen and I have arranged a splendid surprise."

Cecily had supposed that Stephen's visit *was* the surprise, but she now perceived what they were at. Sir Frederick had obviously planned some sort of celebration in honor of her twenty-first birthday and, in view of her childhood attachment to Stephen, had invited him to participate. And despite the imminent start of the Season, Stephen had traveled all the way from London to attend the party. Cecily could not but be touched, and she gulped down a lump in her throat.

"That is very kind of you," she murmured. "Very kind of both of you."

"It was not a question of kindness," Sir Frederick said kindly. "It was the very least I could do. I have been aware for some time that your come-out was long overdue."

"Perhaps so, but I . . ." She belatedly registered his words. "Come-out?" she repeated sharply.

"I knew you would be surprised!" Uncle Frederick clapped his plump hands with delight. "And you needn't tease yourself about a single detail. Esther is planning a grand ball to introduce you into society, and Stephen will have you under his wing from the first moment. From the instant you and he leave for London tomorrow morning."

"Tomorrow morning?" Cecily gasped. "Stephen is to take me to town?"

"I quite understand your objection, Cecily," Stephen said, clearly not understanding at all. "You are naturally reluctant to travel in the company of an unmarried man. I considered that circumstance myself, but I believe no one will judge it amiss inasmuch as we are—if only distantly— related. And in any event, there was no alternative. Frederick has urgent business in Liverpool, and I could not persuade Aunt Esther to come to Derbyshire."

"That is scarcely astonishing," Sir Frederick growled. "Esther declared on the day she left that she would not return to this house till I was dead. And as I recall, she

added her wish that that joyful event would not be long
delayed.''

"Umm." Stephen's single grunted syllable fairly dripped
with disapproval.

"But let us not dwell on Esther's unforgivable conduct," Uncle Frederick said nobly. "Let us overlook her
innumerable past transgressions and be happy that she has
at last agreed to bring Cecily out.''

Sir Frederick wolfed down the final bite of his unidenti-
fiable meat and signaled Hedges to remove the entrées and
bring dessert and brandy. Though Cecily's plate remained
nearly full, she had altogether lost her appetite, and she
welcomed the lapse in conversation. She had no intention
of going to London, of course, but she judged it best to
tender an excuse which did not involve Dennis. By the
time Hedges completed his chores, she had conceived just
such an excuse, and she pushed Mrs. Gillman's watery
blancmange aside and cleared her throat.

"It is very, *very* kind of you," she reiterated, "and I do
most sincerely appreciate your thoughtfulness. However, I
fear it has escaped your attention that I am far too old for a
come-out.''

"Nonsense!" Uncle Frederick said cheerfully. "Many
girls' debuts are delayed by a death in the family or some
other unfortunate circumstance. Indeed, I well recollect a
case in my day—a young woman who did not come out till
she was three and twenty. She had been brought up in
North America or India or some such uncivilized place.
And *she* ultimately wed a duke! No, my dear, twenty-one
is by no means too old for a come-out.''

Is that what they had in mind for her? Cecily wondered
distantly. Did they expect her to marry a duke? She groped
toward her brandy glass, and as she did so, the lace trim at
her sleeve slipped into her pudding. She jerked her hand
back, swabbed the lace with her napkin, and glimpsed
another avenue of escape.

"What a relief!" she said. "This afternoon, by sheer
coincidence, I was reflecting on my come-out, and I realized that my wardrobe is altogether inadequate for a Season in London. So I am enormously comforted to learn we

can postpone my debut another year. As Miss Lane is prodigious slow, I shall put her to work at once—''

"Wardrobes!" Sir Frederick interrupted testily. "That is all I hear from Esther; she writes of nothing but the presumably lamentable state of her clothes. I am thoroughly tired of the subject."

Cecily repressed a grin of triumph.

"But I have resigned myself to the inevitable." Sir Frederick heaved a martyred sigh. "As soon as you arrive in town, Esther will take you to her seamstress, and the two of you will be properly rigged out for the Season."

This was such an astounding concession that Cecily briefly suspected her uncle had suffered some kind of mental collapse. But his brown eyes seemed quite sane, and she concluded that he had simply and absolutely determined to bring her out at last, whatever the financial or emotional cost. Whether his decision had been prompted by genuine concern for her welfare or a deeper, more devious motive, she couldn't begin to guess; she was only certain he would not entertain any other casual objection she might manufacture. Much as she misliked the prospect, she would have to tell him the truth, and she once more cleared her throat.

"The fact is, Uncle Frederick, that I am in no position to go to London. I had hoped to discuss the matter in somewhat more private circumstances"—she could see Stephen's startled gaze from the corner of her eye—"but I can wait no longer. I have decided to wed Dennis Drummond."

"In no position . . ." Stephen's pale eyes widened with horror. "Good God, Cecily, you cannot mean—"

"Of course not!" she screeched. "I do not *have* to marry Dennis; I have simply decided to do so."

"You wish to marry the son of an *innkeeper*?" Sir Frederick's words were precisely those Cecily had predicted, but she had erred about his tone, for his voice was pitched not one whit below a roar. "You? The daughter of a baronet?"

Cecily parted her lips to deliver the rebuttal she had rehearsed, but she realized at the last instant that it wouldn't do at all. She could hardly complain of her social isolation when they had just offered her a magnificent London come-out, and she reluctantly reverted to her alternate argument.

"Mr. Drummond is far from being a mere innkeeper," she said stiffly. "As you yourself have frequently pointed out, he is probably one of the wealthiest men in the county."

Actually, insofar as Cecily could recall, Uncle Frederick had *never* pointed this out. However—since he fancied himself an authority on virtually all subjects and much enjoyed hearing his alleged wisdom cited by others—she perceived no harm in this small fabrication.

"As he is," Sir Frederick snapped. "But I daresay I should be the wealthiest man in *England* if I engaged in Henry Drummond's sharp practices. He charges exhorbitant rentals for his properties and usurious rates of interest on his loans. And Dennis has made it abundantly apparent that he has every intention of following in his father's greedy footsteps."

Cecily stifled a sigh of her own. Dennis had recently been placed in charge of a number of his father's rental properties, and he had aroused the wrath of the entire community by evicting several tenants from a row of small cottages on the fringes of Buxton. Which was monstrous unfair because no one had been more overset than Dennis himself. Indeed, his eyes had glistened with tears when he explained to Cecily the complex financial considerations which had forced him to cast one particular family of seven literally into the street.

But as she had feared, Sir Frederick was irrationally prejudiced against the Drummonds, and Cecily judged it futile to repeat Dennis's explanation. "I shan't debate with you," she said instead.

"Excellent." Uncle Frederick nodded. "I am delighted you perceived the error of your ways before I was compelled to *forbid* you to wed Drummond. Which, of course, I should have done without a moment's hesitation. I can scarcely conceive a more unsuitable alliance."

"But . . . but . . ." He had utterly misinterpreted her statement. "But I—"

"You needn't apologize, my dear," Sir Frederick interposed soothingly. "I myself conceived more than one ridiculous *tendre* in my salad days. In fact, if memory serves me right, I was passionately in love with a scullery maid for one whole summer."

"But I—"

"And it is not your fault you developed a misguided affection for Dennis Drummond. It is Esther's fault." Uncle Frederick scowled at his blancmange. "Had you been brought out at the proper time . . . But I have resolved not to dwell on Esther's deficiencies. You will go to London tomorrow, and I am persuaded you will be engaged—*suitably* engaged—before the Season is half over."

"But . . ."

But Sir Frederick had left no room for discussion. He had made it unmistakably clear that he would never consent to a union between the Osbornes and the Drummonds, and Cecily's mind began to churn. It was obvious she and Dennis would have to elope, and as she saw no way to organize their escape before tomorrow morning, she must somehow delay her departure.

"You are right," she said humbly. "I daresay there are other young men who might be more suitable." She was pleased to be able to utilize at least this portion of her planned speech. "However, I can't possibly leave for town tomorrow. I shall require a day to . . . to . . ." What activity could credibly take a day? "To pack," she finished lamely. She hoped neither of them would remember her recent remarks about her wardrobe, which—in an emergency—could readily be packed up in half an hour.

"That would be highly irregular," Stephen said. "Unless Frederick can also postpone his journey to Liverpool."

Cecily had forgotten Uncle Frederick's business trip and, in any case, she could not perceive that it had any bearing on her own request.

"No." Sir Frederick shook his outlandish orange head. "No, as I told you, Stephen, I must go to Liverpool tomorrow without fail. I have packed already, and I intend to depart as soon as the sun comes up."

"As had I," Stephen said. "That is what renders the situation irregular. Were Cecily and I to remain here for four and twenty hours, we should be alone together in the house—"

"For God's sake, Stephen!" In other circumstances, Cecily might have been amused; as it was, his prudishness threatened to complicate her already precarious situation. "We shall scarcely be alone with half a dozen servants about. If you do not regard them as sufficient protection, I shall promise not to attack you in the middle of the night."

"I do not find that amusing, Cecily," Stephen said frostily. "If your crude notion of humor results from your association with Mr. Drummond, I count it excessively fortunate that you will soon be removed from his influence."

How could such a hopeless prig be so attractive? she marveled. The stern set of Stephen's mouth, the icy glitter of his eyes, perversely enhanced his handsome demeanor . . .

"Well, it is settled then," Uncle Frederick interjected hastily. "I shall leave for Liverpool tomorrow, we shall grant Cecily an extra day to pack, and the two of you will proceed to London Friday morning."

"Very well," Stephen agreed tersely.

"Very well," Cecily echoed.

By Friday morning, she calculated, Sir Frederick would be in Liverpool, and she and Dennis would be well along the road to Gretna Green. When Viscount Trowbridge awakened, he would discover himself very much alone indeed, and Cecily only regretted she would not be present to witness the moment of his enlightenment.

⚜ 2 ⚜

"Good morning." Mr. Drummond's chief groom emerged from the shadows at the rear of the stable and lovingly patted Cecily's mare. "And a good morning to you too, Miss Osborne."

"Good morning, Sewell," Cecily said solemnly.

During the early days of their acquaintance, she had been alternately amused and annoyed by the groom's clear preference for equine rather than human companionship. However, she had soon come to realize that she and Dennis could not wish for a better, more discreet ally to assist in the conduct of their courtship. Sewell uncomplainingly fetched Dennis each time Cecily rode to town, then guarded the stable against intruders while they conversed in the back stall. But Sewell was so very disinterested in the affairs of his fellow man that Cecily doubted he understood, or cared to understand, the nature of the relationship between herself and his young master. She was certain he would never idly gossip about their meetings, and she optimistically suspected that even if some whisper of scandal prompted Uncle Frederick to interrogate the groom directly, Sewell might well fail to recollect the frequency or duration of Miss Osborne's visits to the King and Dragon.

"And how is Moonbeam's leg?"

The groom's anxious inquiry served to confirm Cecily's theory, and she gritted her teeth against a familiar flood of impatience.

"Moonbeam's condition is quite perfect," she responded politely. "So if I could prevail on you to summon Dennis . . ."

"Umm."

As was invariably the case, Sewell declined to accept Cecily's uneducated opinion as to the health of her horse: he squatted on the stable floor and carefully inspected Moonbeam's right front leg. Apparently satisfied, he rose but—for good measure—prodded the mare's flanks, checked her teeth, and peered critically into her great dark eyes.

"Umm," he muttered again. "I doubt Mr. Dennis is yet awake."

Cecily doubted this as well, for she had left Osborne Hall at an excessively early hour. She would much have preferred to sleep late in order to be thoroughly rested for her elopement, but she had judged it imperative not to risk a confrontation with Stephen, who—in view of his ludicrous sense of propriety—might well have insisted on accompanying her to town. She had consequently risen just after dawn, when she heard the clatter of Sir Frederick's hired post chaise in the drive. She watched from her window as Uncle Frederick settled himself inside the coach, the postilion secured his baggage to the roof, and the carriage rolled back down the drive and out of sight.

Assured that her primary obstacle was speeding toward Liverpool, Cecily dressed, gulped down one cup of lukewarm coffee and one of Mrs. Gillman's horrid, soggy muffins, saddled and bridled Moonbeam herself, and struck out toward Buxton. The clock in the church tower had been chiming eight as she passed it, and she did, indeed, doubt that Dennis was yet awake. Dennis had many virtues, but early rising could not be numbered among them.

"Probably not," she agreed aloud, "but I should very much appreciate it if you would wake him and advise him I am here. I've a matter of grave importance to discuss with him."

"Very good, Miss Osborne."

Sewell trotted out of the stable, characteristically forgetting to help Cecily dismount, and she sighed and clambered down from the saddle unassisted. She led Moonbeam to the nearest vacant stall and closed her inside, and the mare happily began to munch the fodder in the trough. Cecily sat on a bale of hay situated just outside the stall and gazed about the gloomy, malodorous building in which she had met Dennis Drummond, her dear love and future husband.

Well, she had not actually met Dennis in the stable, Cecily amended. She had encountered him any number of times during her childhood and adolescence, for Buxton was, after all, a small community. She had nodded at Dennis in the street and exchanged a few words with him in the dining room of the inn, where she and Aunt Esther had occasionally gone for lunch. But she had not really *known* him till the wonderful day, some six months ago, when Moonbeam had gone lame immediately in front of the King and Dragon.

Cecily cast the mare a glance of silent apology; she would never have *wished* an injury on her beautiful white horse even in such a magnificent cause. But, wishes notwithstanding, Moonbeam had mysteriously begun to limp as they approached the fringes of the town, and by the time they reached the inn, the poor mare could scarcely walk at all. Cecily, sniffing back tears of panic, reasoned that the stable hands at the King and Dragon would know as much about horses as anyone in the county, and this proved to be the case. After the briefest of examinations, Sewell spotted a nasty gash in the vicinity of Moonbeam's right front fetlock, cleansed the wound, applied a magical ointment of some sort, and advised Cecily that the mare's injured leg would require a week of rest to heal.

Much as Cecily admired and appreciated the groom's veterinary expertise, she found herself considerably distracted by the presence of Dennis Drummond, who had entered the stable just as Sewell initiated Moonbeam's treatment and—whatever his original errand—remained to observe the proceedings. Dennis's light brown eyes darted back and forth between Moonbeam and Cecily, clouding with sympathy in the former case and signaling warm encouragement in the latter. Cecily shortly noticed that his eyes were almost the same color as his sandy hair, and she wondered how—after dozens of chance meetings—she could possibly have failed to perceive how attractive he was. His nose was a trifle crooked, as were his teeth, but he was a tall, stocky man brimming with health and surely no older than five and twenty. All of which rendered him infinitely superior to Sir Robert Norcott—the only "eligible" prospect in this part of Derbyshire—who was a fat widower well in the gout and far closer to fifty than thirty.

"A week?" Dennis echoed. "Then Sunlight must certainly remain here while she recovers."

"Moonbeam," Cecily corrected.

"Moonbeam." Dennis bobbed his pale brown head. "She must remain here—at no expense to you, of course— and with your permission, I shall drive you back to Osborne Hall. I shall return for you a week from today and bring you back to town to retrieve Moonlight."

Cecily elected not to issue a second correction, for despite his confusion about the name, Dennis had evinced a truly touching concern for her and her beleagured horse. She gave him a grateful nod, and with the merest snap of his fingers, Dennis summoned two assistant grooms to hitch his father's curricle, which proved to be years newer and vastly more elegant than Sir Frederick's. Cecily had an uncomfortable feeling that Uncle Frederick would not much relish the spectacle of a vehicle so far surpassing his (to say nothing of the perfectly matched bay team, which put Sir Frederick's aging horses quite to shame), and she was relieved to find her uncle from home when they reached Osborne Hall. By a stroke of fortune, Sir Frederick was also away when Dennis returned a week later to drive her back to Buxton. Upon their arrival at the King and Dragon, Cecily discovered Moonbeam entirely recovered from her injury, and that should have been the end of her association with Dennis Drummond.

But it was not, for in the course of a few short hours, Cecily had learned that she and Dennis had a great deal in common. Both Dennis's parents were still alive, but—he sorrowfully confided to Cecily—he often thought of himself as an orphan. An orphan like Cecily herself. Everyone in the community knew that his father was a heartless tyrant. Less widely known was the fact that his mother had long since developed a fondness for the wares of the taproom and spent most of each day staggering about in a heavy wet. Cecily was exceedingly shocked by the latter revelation inasmuch as she had encountered Mrs. Drummond on numerous occasions and judged her—though undeniably coarse in both behavior and attire—a woman completely in control of her faculties. However, when she mentioned this observation to Dennis, he reminded her that rumpots were notoriously adept at hiding their shameful weakness.

In any event, after their drives to and back from Osborne Hall, Cecily was utterly enchanted by Dennis Drummond and more than willing to entertain his suggestion that they arrange to meet again. While neither of them specifically alluded to the necessity for such meetings to be conducted in secret, it was tacitly understood that Sir Frederick Osborne would look with a very jaundiced eye indeed upon any relationship between his niece and the son of Henry Drummond, and Dennis further proposed they use Sewell as their intermediary. Whenever Cecily could escape from Osborne Hall, she was to come to the stable; and the chief groom, who would always be apprised of Dennis's whereabouts, would fetch his young master at once.

Cecily was well and uneasily aware that this system rendered her the aggressor in their courtship—a situation very far from Aunt Esther's memories of eager *partis* fairly battering down her father's front door in hopes of being granted a cup of tea in the saloon. But it had worked for nearly six months now, and she had never seen any viable alternative—

"Cecily?"

Dennis strode through the stable entry, and Cecily leaped up and hurried forward to meet him.

"What the deuce is amiss?" he asked irritably. "Do you not realize how early it is?"

"I'm sorry," she murmured.

She had reached his side, and she looked contritely up at him and entertained a peculiar notion that his appearance had undergone a radical change in the five days since their previous meeting. She initially fancied she was merely reacting to his dishevelment; it was clear he had made only the most cursory effort to comb his hair, and there was a sprouting of light brown beard on his chin and cheeks and above his upper lip. However, upon closer inspection, she noticed a deficiency she had somehow overlooked in the past: Dennis was very . . . very *colorless*. Yes, his hair, his eyebrows, his eyes, his skin were so nearly the same hue that—at least in the dim morning light of the stable—they seemed to run all together. But she was being prodigious overcritical, Cecily chided herself. It was wretchedly unfair to compare Dennis to Stephen, who was blessed with that remarkable gold-shot hair, those astonishing gold-green eyes—

"It is quite all right," Dennis said soothingly.

He slipped his arms around her waist and pulled her close against him, but his unshaven cheek scratched hers most unpleasantly, and Cecily squirmed out of his grasp. To say the truth, she did not much enjoy Dennis's embraces even when he was clean-shaven, properly combed, and fresh from his bath. In the beginning, she had been exceedingly alarmed by this lack of response, but she had subsequently collected that her reaction was not in the least unusual. A few months since, Cordelia—the maid who served as Cecily's abigail on the rare occasions she required some special attention—had wed Pickett, the coachman. While the new Mrs. Pickett had declined to disclose her precise complaints about her conjugal duties, she had made it unmistakably apparent that she found the physical aspect of marriage quite repellent. Indeed, Cordelia had gone so far as to say that "it" was a loathsome chore one simply had to perform, somewhat akin to the task of emptying and washing the chamber pots. Cecily hoped that when the time came, she could submit to "it" with similar fortitude.

"Well, what is it?" Dennis demanded peevishly, dropping his arms. "Sewell said you had a matter of grave importance to discuss."

As if on cue, the groom loomed up in the doorway beside them, and with a snort of annoyance, Dennis seized Cecily's elbow and ushered her—none too gently—to the rear stall in which they customarily held their rendezvous. Months before, they had placed two hay bales side by side so as to form a bench of sorts, and when they were seated, Dennis turned toward her and impatiently lifted his pale eyebrows.

"A dreadful thing has happened, Dennis." Though Sewell remained yards away, just inside the stable entry, Cecily instinctively spoke in a whisper. "Early yesterday evening, my cousin arrived from London." Dennis frowned in puzzlement, then shook his head. "My *cousin*," she repeated. "The one I've told you of. The viscount."

"Ah, yes." He nodded. "Lord Turnbridge."

"Trowbridge," she snapped. Dennis's constant lapses of memory were really rather maddening.

"Trowbridge." He nodded again. "And what is so dreadful about that? Is he ill? Dying?"

"Worse," Cecily hissed dramatically. "He has come to escort me back to the city. He and Uncle Frederick devised the plan entirely behind my back. They have at last decided to give me a come-out."

"And that is dreadful?" Dennis was dismayingly undismayed.

"Evidently I have failed to convey the urgency of the situation," Cecily said stiffly. "They intend me to leave tomorrow morning. Actually, they wished me to depart *this* morning, but I persuaded them to grant me a delay of four and twenty hours."

"So you could come to town and bid me a proper good-bye." This time, Dennis's arms snaked around her shoulders. "You are such a sweet girl, Cecily. I shall miss you; truly I shall."

He lowered his head and laid his bristly mouth on hers, and Cecily once more jerked away.

"I did not come to tell you good-bye!" she screeched. "I came to tell you that in the circumstances, we must elope at once."

"Elope?" Dennis released her so hastily that Cecily momentarily lost her balance and nearly toppled off the hay bale and onto the stable floor. "Be married, you mean?"

"I believe an elopement normally culminates in a wedding," she confirmed dryly.

"But . . . but . . . but I . . ."

His voice sputtered off, and Cecily ground her fingernails into her palms. She had been prepared for him to question the logistical details of her plan—to debate the time and place of their meeting and their ultimate destination—but she had not expected him to balk at the very *idea* of an elopement. Perhaps Dennis was more conservative than she'd judged, the sort of man who desired a proper ceremony in the parish church with every relative of both families watching approvingly from the pews. But it was too late to ask his specific objection. Cecily had already made a fearful cake of herself, and she could only try to exit the scene with some small degree of dignity.

"Please do not tease yourself about it." She stood and gave him a tremulous smile. "As you are obviously reluctant to be wed in secret, I shan't trouble you again—"

"No!" Dennis sprang to his own feet and seized her elbow again. "No, you simply . . . ah . . . caught me by surprise, and I shall require some time to . . . to consider the matter. Yes, that is it; you caught me entirely by surprise. As you well know, I very much *want* to marry you, but I have always recognized that your family would never consent to such a union. No, I perceived from the start that Sir Frederick would not agree, and inasmuch as your cousin is a viscount . . .''

He stopped, his brown eyes briefly narrowing, then squared his shoulders. ''But I have considered long enough,'' he continued firmly. ''I quite concur that we must elope at once. In fact, since Lord Trowbury intends to spirit you to London tomorrow, we must go tonight.''

Cecily had never before witnessed such a rapid and amazing reversal of opinion, and she could only surmise that her abrupt proposition—far from merely surprising him—had temporarily unhinged his mind. At any rate, she herself was so startled that she sank weakly back on the hay bench, altogether forgetting to correct his latest distortion of Stephen's name.

''I . . . I had thought we should go to Gretna Green,'' she stammered. ''Though I shall be twenty-one tomorrow and legally entitled to wed without Uncle Frederick's consent, there might be some delay in obtaining a license in England. Whereas, or so I am given to understand, there are no formalities whatever in Scotland.''

To Cecily's further astonishment, Dennis offered no objection to this or any other particular of the tentative plan she had devised. He agreed it would be best for Sewell to drive them to Sheffield—the nearest major town, located some twenty miles up the road—where they could readily purchase places in a public coach traveling to Scotland. Dennis shared her view that the groom was unlikely to question the reason for their journey and assuredly wouldn't mention it till someone took note of their disappearance and launched an investigation. ''Someone'' being, Cecily thought darkly, her priggish cousin Stephen. However, by the time Viscount Trowbridge realized she was missing and ascertained the direction of her escape, she and Dennis would have gained so many hours' advantage that pursuit would be quite fruitless.

That left only the time and place of their meeting, and Cecily had decided at the outset that the ideal hour for her escape was nine. She and Stephen would finish their dinner by five, she calculated, and her cousin would thus have four full hours in which to drink a glass or two of brandy, ready himself for bed, and retire. By nine o'clock, when it would be fully dark, Stephen should be safely and soundly asleep, and she and Dennis could still reach Sheffield before midnight.

The site of the rendezvous posed a substantially more difficult problem. The safest course, and the one Cecily had initially favored, was to meet Dennis at the bottom of the drive, which was situated nearly half a mile from the house. However, she soon realized that she couldn't possibly transport her luggage so far, and she dared not ask one of the footmen to carry her trunk the whole length of the drive and hide it in a hedge or stand of weeds beside the road. She had consequently determined to meet Dennis in the coach house behind Osborne Hall, and she now issued the requisite instructions: he was to leave his carriage at the *top* of the drive, just where it branched into the circle that arced in front of the house, and he and Sewell were to steal round to the coach house. The three of them would then creep back to the carriage, Dennis and Sewell bearing her trunk between them. Described aloud, the scheme sounded frightfully dangerous even to Cecily, but Dennis did not voice a single syllable of opposition.

"Very good." He once more bobbed his pale brown head. "I shall meet you at the coach house at ten."

"Nine," Cecily hissed. "If only this once, Dennis, you must remember the details. We are to meet at the coach house at nine."

He nodded again, rose, and drew her up beside him, and this time—since they were, at last, formally engaged—Cecily allowed him to kiss her. But when she and Moonbeam were well out of sight of the King and Dragon, she scrubbed her mouth with the back of her hand and shuddered a bit at the recollection that she would shortly be compelled to endure "it."

Cecily had expected the remainder of the day and evening to drag interminably, but in the event, her packing required far longer than she had anticipated. Not the packing of her clothes; as she had guessed, it took her under half an hour to transfer her minuscule wardrobe to her trunk. However, after she had placed the final gown in her case, it occurred to her that Uncle Frederick might be so overset by her elopement that he would refuse to permit her to return to Osborne Hall for the rest of her things. She couldn't possibly take them all, of course, all the books and bric-a-brac and souvenirs she had accumulated in one and twenty years. She was consequently forced to examine and evaluate every one of her possessions, and by the time she finished, the corridor clock was striking half past two.

Cecily closed the trunk and attempted to lift it off the bed, but the addition of her various memorabilia had rendered the case much too heavy for her to manage. Indeed, she calculated that it weighed at least five stone, and it was clear she couldn't drag it—much less carry it—even so far as the coach house. She opened the lid with a sigh, prepared to remove the items she had sorted through so carefully, but as she plucked out the shellwork dolphin Aunt Esther had brought her from Margate, there was a knock on her bedchamber door. Cecily stiffened, then remembered that she was *supposed* to be packing, albeit for an altogether different journey.

"Come in," she called.

"Ah, here you are, Miss Osborne." Cordelia peered over the threshold. "I came earlier this morning, but you were out."

The maid paused expectantly, but Cecily said nothing. Unlike Sewell, Cordelia was immensely interested in the activities of others and monstrous wide in the mouth, and Cecily had learned long since to trust her with no confidence more intimate than an observation about the weather.

"Humph." Cordelia emitted a wounded sniff. "Well, at any rate, before he left, Lord Trowbridge desired me to assist your packing."

"Before he left?" Cecily echoed.

"Yes. He borrowed Sir Frederick's saddle horse and one of his guns and rode out—at seventeen minutes past nine, it was—to hunt in the woods round Bakewell. He said he wouldn't be back till late this afternoon."

"Excellent!" Cecily said, glimpsing the solution to her

dilemma. Cordelia frowned. "I mean," Cecily elaborated hastily, "that it is excellent Lord Trowbridge has a chance to enjoy a bit of recreation, is it not? As it happens, I have packed my trunk already"—she tossed the dolphin back in as unobtrusively as she could and snapped the lid closed— "and I should like you to summon a footman to take it to the coach house."

"Now?" Cordelia's frown deepened.

"Yes, now," Cecily snapped. "I am sure his lordship won't want to waste a single moment tomorrow morning."

Cordelia granted her a dubious nod and backed into the hall.

"And I wish it to be a surprise," Cecily added. "For Stephen, I mean. You know how men are. He won't expect me to be ready on time, and he'll be pinching at me about my luggage, and I shall . . . I shall surprise him," she reiterated lamely.

"Yes, men *are* like that, aren't they?" Cordelia shook her head in sorrowful resignation and raced away to fetch a footman.

Unfortunately, the footman Cordelia produced was a puny specimen, hardly more than a foot*boy*, and it soon became apparent that he couldn't carry the trunk either. Cordelia volunteered her opinion that the best course was to find a second footman to aid the first, but the corridor clock was chiming three by now, and Cecily judged that speed was of the essence. She therefore decreed that she and Cordelia would support one end of the trunk while the footman bore the other, and—with much puffing and groaning and several shocking curses on the part of the footman— they succeeded in wrestling it into the hall, down the back stairs, along the lower rear corridor, and out to the coach house. Upon their arrival, Cordelia announced in a prodigious loud voice that they had brought the trunk early so as to surprise Viscount Trowbridge and expedite his and Miss Osborne's departure for London.

"Then I shall tie the trunk to his lordship's carriage at once," Pickett said helpfully.

"No!" Cecily protested. "No, Stephen is excessively particular about the arrangement of the luggage." She had seized upon the first remotely logical objection that came to mind, but, upon reflection, she thought it quite likely she was right. "Leave the trunk here." She indicated the spot just inside the coach-house door where they had crashed the trunk to the floor. "Lord Trowbridge will direct you how to load it tomorrow morning."

Evidently Pickett concurred in her assessment of Stephen's meticulous habits, for he nodded and carefully began to remove a few wayward pieces of straw which had festooned themselves around the bottom of the trunk.

So much for her interminable day, Cecily thought wryly, tugging Cordelia out of the coach house. It must be approaching half past three, and she had yet to dress for dinner. *Bathe* and dress, she amended: her morning ride, her struggle with the trunk, her underlying anxiety had left her damp and feeling altogether unclean.

"I must have a bath immediately," she announced as she and Cordelia stepped through the back door.

"Now?" the maid whined.

Cecily bit back a sharp retort because, to say the truth, Cordelia had a valid point: even if the tub was brought to Cecily's bedchamber and filled with unprecedented speed, she couldn't complete her toilette by four o'clock. On the other hand, she couldn't conceivably go to dinner in her present lamentable state, and she essayed a patient smile.

"I am well aware I shall be late," she said. "Dinner will simply have to be held—"

"Dinner!" Cordelia clapped one hand over her mouth. "That was the other thing Lord Trowbridge desired me to tell you. Because of his hunting expedition, he ordered that dinner be postponed till seven."

"Seven!" Cecily gasped. "But he can't . . . I can't . . ."

Her first inclination was to claim that she had taken ill, which—in view of the fact that her stomach had started to churn and her hands were trembling most alarmingly—was far from being a lie. But she realized that, at the least, Stephen would demand to speak with his allegedly ailing cousin, and he might well insist on summoning Dr. Erskine from Buxton to conduct a complete examination.

In short, a mythical attack of ill health offered no salvation, and Cecily's mind began to spin in calculation. If she and Stephen started dinner at seven, they would finish no later than eight, and—with Cecily's clever, subtle manipulation—Stephen could still be in bed by nine. Furthermore, the delay would afford her the opportunity to compensate for the hours of rest she had lost that morning.

"Very well, Cordelia." Cecily regally inclined her head. "Please be sure to have my bath drawn at six o'clock precisely."

She walked up the steps, down the hall, and into her bedchamber and collapsed upon the counterpane. And, miraculously, fell at once into a deep, untroubled sleep.

❧ 3 ❧

"What the devil is that . . . that *thing* you are wearing?" Stephen snapped.

Cecily repressed a sigh, for she had hoped against hope that her cousin would fail to notice her admittedly peculiar attire. But the moment she entered the dining room, he had begun to stare at her again, his green eyes raking her from head to toe and side to side in the same unnerving manner they had the night before. As she had then, Cecily detected the symptoms of an inexplicable, maddening blush; and she willed herself not to gaze at the carpet and shuffle her feet like a skitter-brained schoolgirl.

"It is my riding costume," she replied with as much dignity as she could muster.

"It resembles no riding habit *I* have ever seen," Stephen said frostily.

Insofar as Cecily knew, it resembled no other riding habit on the face of the earth because she had designed it herself. When—on the occasion of her fourth birthday—she had received her first pony, she had insisted on learning to ride astride and persuaded Aunt Esther to make her a miniature pair of buckskin breeches exactly like Uncle

Frederick's. Lady Osborne fashioned a new and larger pair
of breeches year after year until Cecily turned fourteen, at
which juncture her ladyship declared that she could no
longer permit her niece—now nearly a woman grown—to
dress and behave like a man. No, Cecily must henceforth
use a sidesaddle and wear a proper habit, and Aunt Esther
escorted her to Miss Lane's establishment in Buxton to be
measured for an elegant emerald-green riding dress.

Cecily was hard put to determine whether she or Moonbeam was more distressed by the new arrangement: Cecily
could scarcely control the horse with one leg rendered
effectively useless, and Moonbeam was forever snapping
at the gratuitous folds of fabric flapping round her neck. In
any case, as soon as Lady Osborne removed to London,
Cecily began casting about for a way to rectify the situation. She probably was too old to wear breeches, she
conceded, but she soon conceived a splendid compromise:
a unique mating of breeches and a skirt. She prevailed on
Mrs. Hedges, the housekeeper, to cut one of her old
dresses up the middle and reseam the resulting halves. The
finished garment allowed Cecily to ride quite comfortably
astride, but she had always fancied that when she was
standing, it would be mistaken for a very short gown.
Which was, of course, the only sort of gown Miss Lane
knew how to create.

However, it now appeared her hypothesis had been
wrong, for she hadn't deceived Stephen an instant. Not
that she had deliberately contrived to test her theory on her
priggish cousin. The truth of the matter was that in her
haste to pack, Cecily had reserved only a fresh set of
underthings, altogether forgetting the need for an appropriate dress to wear to dinner. She had not recognized her
error until a quarter before seven, and by that time, it was
far too late to race out to the coach house and begin
rummaging through her trunk. She had consequently been
compelled to use Cordelia's hairbrush and comb, and—
had the maid not been three full inches taller and at least
two stone heavier—Cecily might well have asked to borrow her Sunday gown as well.

"And at any rate, one does not wear one's riding clothes
to dinner," Stephen continued. He had avoided any such

shocking *faux pas* by donning mustard-colored pantaloons, a canary frock coat in the finest Bath, a lemon-yellow waistcoat, and an ivory neckcloth that threatened to strangle him should he turn his head too quickly.

"No, one does not," Cecily snapped. As had also happened last night—last night and many years ago—his insufferable priggishness was starting to dilute his physical charm. "In normal circumstances, I shouldn't have worn it, but I have packed everything else."

"Everything?" Stephen echoed. "You intend to travel to London in . . . in . . ." Words failed him; he could only wave his hand from her neck to the divided hemline of her skirt.

"Of course not," Cecily said. "I saved a carriage dress for the journey."

In point of fact, she did not even *own* a carriage dress, and she belatedly feared Stephen would command her to change at once, lest his digestion be overset by prolonged exposure to her scandalous ensemble. But he nodded— albeit grudgingly—seated her in her customary chair, and occupied Sir Frederick's vacant place at the head of the table.

"I must confess," Stephen said, "that I am relieved to learn you completed your packing so expeditiously. Following our previous conversation—"

"Shouldn't we direct the soup to be served?" Cecily interrupted nervously. She glanced toward Hedges, who was poised expectantly in front of the sideboard.

"Are you too hungry to wait another moment?" There was the merest ghost of a smile at the corners of Stephen's mouth.

She *should* be hungry, Cecily thought, because she had eaten nothing all day since that wretched morning muffin. But tension had quite destroyed her appetite, and she wanted only to end the meal as rapidly as possible.

"I am fairly starving," she lied. "And I'm most eager to finish dinner and retire early so as to obtain a good night's sleep before our departure. A *long* night's sleep," she emphasized. "I daresay you also wish to retire early."

"Well, I do want to leave at six, which means we shall have to rise at five—"

"Then we must *certainly* be in bed by nine," Cecily said firmly.

She signaled Hedges, and the butler ladled out two bowls of soup from the tureen on the sideboard and brought them to the table. Having claimed to be ravenous, Cecily judged it imperative that she pretend to eat, and she seized her spoon and noisily gulped down several mouthfuls of the . . . the . . . She charitably elected to term it a broth though she honestly could not detect any ingredient except lukewarm water.

"As I was saying"—Stephen laid his own spoon aside with a moue of distaste—"I am much relieved by your attitude. I—"

"Are you not going to eat your soup?" she interposed.

"I believe not," he said wryly.

"I can't finish mine either." Cecily shoved her bowl away. "So let us have the main course."

"Good God, Cecily! We have been at table under ten minutes . . ."

He bit his lip and nodded at Hedges, and the butler whisked away the soup bowls and delivered the entrées. Cecily began to cut her meat and boiled potatoes and asparagus into tiny pieces, calculating that if she distributed the pieces artfully round her plate, she would not be compelled actually to consume a single bite.

"Pray forgive my objection to your haste," Stephen said. "The fact is, as I've been attempting to explain, that I am surprised and delighted by your enthusiasm for your come-out. Evidently you have come to realize that a match with Mr. Drummond would have been most unsuitable indeed."

"Umm." Cecily moved her jaws energetically up and down as though her mouth were full of food.

"Did you advise him of your departure?" Stephen asked. "Drummond, that is?"

Cecily continued her careful chewing, pondering the best response. Even if Stephen had learned of her ride to Buxton—and there was no reason to suspect he had—he couldn't possibly know she had met with Dennis. Her admission that such a meeting had taken place could only have unpleasant consequences: a ripping-up for her impropriety or, worse, a lengthy interrogation about the details of their conversation. She swallowed her imaginary food.

"No," she murmured. She couldn't meet his probing green eyes, and she peered studiedly at her plate. "No, after I perceived how very unsuitable Dennis was, I decided not to see him again."

"You needn't be embarrassed, Cecily," Stephen said kindly. He had obviously misinterpreted her downcast eyes. "As Frederick pointed out last evening, everyone conceives a ridiculous *tendre* at one time or another."

Everyone but you, Cecily thought. She doubted Stephen had ever conceived a *tendre* of any sort, much less a ridiculous one. "I fancy you are right," she muttered aloud.

"And as Frederick went on to say, you'll surely be engaged to a suitable *parti* before the Season is half over."

His voice was curiously hollow, and when Cecily glanced up, she found him watching her again, his pale eyes narrowed in speculation. But, to her vague astonishment, he looked away at once, clearing his throat and returning to his meal with far more eagerness than she supposed it could possibly warrant. Indeed, Stephen now seemed as anxious to finish as she was, and the ormolu clock on the dining-room mantel had not yet chimed eight when he devoured the last bite of his bilberry pie, patted his lips with his napkin, and rose.

"Well." Cecily sprang from her own chair and negotiated a great yawn, as if she had suddenly discovered herself quite exhausted. "I believe I shall retire immediately."

"As you will." Stephen inclined his chestnut head. "I trust Frederick will not object if I repair to the library and sample a glass or two of his brandy."

"No!" Cecily protested. Stephen frowned. "I mean," she went on quickly, "that Uncle Frederick would not object, but I wonder if you should drink spirits so shortly before bedtime. Remember that you must be asleep by nine."

"I'm deeply gratified by your concern for my health," Stephen said dryly. "However—as you'll learn all too soon for yourself—the older one grows, the less sleep one requires."

"But . . . but . . ." But she dared not press the issue any further; her alleged concern for his health already appeared a trifle obsessive. "Very well," she said lightly. "But I do hope you will get an adequate night's rest. I should hate you to be tired and grumpy all the way to London."

Cecily hurried up the stairs and along the corridor to her bedchamber and sank on the bed to review the situation. She soon realized that if Stephen had known of her elopement and intentionally devised a counterplan to thwart it, he could hardly have conceived a better one. Had he elected to take his brandy in the dining room or the saloon or, in fact, virtually any other room in the house, Cecily would have stood some chance of slipping out either the front or the rear door. But the library ran the full width of the house, and there was an entry at either end—one off the vestibule, mere feet from the front door, and the other off the back hall, just adjacent to the *rear* door. Cecily couldn't use either exit so long as Stephen remained in the library, and she gazed a moment at the window, then shook her head. Even were she bold enough to tie her bedsheets into a rope and descend the twenty or so feet to the ground, she would come to rest immediately outside the front window of the library, and Stephen would surely see her. Actually, she judged it far more likely that she would *fall* to rest in this location, in which case Stephen's view would be that of her crumpled corpse.

In short, escape was out of the question; she could only wait as patiently as possible till Stephen tired of Uncle Frederick's brandy and went to bed. And hope, she added grimly, that Dennis would wait with equal patience when he reached their rendezvous and found her not yet there. She took some slight comfort in the recollection that the library had no side windows—a gallery stood between it and the outside wall of the house—so Stephen could not spot Dennis and Sewell as they crept from the drive to the coach house. And perhaps, she thought optimistically, Stephen would have but one glass of brandy before he retired. Perhaps she would not be very late after all.

*   *   *

"Where the *deuce* have you been!"

"Shh!"

Cecily instinctively raised one finger to her lips, then realized that Dennis was whispering already. However, in view of the fact that his voice was literally shaking with rage and his eyes gleaming like two furious beacons in the darkness, it was easy to form an impression that he was shrieking at the top of his lungs.

"Are you aware that it is *midnight?*" he hissed.

Cecily was most dismally aware of this inasmuch as she had counted every stroke of the corridor clock for nearly four hours. At a quarter past eight, she had taken the precaution of cracking her bedchamber door so she would be certain to hear Stephen when he left the library and ventured upstairs. At nine, judging this measure inadequate, she had additionally opened her window, enabling herself to lean out and determine whether a lamp still burned in the library. At half past nine, she had commenced to pace between the open door and the open window—now peering into the hall and listening for the sound of Stephen's footfalls, now gazing down at the light which streamed from the window just below.

By half past ten, Cecily was persuaded that despite her vigilance, Stephen had managed to ascend the stairs without her knowledge, neglecting to extinguish the library lamps when he left. Or perhaps he had fallen asleep in the library with the lights still blazing; indeed, this was by far the likelier circumstance. And if he *was* asleep, whether in his bedchamber or in the library, she might spend the remainder of the night needlessly trapped in her own bedroom.

It was clear she would have to check, and, scarcely daring to breathe, she stole into the corridor and down the front staircase. She was halfway to the bottom before it occurred to her to wonder what explanation she could credibly offer if her cousin chose that very moment to emerge from the library. Why—when she'd been frantically eager to retire at eight—was she creeping round the house, fully clothed, at half past ten? Fortunately, just as she reached the vestibule, Stephen cleared his throat, confirming that he was still in the library and still awake; and Cecily scurried back up the stairs and resumed her incessant pacing.

Her patience—to use the term prodigious loosely—was rewarded at half past eleven by the tap of footsteps on the marble staircase, the creak of a floorboard in the first-floor hall, the slight rattle of the knob as Stephen opened his bedchamber door, and the click of the latch as he pulled it closed behind him. Having been delayed so excessively long already, Cecily decided to grant him a few minutes more to fall asleep, and she stationed herself at her own door and waited for the sound of his snoring. But no such sound ensued, and at a quarter before midnight, she was compelled to consider the possibility that—unlike Uncle Frederick, who could fairly rouse the dead during his more impressive performances—Stephen did not snore. She stepped cautiously into the corridor, tiptoed to the rear stairs and down them to the back door, slipped outside, and stumbled through the darkness to the coach house.

"I have been waiting two full hours," Dennis continued testily.

Cecily collected from this complaint that he had confused the time of their meeting after all and not appeared at the rendezvous till ten. However, in the circumstances, she counted it best not to mention his error.

"I am sorry," she whispered instead. "But let us not waste time in argument. You and Sewell must take my trunk—"

"We have already done so," he snapped. "*Hours* ago. Are you ready then? Ready *at last?*"

Cecily nodded, and Dennis clamped his fingers round her elbow and tugged her toward the side of the house. His grip was really most painful, but Cecily doubted he would appreciate a remark on this head either. Furthermore, or so she surmised, his eyes had adjusted to the night far better than hers because it took them under ten minutes to reach Mr. Drummond's traveling carriage and settle themselves inside. The coach lurched forward with a fearful clatter, and Cecily looked apprehensively over her shoulder, fully expecting to see a sudden flash of light in Stephen's bedchamber window. But Osborne Hall remained reassuringly dark and, within a few minutes more, was altogether out of sight.

"It will be nearly three o'clock by the time we arrive in Sheffield," Dennis said irritably.

"I am *sorry*." Her words to the contrary, Cecily's tone was not in the least contrite, for she was beginning to grow exceedingly vexed herself. "I did not deliberately keep you waiting. My cousin postponed dinner from four until seven, and after that, he stayed awake in the library for hours—"

"Ah, yes, your cousin," Dennis interposed forgivingly. "I had nearly forgotten your cousin. You need apologize no more." He patted her knee. "We can sleep en route to Sheffield, and I daresay we'll be quite rested by tomorrow morning."

Cecily had somehow fancied they would spend these first thrilling hours of their life together joyfully discussing the future. In fact, she recollected with a start, they had planned their elopement so hastily that they had not even determined where they would live upon their return from Scotland. She turned to Dennis, intending to remind him of this rather grave oversight, but he had already laid his head against the seat; and she further recollected that the many hours of travel ahead would afford them ample opportunity for conversation. She dropped her head to the squab as well and fell into a fitful sleep, waking enough from time to time to discover that Dennis *did* snore.

As Dennis had predicted, it was almost three o'clock when they reached the White Lion, the principal inn on the near side of Sheffield. At this juncture, Cecily additionally discovered that Dennis was extremely groggy when first he woke: it was left to her to enter the inn and summon a footman to assist Sewell with the luggage. When their bags had been unloaded and borne inside, she directed the groom to arrange overnight accommodation for the carriage, the horses, and himself. But Sewell insisted he had a mare due to foal at any time and must return to Buxton immediately. Cecily judged the expectant mare a very fortunate circumstance indeed—one certain to divert the groom's attention so completely that he would not give his midnight drive to Sheffield another moment's thought.

During Cecily's discussion with Sewell, Dennis had bestirred himself sufficiently to ring for the night clerk, who advised them that they had narrowly missed the late-night stage for the northwest; the next would depart at ten a.m. Cecily had hoped to be considerably farther along the road by then, but there was nothing to be done about the coaching schedule. And by now, she was quite as exhausted as she had pretended to be after dinner and desperately in need of proper rest in a proper bed.

"Very well," Dennis said. "Please see we're knocked up at half past nine. Now, if you could assign us a room—"

"Two rooms," Cecily interjected firmly.

"For God's sake, Cecily! We are practically—"

"We shall be soon, but we are not yet."

The clerk's eyes darted back and forth between them, and he evidently judged Cecily the victor in their debate, for he pulled two keys from the board behind his desk and passed one to each of them. Dennis accepted his with excessively poor grace—scowling at the clerk and Cecily in turn—and stalked up the stairs without a further word. By the time Cecily herself reached the top of the staircase, Dennis was already entering his room, and he slammed his door in a decidedly mifty manner.

But he would shortly forgive her, Cecily thought. And, to say the truth, she was almost too tired to care whether he did or not. She glanced at her trunk, which the footman had deposited on the floor of her room, but she was too tired to change for bed either. She removed only her bonnet and shoes before collapsing on the counterpane, and she tumbled at once into oblivion.

4

Cecily had scarcely fallen asleep when she began to dream of a great pounding at her bedchamber door. It wasn't clear what person or thing was seeking entrance because the pounding was not accompanied by a human voice or any other sound. But it continued rhythmically, relentlessly, on and on . . .

Cecily's eyes flew open at last, and she discovered herself in a strange room and recollected where she was. She was quite persuaded she had slept only a few minutes, but, in fact, a river of brilliant sunlight coursed through the open draperies at the window and splashed across the bed. So it must be half past nine, she surmised, recalling Dennis's instructions to the clerk, and the landlord had dispatched someone to knock her up.

"Yes, I am awake," she called. "I shall be ready by ten." The pounding went on. "I am awake!" she repeated, raising her voice considerably. "Thank you!" Knock, knock; pound, pound. "*I am awake!*" she fairly shrieked. "*You may . . .*"

But it was obvious the idiotish servant at the door was pounding so very loudly that he couldn't hear her, and Cecily climbed irritably out of bed. She glanced around, wondering where she might have left her dressing gown, then remembered that she was still wearing her riding costume. She marched to the door and threw it open.

"I have been trying to advise you . . ." She felt the blood drain from her face. "Stephen!" she gasped. "When . . . how . . . where . . ."

"I shall attempt to answer your questions in sequence," he said furiously.

His fingers snaked around her arm, and she distantly

noted that despite his leanness, he was excessively strong. He jerked her to one side, stepped into the room, slammed the door behind him with a fearful crash, and dragged her to the side of the bed. He moved his hand to her shoulder, and for a moment, she fancied he was going to shake her, as Aunt Esther had occasionally done when her childhood conduct was particularly odious. But he executed a little shove instead and sent her tumbling most unceremoniously onto the counterpane.

"The *when*," he said through gritted teeth, "was five o'clock this morning when I desired Cordelia to wake you and she reported you were not in your bedchamber. Cordelia helpfully suggested that perhaps you had gone to the coach house to add some forgotten item to your trunk. When I inquired why your trunk was already in the coach house, she told me of the grand surprise you had planned. Which, indeed, you had."

Perversely enough, his anger rendered him even more attractive than usual—lending a slight flush to his cheeks and a glitter to his green-gold eyes. Cecily realized that in all the years of their acquaintance, she had never before seen him in the grip of deep emotion; and, to her astonishment, she found herself wondering how he would look if he were stirred by passion rather than rage.

"As to the *how*," Stephen continued, "I soon recollected your prodigious eagerness to send me to my bed. Given the same circumstances, I daresay a clever three-year-old could have deduced your intentions."

Cecily bit her lip and tried to avert her gaze, but she could not. There was something about him—in the way he was towering over her, his eyes blazing down at her—that held her quite in thrall.

"In any case, I perceived at once that you had eloped with Drummond, borrowed Frederick's horse again, and rode to *where:* the inn in Buxton. By a great stroke of luck, one of the employees—a certain Sewell—was pulling into the innyard just as I arrived."

So the expectant mare had not been a fortunate factor after all, Cecily reflected grimly. Had Sewell not been worried about one of his beloved horses, he would no doubt have spent the night in Sheffield and been unavailable to tell Stephen where she and Dennis had gone.

"I cannot conceive why you and Drummond did not counsel Sewell to keep his silence," Stephen said. "I was prepared to pay him handsomely for his information, but in the event, I was put to no expense whatever. Sewell told me quite willingly that he had driven you to the White Lion in Sheffield. I got the impression he did not even recognize what you were at."

"We . . ." But there was no reason to embark upon a lengthy explanation of Sewell's uncurious personality. Nor to mention that she had thought to be many miles up the road by now and far beyond pursuit.

"At any rate, when Sewell advised me of your destination, I calculated that you planned to take a public coach to Gretna Green. My own course was clear: I could only ride to Sheffield as fast as possible and hope to catch you up. And that, I trust, answers your questions to your entire satisfaction."

His wrath seemed to have cooled a bit: his tone was exquisitely polite, and he had raised his brows as if to indicate that he would be delighted to entertain any further inquiries she might care to pose. But she had none, for this was hardly the way she had intended to celebrate her twenty-first birthday . . . Her birthday! Cecily had forgotten it until that very instant, and with a great flood of relief, she realized that Stephen was powerless to prevent her marriage. Powerless, that is, if she could escape his spell—the peculiar physical spell he had wrought—and she tore her eyes away.

"No, I've no more questions," she said, her inflection quite as courteous as his. "However, I must inform you that you have altogether wasted your time. Apparently it slipped your mind that I am one and twenty years of age and can wed whomever I wish. There is no way you can stop me."

"To the contrary, my dear, I *have* stopped you. Drummond is even now en route to Lincoln."

"Lincoln?" Cecily echoed. "But why—"

"Because he and I had a brief chat before I came to wake you. We agreed it would be best for Drummond to remove himself from the scene at once, and the next departing stage chanced to be traveling to Lincoln. I should guess he'll leave the coach at the first stop and proceed back to Buxton, but his ultimate destination was of no concern to me."

"You . . . you talked to Dennis?" Cecily stammered. "And he . . . he agreed to . . . But why?" she repeated lamely.

"Surely it occurred to you . . ."

He stopped and shook his head, and the movement appeared to dislodge the last traces of his anger. His eyes turned gentle, gentle and oddly dark, and he sank on the bed beside her and took one of her hands in both of his.

"Did it never occur to you"—he rephrased his words—"that Drummond's affection was largely inspired by the wealth and position of your family? Specifically—and I take no pride in pointing it out—he was most enamored of the prospect of being connected to a viscount. He planned to bring you to London immediately after your marriage and reside with me throughout the Season. And I cannot suppose that would have been the end of it. No, I believe he had visions of living quite comfortably on my largesse for the remainder of his life."

Cecily parted her lips to deny his charge, but before she could find her voice, she recalled that Dennis had consented to wed her shortly after being reminded that her cousin was a viscount. Had forgiven her tardiness last night the instant she referred to Stephen. "Go on," she said weakly.

"I made it abundantly clear to Drummond that if he wed you, he could not anticipate a single groat from me."

"And he . . . he left."

Stephen hesitated a moment, then drew a deep sigh. "No, he did not leave. Not then. He mentioned that it would be exceedingly unfortunate if your elopement became public knowledge. That no gentleman would wed a girl of such tarnished reputation."

He paused again, his eyes expectantly searching her face, but Cecily had no notion what it was he expected, where the conversation was leading. She gazed blankly back at him, and he heaved another sigh.

"Drummond went on to say that it would surely be in your best interest if he retired discreetly from the scene and—as he put it—'forgot' the incident entirely. Which he was prepared to do. For a price."

"He demanded a bribe," Cecily said dully.

"Yes, he asked a thousand pounds." Cecily's mouth dropped open. "However, he settled for five hundred. Five hundred pounds plus 'expenses': your rooms last night, his coach fare to Lincoln and back to Buxton, his meals and accommodations during the journey . . ."

Stephen's voice trailed off, and his eyes roved her face again, clearly seeking her reaction. And just what *was* her reaction? Cecily wondered. Humiliation, of course: she could only be mortified to learn that Dennis had never cared for her; had, in effect, sold her for the sum of five hundred pounds. Dennis's betrayal would have shamed her in any circumstances, and the fact that Stephen had witnessed the whole sordid sequence of events rendered the situation infinitely worse.

But mingled with the humiliation, Cecily detected a distinct sense of relief. Perhaps, she admitted, much of Dennis's charm had stemmed from her awareness that he was, indeed, a most unsuitable *parti*. She had always fancied most the things she was told she couldn't have— from the monstrous expensive doll she had wept for as a tiny child to the half-wild stallion she had wanted when Uncle Frederick bought her Moonbeam to . . . to Dennis. Now she thought on it, she realized that she and Dennis had bickered nearly as much as Sir Frederick and Lady Osborne, and she could not suppose their marriage would have been any happier than the latter union. No, it was best to put Dennis Drummond altogether behind her, and Cecily disengaged her hand from Stephen's and assumed her brightest smile.

"Well, that is that then," she said cheerfully. "And no real harm was done. If we exert ourselves a bit, we can still reach London by tomorrow evening."

"I fear it is not that simple, Cecily." Every vestige of emotion had left him now—the rage and the gentleness as well—and he had reverted to his familiar stern self. "I fear that in one respect, Drummond was right. You have compromised yourself quite shockingly—''

"I have not compromised myself in the least!" she screeched. "You know very well that Dennis and I occupied separate rooms."

"That is immaterial," Stephen said frostily. "The fact is you did elope, and while that alone is sufficiently scandalous, you eloped with a man of no quality and dubious character. After many unchaperoned hours together, the two of you were discovered at the same inn. I assure you that no *on-dit* will include the information that you slept in different bedchambers. To the contrary, gossip invariably exaggerates the truth, and rumor will have it that you were caught in the very act of . . .'' He coughed and picked an imaginary speck of lint from his chocolate-colored pantaloons. "In very compromising circumstances indeed," he finished.

"On-dit?" Cecily echoed. "Gossip? Rumor? Where is it to start? Dennis promised to hold his tongue."

"Ah, yes, so he did." Stephen sardonically bobbed his head. "And Dennis has heretofore shown himself to be totally trustworthy."

"No, he has not," Cecily snapped, "but I shall have to take my chances. Even if Dennis doesn't keep his silence, Buxton is a long way from London. By the time his tale reached town, I might well be already engaged."

"And that is precisely what I cannot permit," Stephen said. "I cannot present you to my friends and acquaintances as if nothing were amiss and allow one of them to wed you. To do so would be the moral equivalent of ordering a troop of infantry into a dark forest with full knowledge that there was an unexploded shell lying about."

Though Cecily judged his military analogy a trifle melodramatic, she could not but concede that it was apt. The story of her elopement was, indeed, much like an unexploded shell, one which Dennis could detonate at any time. She couldn't possibly accept an offer of marriage without revealing her past, but once she did reveal it, no respectable man would wed her. And he, in his horror and disappointment, might repeat the tale, explode the bomb . . .

"Am I to resign myself to spinsterhood then?" She

spoke lightly, but her stomach had begun to flutter with panic. "Or do you intend to dispatch me to a nunnery? Or have you given the matter any thought?"

"I have given the matter very considerable thought," he replied. "In fact, I thought of little else all the while I rode from Buxton, and I perceived but one solution. I must marry you myself."

"Marry . . . me . . . yourself?" she choked.

"It is the only conceivable course," Stephen said firmly. "For me, it is the only *honorable* course. You were, after all, under my protection when this lamentable episode occurred. Had I performed my duty with proper diligence, you would have had no opportunity to plan an elopement, much less execute the plan."

"But . . . but I . . ."

"For you, it is the *only* course," Stephen went on. "Unless you do, indeed, desire to become a spinster or a nun. To be brutally candid, no other man will have you. If you are ever to wed, you will have to wed me."

His proposal, if such it could be termed, had rendered Cecily literally dizzy, and she closed her eyes and gripped the mattress lest she grow quite ill with shock. At length, her head stopped spinning, but she continued to sit with her eyes tightly shut, pondering his words. She had no doubt he was right about her dismal marital prospects; she had reached much the same conclusions herself a few minutes since. So the real question to be resolved was whether it would be better to wed Stephen than not to marry at all.

He was certainly, as Aunt Esther would have phrased it, a "splendid catch": he was a viscount, and he was wealthy. Well, Cecily amended, she did not know for an absolute fact that he was wealthy, but she judged it reasonably safe to infer—from his clothes and his carriage and his five-hundred-pound donation to Dennis—that he was. Which meant that even had her reputation not been "tarnished," she could not realistically have expected to make a better match.

Indeed, she might well have done worse, for she could not suppose there were many men in London—in the *world*—as handsome as Stephen. It came down to that, of course: to whether she could bear "it." There was no way to be sure until the moment arrived, but she had come to recognize during the preceding forty-odd hours that she was still attracted to her cousin. Yes, she could admit that now. Now that she owed Dennis no further loyalty, she could admit that—if not the flames—at least the coals of her girlhood *tendre* still burned.

The only remaining obstacle was Stephen's insufferable priggishness, and Cecily decided that in this regard she would simply have to hope for the best. Perhaps, in time, she could breach that inexplicable wall he'd erected and find the gay companion of her youth. Perhaps marriage would mellow him—

"Are you all right, Cecily?" Stephen asked sharply.

"Yes." She forced her eyes open. "Yes, I was but thinking."

"And?" He sounded curiously anxious.

"And . . . and I agree that I shall have to wed you."

It was a singularly unromantic acceptance, but his offer had not exactly been the stuff of fairy tales. And in any event, he did not appear distressed: he nodded with more enthusiasm than she had any right to expect and leaped to his feet.

"Excellent. I trust you will further agree that we should marry immediately. Before we proceed to town. I shall make the arrangements at once."

To say the truth, Cecily did *not* agree, for she had counted on a delay of several weeks to accustom herself to her startling new situation. She had assumed they would travel to London, have the banns posted and the invitations printed and delivered, order proper wedding attire . . . But he was probably right on this head as well, she owned. If they arrived in town already wed, any rumor of her elopement was likely to be dismissed as sheer fabrication.

"Very well," she said. "As we have already missed the ten o'clock coach, perhaps you should send to Osborne Hall for your carriage. I daresay it will get us to Gretna nearly as fast and far more comfortably—"

"Gretna?" he interposed. "Why the devil should you wish to go to Scotland? We shall be married here in Sheffield."

Cecily repressed a sigh of relief; she was to have her

delay after all. "Then you must advise the landlord we'll be staying on. I fancy it will require some days to procure a license."

"So *that* is why you wanted to go to Gretna." Stephen looked quite pleased; he actually flashed a tiny smile. "Do not tease yourself about it a moment more. I shall have a special license by noon."

"Noon!" Cecily echoed shrilly.

"But you needn't be ready so soon." Fortunately, he had misinterpreted the reason for her dismay. "I shall schedule the ceremony for . . . Shall we say four o'clock?"

"Yes," she muttered. "Yes, four o'clock will be fine."

"Excellent," he said again. He strode to the door, opened it, turned once more to face her. "I do hope," he added severely, "that you do not intend to wear that . . . that garment to our wedding." His eyes swept disdainfully over her riding costume. "I trust you've something more suitable in your trunk."

She wondered what he would do if she claimed she had no other garment with her. Drag her to the nearest mantua-maker? Dispatch someone to Osborne Hall to bring back the entire contents of her wardrobe? She was sorely tempted to lie, to find out, but it wasn't the time to bait him.

"Yes, I shall wear something more suitable."

Stephen nodded and stepped into the hall, then turned back round. "I suggest you leave your . . . ah . . . riding costume here," he said. "You'll have no further use for it because I shan't permit you to wear it again."

He closed the door, and Cecily glared in his wake. Permit indeed! She would wear something "suitable" to her wedding, but she would not leave her riding costume behind. No, her dear husband would soon learn that she was not his to order about as he pleased.

Though Cecily had not thought of it for many years, she recollected during the course of the day that she had once entertained visions of her wedding to Stephen. Indeed, while in the throes of her childhood *tendre*, she had imagined the scene so many times that the details had grown quite clear in her mind. Since she would, by then, be the most glamorous belle in Britain, they would naturally be married at St. George's, Hanover Square—the premier church in London. Cecily had never actually seen St. George's, so in her visions, it became progressively larger and grander until its splendor far exceeded that of the cathedral in York.

On the day of her wedding, this magnificent edifice—enormous though it was—was overflowing with guests. The most important of these was King George himself (the poor old man had not yet gone mad), who had been excessively impressed with Miss Osborne when she was presented at court. The king's presence inspired much envious whispering among the other guests, and he was the center of attention until Cecily herself entered the nave. At that juncture, everyone quite forgot his majesty because the bride—clad in an ivory gown of satin and lace, sewn all over with tiny pearls—was utterly breathtaking in her beauty. *Literally* breathtaking: the congregation emitted a gasp of awe as they leaped to their feet and watched her float down the aisle on Uncle Frederick's arm.

There was another gasp when Cecily reached the altar and Stephen stepped forward to meet her, for he was as handsome as she was beautiful. Attired in full-dress uniform, fairly glittering with medals, his hair gleaming gold in the sunlight which streamed through the stained-glass windows, he put the numerous princes and dukes in attendance entirely to shame. He and Cecily looked so very well together that—though it was rather rude to do so—the guests could not refrain from commenting to one another about the remarkable pair. There was universal agreement that General Chandler (this was the rank Stephen now held) and his bride were certainly the handsomest couple anyone had ever seen. The conversation grew so enthusiastic that the Archbishop of Canterbury was compelled to raise his hand for silence before he could conduct the ceremony.

But conduct it he did, and Cecily and Stephen were shortly married, her new status confirmed by a wide gold band set with dozens of enormous diamonds. Arm in arm, they sailed back up the aisle and out of the church and climbed into Stephen's resplendent new coach. The vehicle, drawn by four white horses, conveyed them to their new home, which was the size of a smallish palace and furnished accordingly. Here the newlyweds hosted a gala reception for their hundreds of guests, sipping champagne and accepting congratulations well into the night. Cecily was told over and over that it had been the loveliest wedding ever, and, of course, she quite concurred—

"Cecily?" Stephen rapped at the chamber door, shattering her reverie. "Are you ready? It lacks but fifteen minutes to four."

So much for visions, Cecily thought wryly, turning this way and that in a vain attempt to inspect her appearance. Though her imaginings had never included the preparations for her wedding, she felt sure she would have had the use of a splendid cheval glass in which to admire her reflection. As it was, she had nothing but a tiny, warped mirror nailed to the inside of the wardrobe door, and this was cracked directly down the center. The only thing she could determine for certain was that her primrose dress bore no similarity whatever to the ivory gown of her dreams, and she dismally suspected this would be but the first of many discrepancies between vision and reality.

Naturally Stephen was not rigged out in full-dress uniform, but he cut a prodigious handsome figure nonetheless. Evidently he had instructed his coachman to follow from Osborne Hall with his luggage because he had changed from his morning attire to the ensemble he had worn the night before. As well as he looked, Cecily could not but wish he had chosen some other costume; for she feared that the two of them—both clad predominantly in yellow—resembled nothing so much as a pair of very large canaries. But it was too late to suggest he change again: he seized her elbow and began propelling her along the corridor.

"I engaged one of the curates from St. Mark's to perform the ceremony," Stephen announced as they approached the head of the staircase.

"Not the Archbishop of Canterbury," she murmured.

"I beg your pardon?"

"Never mind." Cecily sighed. "Never mind; it doesn't signify."

They descended the stairs to the lobby of the inn, where Cecily found the landlord, his wife, and the night clerk clustered round the main desk. She collected from the ensuing conversation that Stephen had invited Mr. Milner, the innkeeper, and Mrs. Milner to serve as witnesses to their marriage and that Mr. Milner had subsequently requested the clerk to take his place at the desk while he was gone. If the clerk counted it odd that Cecily had arrived in the middle of the night with one man and—a scant half-day later—was setting out to marry another, he was kind enough to betray no sign of his puzzlement. He seated himself on the stool behind the desk, and the wedding party trooped across the lobby and out the front door.

"We are to be married at Mr. Henley's home," Stephen said as they stepped into the innyard. "Since it is located only a few streets away, I fancy it would be most convenient to walk."

His lordship's pronouncement eliminated any possibility of a carriage drawn by four horses, white or otherwise, and Cecily struck grimly out beside him, the Milners marching along just behind. Whether fortunately or un-, she had little opportunity to dwell on this latest flaw in her dream, for she soon became aware that her slippers—which she had heretofore worn only to church—were chafing her feet most painfully. By the time they reached the curate's cottage, she was more nearly hobbling than walking, and she could feel the first twinges of a blister on both heels and the top of her right great toe.

The ceremony, it shortly proved, was to be conducted in Mr. Henley's parlor, which was slightly larger than the butler's pantry at Osborne Hall. In fact, Mr. Henley, assisted by Mr. Milner, had to move the armchair into the minuscule foyer before he could arrange the wedding party in front of the hearth, and even then, Mrs. Milner's outside leg was awkwardly jammed against the sofa. The scene was far removed indeed from the magnificent cathedral Cecily had pictured, but at least she needn't lament the absence of guests. There was no room for guests. Had the Prince Regent himself arrived, begging to attend the wedding, she would have been forced to turn him away.

In the full flush of her adolescent romanticism, Cecily had fairly memorized the marriage ritual in the prayer book, and she was able to follow almost word for word as

Mr. Henley began to read it. He did quite well at the outset, but he altogether omitted the portion in which he was supposed to ask who gave "this woman" to be married to "this man." Cecily was debating whether to bring this oversight to his attention when it occurred to her to wonder who, in the circumstances, could possibly give her away. Uncle Frederick wasn't here, and Stephen was her only other male relative. Could the groom give the bride to himself? Surely not, she decided; Stephen had obviously counseled the curate to eliminate that part of the rite.

"Ahem."

Mr. Henley coughed, and Cecily surmised that he had posed some critical question.

"I . . . I do," she stammered, hoping this was the correct response. Apparently it was because with a sympathetic, encouraging smile—the curate flew on.

Armed with the knowledge that Stephen and Mr. Henley had discussed the particulars of the ceremony, Cecily expected the curate to eliminate any reference to a ring as well, but when he reached the familiar passage, he started to read it without hesitation. Cecily was oddly touched that Stephen had taken the time to purchase a ring, and her reaction turned to one of astonishment when he slipped it on her finger. She had anticipated a simple band of gold, but, in fact, the ring was not vastly different from the one in her visions. The diamonds were not so large, of course, but Cecily had long since come to realize that few diamonds in the world were as large as the ones she'd pictured. She tore her eyes away from it only when Mr. Henley emitted another cough, and swallowed a peculiar little lump in her throat.

No coach had magically materialized during the ceremony, so after thanking the curate and bidding him farewell, the wedding party walked back to the White Lion. When they arrived, Cecily was touched all over again to discover that Stephen had arranged a wedding dinner in Mr. Milner's best private dining room. To say the truth, she judged this far preferable to the grand reception she had imagined, for her feet were hurting so badly by now that she did not believe she could have continued to stand even to greet the royal family. The landlord assisted her

into her chair, and as soon as her feet were safely out of
sight beneath the table, she reached discreetly down and
removed her shoes.

Apart from the ring, the only other detail of Cecily's
vision which proved remotely accurate was a great abundance of champagne. To her immense surprise, Stephen
had desired the Milners to share their dinner, and the
innkeeper would not allow their glasses to remain empty a
moment. Cecily soon collected that Mr. and Mrs. Milner
were quite overwhelmed to find themselves at table with a
viscount and sought to ease their discomfiture with the
only weapons at hand: an excessive quantity of spirits and
an incessant stream of chatter. Before the meal was
over, Cecily knew more about the Milners than she did
about the Osbornes—every fact about the living brothers
and sisters and cousins and every legend concerning
the previous generations of the family, all the way
back to one Harold Milner, who had allegedly accompanied Richard Lion-Heart on the Third Crusade.

Cecily had initially fancied Stephen's invitation to be
one of mere courtesy, a gesture of appreciation for the
Milners' considerable assistance. However, as the evening
progressed, she began to speculate that he, like Cecily
herself, had feared to spend these first hours of their
marriage alone. She and Stephen had been acquainted for
years, but they did not *know* one another at all. Her
ill-advised elopement behind them, what the deuce would
they have talked about? As it was, they were not required
to utter a single word: an occasional nod or shake of the
head, an "ooh" or "ah" of interest, was sufficient to
launch one or both the Milners on yet another tale.

This one-sided discourse could not go on forever, of
course, and at length, Mr. Milner drained his glass and got
unsteadily to his feet. An invisible clock was chiming
somewhere nearby, and Cecily believed she counted eight
strokes. However, inasmuch as she had consumed at least
half a dozen glasses of wine herself and was more than a
trifle giddy, she could not be certain. It might be seven; it
might be nine; it really didn't signify. She giggled and
struggled out of her chair, and with a frown of disap-

proval, Stephen took her arm and ushered her out of the dining room, across the lobby, and up the stairs.

Though she had not thought on the matter before, Cecily now realized that Stephen must have taken a room; he would have needed a place to store his baggage and change his clothes. So, she wondered—stumbling against him as she tripped on the top riser—which room was to serve as their nuptial chamber? Hers apparently, for he was guiding her along the corridor in that direction. The wooden floorboards felt very cold beneath her feet, and she belatedly remembered that she had left her shoes under the dining-room table.

Stephen opened the door of her room and propelled her in ahead of him, released her arm, closed the door, and leaned against it. He was silent for such a long time that she was reminded of their wedding; perhaps he had posed an inquiry she hadn't heard. But eventually he straightened and cleared his throat.

"Well." Insofar as she could recall, this was the first word he had spoken directly to her since their marriage. "Well, we are wed." She could not but nod in agreement. "Do you have any notion what that . . . ah . . . entails?"

"Y-yes," Cecily croaked.

"Please don't be frightened," he said softly. "Whatever you may have heard, I promise not to hurt you."

Hurt her? Good God. Was that Cordelia's objection? Was "it" actually painful? Cecily's giddiness abruptly evaporated, and her eyes darted about the room, seeking some avenue of escape. But if she retreated, she could only retreat toward the bed, which was precisely the place she wished to avoid. Her stomach constricted with panic, and before she could act, Stephen stepped forward and took her in his arms.

She perceived immediately that he was altogether unlike Dennis. Dennis had never held her like this, simply held her—his heart beating steadily against her, his breath barely stirring the hair at her temple. Despite her terror, she felt strangely secure, and after a time, she gained sufficient confidence to raise her own arms and clasp them tentatively round his neck. Stephen's breath quickened, and—

though she wasn't sure exactly how—he shifted their positions and laid his mouth on hers.

Cecily had hoped to find Stephen's kisses only moderately distasteful, and the reality quite stunned her. She had never imagined, in her wildest dreams, that the mere touch of a man's lips could create this delicious, throbbing ache in her midsection, could turn her knees to water, could fairly melt her bones. Her mouth opened against his—she wasn't sure how that happened either—and she moaned deep in her throat as she felt his tongue.

Stephen moved his lips to her ear, her neck, and Cecily writhed against him, shuddering with pleasure; but it was not enough. His hands began to explore her body—the lean fingers somehow gentle and hungry at the same time— but still, it was not enough. She couldn't have said what it was she wanted. She only knew she wanted more of him, and she wrapped her own fingers in his hair, tugged his head up, and brought his mouth back to hers.

At length, Stephen started to maneuver her toward the bed, but Cecily was now quite willing to go, and it was purely by accident that he trod on her right foot. No amount of passion was sufficient to dull the pain of a heavy Hessian slamming down upon a fresh blister, and she couldn't stifle a little groan of agony.

"What is it?" Stephen murmured hoarsely. "I can't possibly have hurt you."

"Well, you did." Her voice was as thick as his. "But just my foot. I am wearing no shoes, you see. I took them off in the dining room and forgot them."

"You are *barefoot*?" His tone suggested that she had been disporting herself about the town altogether unclothed— à la Lady Godiva—and he cast a horrified glance of confirmation at her naked feet. "You've been walking barefoot round the inn?"

"Only from the dining room to here," Cecily said defensively. "And only because my shoes were most dreadfully uncomfortable."

"Then I shall overlook it." Stephen had never entirely released her, and he pulled her close again and buried his face in her hair. "You've a great deal to learn about proper behavior, but with my instruction . . ."

His voice trailed off, and he sought her lips again, but Cecily wrenched her head away.

"With your instruction, I shall learn what you'll permit and what you won't?" she prompted.

"Precisely."

He took her chin in his fingers and raised her mouth to his, and Cecily willed herself not to respond. She knew even less about the mysterious connection between men and women than she did about "proper behavior," but she fancied this was the key: Stephen intended to use his undeniable physical magnetism to bend her to his wishes. And if she succumbed tonight, her riding costume and her bare feet would be but the beginning; he would soon conjure up a whole host of other things she was not allowed to wear or do, to discuss or even to think. She kept her lips tightly closed, and he shortly lifted his head.

"Are you that overset that I stepped on your foot?" he said lightly.

"No." She managed a cool smile. "No, I have merely recovered from a slight excess of champagne. However, you must not regard that as an obstacle. You forced me to marry you, and I perceive no reason you shouldn't force a consummation of the marriage as well."

He did release her then, released her so abruptly that she staggered backward and nearly lost her balance. His face had gone dead white, leaving his eyes to glitter like two great emeralds below his brows.

"I have never taken a woman against her will." His voice was so soft she could barely hear him. "No woman ever, so I certainly won't force myself on a *child*."

He spun around and strode to the door, flung it open, stalked into the corridor, crashed the door to behind him. She had won, Cecily judged; she had demonstrated beyond doubt that she would not be the sort of wife he could casually order about. She had won, and she wondered why her victory seemed so very hollow, why she felt so terribly empty inside.

❧ 5 ❧

"We are here," Stephen growled.

During the two interminable days of their journey to London, Cecily had taken to amusing herself by counting all the words her husband spoke directly to her. According to her tally, these were numbers seventy-two through seventy-four. The great majority of his previous remarks had been delivered at mealtimes and addressed the quality of their food. Was her sole satisfactory? Did she not think the kidneys a trifle underdone? However, the most words he had uttered in a single, uninterrupted sequence—sixteen—concerned their travel plans: he had advised her last night that he wished to depart at six this morning and would therefore desire the landlord to wake her at five. Cecily inferred from this lengthy soliloquy that they were not to share a room, and this proved to be the case.

The rest of his comments had actually been grunts instead of words, and Cecily was compelled to own that she probably shouldn't have included them in her count. "Is it not a lovely day?" "Umm." "I never realized Northamptonshire was so hilly." "Umm." "I believe we are making excellent time. Your coachman is to be commended." "Umm."

In short, the two days of her marriage had surely been the longest of Cecily's life, and when the carriage came to a stop at last, she peered eagerly out her window. Stephen's home—her home now, she reminded herself—was hardly the palace she had imagined, but it was a handsome townhouse nonetheless. Plainer than the neighboring homes, with tabernacle windows above a rusticated arcade and no pilasters at all. But Cecily rather liked its simplicity, and as Aunt Esther had once pointed out, it was splendidly located: on Brook Street between Davies and Duke, very near to Grosvenor Square.

As was his custom, Stephen opened the coach door himself, pushed the steps out, and clambered nimbly down from the carriage. Cecily didn't know whether it had always been a part of his custom quite to ignore any passenger who might be with him in the coach; she only knew that during the two days of their journey, he had yet to tender her the first finger of assistance. She could have waited for the coachman, of course, but she had an absurd fear that Stephen might stride into the house and deliberately lock her out; and she stumbled down the steps unaided and caught him up just as he opened the front door.

"Mr. Stephen!"

The butler—or so Cecily presumed him to be—was an excessively elderly man, and she surmised from his familiar form of address that he had known his master since the latter's infancy. As if to confirm her conjecture, the butler hurried forward and threw one of his arms round Stephen's shoulders.

"We were growing quite worried about you, sir. We expected you to return last evening."

"I'm sorry for your alarm, Evans." Stephen smiled down at the butler, who scarcely reached his chin, and Cecily wondered if he would ever smile half so kindly at her. "The fact of the matter is that I was . . . ah . . . unavoidably detained."

"I understand."

Evans patted Stephen's shoulder, stepped away, and transferred his gaze to Cecily. Old as he was, his eyes were still a brilliant blue, and they darted over her like the eyes of a busy bird.

"And this must be Miss Osborne," he said.

"Not exactly." Stephen cleared his throat. "That, you see, was the nature of the . . . er . . . delay. I daresay you'll be delighted to learn that Miss Osborne and I were married in Sheffield on Friday afternoon."

"Married?"

Evans staggered backward but fortunately collided with the gilt pier table before he could topple altogether to the floor. Cecily was relieved to observe that he did not appear to be injured, and she wished Jordan, the coachman, had been so lucky. When Jordan was informed of the marriage, he had dropped Stephen's valise on his foot, and he'd been noticeably limping ever since.

"I . . . I *am* delighted, sir." His statement to the contrary, Evans was now staring at Cecily as though she were an evil sorceress who had trapped his master by means of some unspeakable spell. "Pray do accept my very best wishes. And you too, Miss Osborne. Miss Trowbridge, that is. *Lady* Trowbridge, I meant to say . . ." His voice expired in a little moan of confusion.

"I am certain you will soon accustom yourself to the notion, Evans." Stephen's grim tone suggested that he himself was valiantly striving to accept his wretched fate. He glanced around the vestibule. "Where is Lucy?"

"Lucy?" the butler echoed blankly. His eyes were still wide with shock, and he was clutching the pier table for support.

"My sister," Stephen prompted wryly.

Cecily had forgotten until that moment that Stephen had a sister. Well, a half sister, she amended, for Lucy Chandler was the daughter of his father's second wife. Cecily had not yet been born when the first viscountess died and the elder Lord Trowbridge took another bride, but Aunt Esther had given her to understand that his lordship's interval of mourning had been appallingly brief.

"Six months." Lady Osborne addressed the subject often and invariably with a wounded sniff. "My dear sister had been in her grave only six months when *he* remarried." Anyone who offended Aunt Esther was doomed to permanent anonymity: she would never again refer to him or her by name.

At any rate, while Lady Osborne's dear sister had delivered two strapping sons, "his" second wife had produced only one daughter. And she, according to Aunt Esther, was certainly no prize. No, the girl was prodigious homely and extremely reclusive, and it was even rumored she might be a trifle mad. In view of her aunt's violent prejudice against "him" and the second Lady Trowbridge, Cecily flavored this information with a generous grain of salt.

"Ah, yes. Miss Lucy." Evans nodded, and the movement apparently settled his wits sufficiently to enable him to stand unaided. He released his grip on the pier table and drew himself up. "Miss Lucy is in her bedchamber, sir. However, as she is working, she desired me not to disturb her till dinner."

"Working?" Cecily gasped. The daughter of a viscount would not be employed unless she had fallen on very hard times indeed, and Cecily wondered if Stephen—far from being wealthy—was so poor he could not support his own sister. "Working in what capacity, Evans?"

"She writes novels, ma'am."

"She is an author!" Cecily clapped her hands with mingled relief and fascination. "Like Miss Austen."

"Hardly like Miss Austen," Stephen said dryly. "None of Lucy's works has yet been published. And until such time as Murray and his various competitors simultaneously lose their senses, none will be. I have had the dubious honor of reading Lucy's manuscripts, and they are . . . indescribable. Precisely the sort of swill one would expect Lucy to write. She lives in a world of dreams . . ." He stopped and shook his head. "But I shall say no more; you'll meet her at dinner."

Though Cecily had neglected to count his words, she estimated that Stephen had said nearly as much in this one speech as he had during the whole two days of their journey. Perhaps, she thought optimistically, he was gradually bringing himself to forgive the debacle of their wedding night. He began issuing instructions to Evans, and Cecily was further encouraged to learn that she was to be placed in the bedchamber adjoining her husband's. She realized that his principal motivation was no doubt a wish to prevent gossip among the servants, but maybe he would eventually thaw so far as to avail himself of the connecting door. Why she welcomed this prospect, Cecily could not conceive; a few days since, she would have hoped to avoid "it" indefinitely. But whenever she remembered those moments in Stephen's arms—and she remembered them constantly—she felt the same throbbing ache she had felt then, followed by a stab of keen regret that she had driven him away. A child, he had called her, and perhaps her behavior had warranted that mocking insult—

"Cecily?" Stephen said sharply.

She started and perceived that during her reverie, a young woman had joined them in the foyer.

"This is Eliza." Stephen's voice remained sharp, and Cecily collected that her inattention had required him to repeat himself. "Eliza is Lucy's abigail, but I fancy she can attend you as well. She will show you to your room."

Evidently Eliza entertained her own dark suspicions of the woman Lord Trowbridge had so abruptly wed, for Cecily was acutely aware of the girl's eyes on her back as they ascended the stairs to the second story. They proceeded abreast along the upper corridor, Eliza casting so many curious sideward glances that at one juncture, she tripped on the edge of the Oriental runner in the center of the hallway and almost lost her footing. However, they reached the last door but one on the right side of the corridor without further incident, and the abigail opened it and nodded Cecily in ahead of her.

The bedchamber was not quite so large as her room at Osborne Hall, Cecily judged, but its furnishings were vastly more elegant. The bedstead—situated on the far wall between the windows—was topped by a great canopy which nearly brushed the ceiling and flanked by matching rosewood nightstands. The dressing table, located to Cecily's right, was also of rosewood, as were the washstand and chest of drawers on either side of it. The wardrobe and writing table, both of mahogany, occupied the wall to Cecily's left, and the connecting door to Stephen's bedchamber was positioned between them.

Cecily's eyes stole from the door back to the canopied bed, and to her considerable mortification, her cheeks began to blaze. She could not go on like this, she counseled herself sternly. She must somehow overcome her idiotish physical obsession—

"Will you be wanting a bath, ma'am?"

Cecily had altogether forgotten the abigail's presence, and she started again and whirled around.

"If you do, you'll have to hurry," Eliza continued. "It's half past six already, and dinner is to be served at half past seven. And his lordship gets all on end when people are late for dinner."

Cecily did not doubt this for an instant, but after two days on the road, she was persuaded she would fairly die without a bath. Fortunately, the tub was delivered and filled within the space of ten minutes, and by the time Cecily finished bathing, Eliza had unpacked her trunk and put everything in its proper place.

"Thank you, Eliza," she said. "As I daresay Miss Chandler needs you, you may go on—"

"Oh, no, ma'am," the abigail interposed. "No, Miss Chandler *never* needs me. So if you will tell me what you wish to wear . . ."

Cecily went to the wardrobe and peered inside, but her clothes had not improved a whit since her last inspection. In fact, hung in the splendid mahogany wardrobe, they looked rather worse than they had before, and she recollected Uncle Frederick's promise of new attire. The situation had radically changed since then, of course; if she was now to have new clothes, Stephen must be the one to pay for them. And she dismally suspected that in his present frame of mind, he would be much inclined to let her go about in rags. If, she amended grimly, he intended to let her go about at all. Perhaps he thought to keep her more or less imprisoned in the house . . .

Eliza emitted an anxious cough, and Cecily sighed. She feared her primrose gown would only serve to remind Stephen of their disastrous wedding night, and she reached into the wardrobe and withdrew her next best dress. This had naturally been styled in accordance with Miss Lane's one and only pattern, but it was slightly more outdated than even the primrose gown, for the bottom panel of the skirt, from the knees to the hem, was made of white muslin so fine as to be almost transparent. As if this deficiency were not enough, the rest of the dress was pink, generously trimmed in black: two colors which, Cecily had belatedly perceived, did not become her at all. But her few remaining evening gowns were more hideous and old-fashioned yet, and she heaved another sigh and allowed Eliza to assist her into the pink.

There was a long-case clock at the top of the stairs, and

Cecily observed, to her relief, that it was just past seven-fifteen when she started down. Given some minutes to spare, she made her way leisurely along the first-floor corridor, pausing to peer into the saloon on one side and the parlor and music room on the other. None of the rooms was as large as those in the spacious country homes she was accustomed to, but—like her bedchamber—all were handsomely furnished. Most of the pieces were in the Adam style Aunt Esther favored, and Cecily surmised that Stephen's mother had decorated the house prior to her death.

Cecily had had no chance to ascertain the plan of the ground story upon her arrival, and she now discovered that the library was situated to the left of the vestibule and the dining room to the right. She proceeded to the latter and found all in readiness for dinner: the long table—though it could surely accommodate a dozen or more—set with three places at one end, and the rest of the chairs moved against the walls. An enormous mahogany sideboard dominated the far wall of the room, and Cecily was intrigued to see a collection of portraits arrayed above it. Small portraits for the most part, their details indiscernible from where she stood, and she stepped forward and around the table for a better view.

She spotted Stephen's picture at once, and it was easy to identify his father and brother as well, for the three men looked astonishingly alike. In fact, Cecily saw as she studied the rest of the portraits, all the Chandlers looked remarkably alike. There was a great predominance of chestnut hair, streaked to some degree with gold, and though the eyes ranged from emerald to aqua to jade, they were almost invariably green. The only portraits not fitting the mold were of women, and Cecily conjectured that these were the viscountesses, whose own eyes and hair and features had been quite overwhelmed by the dominant Chandler attributes. Evidently, she reflected wryly, her children were destined to resemble Stephen. Assuming they had children, which, in the present circumstances, was monstrous unlikely—

"Cecily?"

Her name was spoken so softly that she fancied she had

imagined it, but she shortly heard a rustle of fabric behind her and spun away from the portraits.

"I may call you Cecily, may I not?"

The young woman, for such it proved to be, rushed around the end of the table and hurried across the room, her progress substantially impeded by the skirt of her gown, which was several inches too long. As the girl drew closer, Cecily observed that the dress was also far too large and of a style so outdated as to render Cecily's own wretched gown in the very height of fashion by contrast. Indeed, Cecily guessed the dress to be at least a dozen years old; and as the girl herself could not be above five and twenty, Cecily further surmised that she had inherited the gown from her mother or some other elder relative.

"I am Lucy," the young woman said breathlessly, reaching Cecily's side. "Evans told me the news, and I was so . . . so . . . But you are *beautiful!* Evans didn't tell me how beautiful you are. You look exactly like Athena."

Cecily had no notion who Athena might be, nor was she much disposed to speculate, for she discovered herself quite fascinated by Lucy Chandler. Her initial inclination was to concur in Aunt Esther's assessment that the girl was prodigious homely, but closer inspection compelled her to temper this first harsh judgment. There was no question that Lucy was a trifle too tall—perhaps as much as five feet and eight inches—and she appeared to be excessively thin for her height. However, Cecily soon decided that the thinness was illusory, an effect of the shapeless dress, for the short sleeves of the gown revealed comely, rounded arms.

Cecily gazed upward, past the long, slender neck to Lucy's face, which seemed pinched and disproportionately small. But that might be an illusion too, she realized, because Lucy had the most incredible profusion of hair—a great mane of unruly curls spilling from her temples nearly to her elbows. The hair obscured her brow and cheeks and jaws as effectively as any veil, and her eyes were largely hidden by a pair of gold-rimmed spectacles. In fact, the spectacles hid much of Lucy's nose as well, for they had slid to a point approximately halfway down it. Since Lucy made no effort to push them up, Cecily collected that they were always awkwardly perched in this location.

In short, Cecily now understood Eliza's declaration that Miss Chandler *never* required the services of an abigail, and her fascination stemmed from a tantalizing glimpse of Lucy's potential. The hair, despite its dreadful disorder, was Chandler hair, chestnut laced all through with gold; and the eyes behind the glasses were a brilliant emerald-green. Cecily suspected that—clad in a properly-fitting gown, hair stylishly coiffed, spectacles removed—her sister-in-law would be astonishingly handsome. She was beginning to conjure up a vision of the transformed Lucy when Stephen strode into the dining room.

"Lucy!" He flashed her one of his rare smiles. "I see you and Cecily have met."

"Just now," Lucy confirmed, her eyes shining through her spectacles. "I was telling Cecily how very lovely she is. I perceived at once why you were so smitten. I daresay that when you saw her again, saw her all grown up, you fell over head and ears in love and determined you couldn't live without her a moment longer."

This was so far from being the truth that Cecily was hard put to repress an hysterical laugh, and she glanced at Stephen, wondering his reaction to his sister's wild misinterpretation of the facts. Anger apparently, she observed with a stab of dismay, for his cheeks unmistakably flushed before he turned away.

"Yes, you're quite right," he muttered. "But come; sit down. I'm eager to hear what you've been at in my absence."

Evidently Lucy was equally eager to discuss her recent activities because she had scarcely picked up her soup spoon before she began to talk. "I am in Dover," she announced. "On my way to France."

On her way to France? Cecily dropped her own spoon into her bowl, splashing droplets of turtle soup all over the linen tablecloth. Good God! Lucy *was* mad, and more than just a trifle.

"Yes," Lucy continued with a sigh, "my poor heroine is on her way to France. She's the one I mentioned earlier, Cecily." Lucy's bespectacled eyes darted across the table.

"Athena, the one who looks like you. She's a spy for the Duke of Wellington, and she's on her way to France to infiltrate Napoleon's court. Little does she know that the kind gentleman who carried her trunk from her carriage to the ship is a *French* spy."

"That sounds most . . . most interesting, Lucy." Stephen choked a bit on his last spoonful of soup, hastily patted his lips with his napkin, and signaled Evans for the main course. "However, I'm somewhat confused. I thought Athena had been captured by Indians."

"No," Lucy said impatiently, "that was *Hera*." Apparently all her heroines bore the names of Greek goddesses. "Don't you remember? Hera is Athena's twin sister, but they don't *know* they are sisters because they were separated at birth by their wicked stepmother."

Cecily was at a loss to conceive how the unfortunate twins could have had a wicked stepmother "at birth," but she elected not to comment.

"Hera was sent to Canada," Lucy went on, "while Athena remained in England . . ."

She delineated the plot in excruciating detail, and Cecily was reminded of her and Stephen's wedding dinner. Lucy was filling the conversational void the Milners had filled then, and—though Cecily couldn't begin to follow Athena and Hera's extensive travels and numerous harrowing adventures—she pretended to hang raptly on Lucy's every word. To her immense relief, the end of the tale precisely coincided with the removal of the dessert plates, and she counted it a matter of scant importance that she hadn't the vaguest idea how the denouement had come about. Somehow both sisters had won the heart of a prince (of what nationalities was unclear), all four lovers had made their way to India, and there was to be a double wedding.

Lucy's eyes were bright with expectation, and Cecily cast about for an honest adjective which might also be construed as praise. "Your story is very . . . very unusual," she said at last. "Perhaps you'll allow me to read one of your books someday."

"I shan't let you read this one till it's finished, but you may have one of the others tonight. Come to my bedchamber after dinner, and I shall give it to you. Now, if you'll excuse me, I must return to work."

Cecily's "someday" certainly hadn't meant "tonight," but—as Lucy leaped to her feet—she judged any alternative preferable to being left alone with Stephen. "Wonderful!" she said shrilly. "I shall accompany you to your room." She fairly threw her napkin on the table, but as she started to struggle to her own feet, Stephen shot her a quelling look.

"Not just yet, Cecily," he said coolly. "There are matters we must discuss."

She sank back in her chair and watched with grim foreboding as Lucy cheerfully waved them farewell and bounded into the vestibule. When the tap of her footsteps had faded away, Stephen shook his head.

"I daresay you now comprehend my remarks about Lucy. As you must have perceived for yourself, she inhabits a world of dreams."

"I am sure she is quite different when she is in society," Cecily said nervously, not sure of this at all.

"I can't say yes or no to that because she has never been 'in society.' "

Stephen signaled Evans again, and the latter brought a crystal decanter from the sideboard to the table. Stephen unstopped it, filled the empty glass at his place with brandy, and replaced the stopper. Though Cecily didn't much care for brandy, she could well have used a bracing dose of spirits, but—as had been the case with the primrose gown—she was reluctant to create any similarity to their wedding night. A request for brandy would no doubt prompt Stephen to recollect the "slight excess of champagne" she had consumed then, and she bit her lip and said nothing.

"Lucy is nearly five and twenty," Stephen continued, "and she has yet to come out. Her mother died not long after Lucy's eighteenth birthday, so she was in black gloves the Season she should have been presented, and she has subsequently displayed no interest in a debut. Nor have I made any great effort to encourage her." He sighed and once more shook his head. "Perhaps I have been remiss in that regard."

"No, you're not to blame," Cecily said sincerely. "There must be some female relative who should have brought Lucy out. Does she have no aunts?"

"She . . . er . . . she does have one aunt." Stephen sounded peculiarly nervous himself, and he drowned his discomfiture in a great swallow of brandy. "But enough of Lucy; I wanted to discuss *your* come-out."

"How can I have a come-out?" Cecily protested. "Much as we might both prefer it otherwise, I am now married."

She regretted her remark at once, would have snatched the words back if she could. But she couldn't, of course, and Stephen flushed again.

"My point precisely," he said frigidly. "You must wait upon Aunt Esther tomorrow morning and advise her to abandon any notion of a come-out ball. I shall order out a carriage if you like, but as she lives only a few streets distant, you'd do far better to walk."

Evidently, Cecily reflected dryly, she was never to have her magnificent coach drawn by four white horses. "Yes," she murmured aloud. "Yes, I shall go tomorrow morning." She once more started to rise.

"I have not finished, Cecily," Stephen snapped. She wilted back into her chair. "I perceive no reason you should tell Aunt Esther the circumstances of our marriage. To the contrary." This seemed to be one of his favorite phrases. "While I do not believe for a moment that she would deliberately reveal your elopement, she might inadvertently do so if she knew the truth. Fabricate a suitable tale. You shouldn't find it difficult; you're a marvelously accomplished spinner of tales. Far more talented than Lucy."

Cecily swallowed a furious retort; she would not rise to his fly. "Is that all?" she inquired politely.

"Not quite all. I collect, if this is any indication"—he waved one hand down the bodice of her hideous pink gown—"that your wardrobe is dreadfully inadequate indeed. Frederick promised you new clothes, and I shan't renege on his promise. When you see Aunt Esther tomorrow, ask her to escort you to her mantua-maker."

He didn't intend to imprison her after all, Cecily thought with a fresh flood of optimism. And perhaps, when she was rigged out in splendid new attire—

"You're to order sensibly, of course," Stephen added. "I have never conceived how a woman can pay more for a single gown than I would pay for a fine horse at Tattersall's. Be assured that I shall never consent to any such ridiculous expenditure."

Cecily was inclined to concur in his opinion because she wouldn't have traded Moonbeam for a dress encrusted neck-to-ankle with diamonds. But—whatever her private view—Stephen was "permitting" again, and she granted him a stiff nod. "I understand," she muttered.

"Then you are excused," he said.

As if she were, indeed, a child, Cecily fumed, stalking out of the dining room and up the stairs. Or a servant. Or maybe a slave. She was fairly seething with vexation by the time she reached the second floor and in no frame of mind, if ever she had been, to read one of Lucy's books. But Lucy's bedchamber was situated just at the top of the staircase, the door ajar, and as Cecily attempted to pass it, Lucy glimpsed her and called her inside.

Cecily had never before seen a room in such chaotic disarray as Lucy's, and though she owned it rather rude to do so, she gazed about in sheer amazement. Lucy's desk occupied the whole of one wall, and upon closer inspection, Cecily perceived that it was actually an ancient dining-room table, not much smaller than the one presently in use. Enormous as it was, the table was literally covered with books and papers—the former towering in precarious stacks halfway to the ceiling, the latter arranged (if they were arranged at all) in short piles and tall piles and piles of every size between. The dressing table and chest of drawers were similarly heaped, and on the washstand, the basin and pitcher formed a little island in a great sea of litter.

Cecily stepped forward, stubbed her toe against an obstacle, glanced down, and saw that the floor was nearly covered as well. In fact, it resembled nothing so much as a formal garden—a garden of books and papers rather than plants, with surprisingly neat paths laid out between the various pieces of furniture. Neat but narrow, she soon discovered, for her skirt snagged on several items of debris as she made her way to Lucy's side.

"I have selected the book I think you will most enjoy," Lucy said. To Cecily's dismay, she indicated one of the taller stacks of papers. "The heroine, Iris, is abducted by pirates and taken to Jamaica . . . But I shall let you read it for yourself."

"Thank you," Cecily murmured.

She extended her arms, and Lucy laid the manuscript in them, then clapped her hands.

"Oh, I do hope we are going to be friends, Cecily! And I fancy we are because I liked you from the moment we met. I'm so glad Stephen didn't marry Aunt Priscilla."

"Marry?" Cecily echoed sharply. "Who is Aunt Priscilla?"

"Lady Priscilla Shawcross. My mother's younger sister. They never got on—Mama and Aunt Priscilla—and I don't get on with her either. In any event, her husband, Sir Simon Shawcross, was much older than she, and he died just over a year ago. And Aunt Priscilla has had her cap set at Stephen ever since. Well, to say the truth, she was making sheep's eyes at Stephen even *before* Sir Simon died, but naturally he'd have nothing to do with a married woman."

Naturally not, Cecily agreed wryly, but Lady Shawcross had now been widowed above a year. "What happened after Sir Simon's death?" she asked aloud, not certain she really wished to know. "Did she and Stephen reach some sort of . . . of understanding?"

"I am sure Aunt Priscilla chose to think so, but I don't believe they did. And it doesn't signify, does it? Once Stephen saw you again, he conceived a hopeless *tendre,* and that was the end for Aunt Priscilla."

No, it was not, Cecily feared, suddenly recollecting Stephen's nervous reaction to the mention of Lucy's aunt. "What . . . what does she look like?" she said.

"She is quite tall, like Mama and me, and she . . . Never mind; you will soon meet her for yourself. She's coming up from Hampshire to spend the Season with us. If I remember aright, she'll arrive on Wednesday. Won't she be astonished to learn that Stephen has wed someone else!" Lucy clapped her hands again.

She would indeed, Cecily thought grimly, and she could

not suppose Lady Shawcross would judge the surprise a pleasant one. "Thank you for the book, Lucy," she said. "I shall begin reading it immediately."

Lucy nodded, and Cecily took the narrow path back to the door and continued down the corridor to her bedchamber. Evidently Eliza had been there in her absence, for the bed was turned down, and Cecily's nightgown lay atop the blanket. She removed her pink dress, donned the nightgown, crawled beneath the bedclothes, and picked up the first page of Lucy's book.

As Stephen had warned, Lucy's work was "indescribable": the sentences so long and convoluted as to be virtually incomprehensible, with approximately three adjectives for each noun and as many adverbs per verb. Cecily realized at once that she would never be able to finish the manuscript, and she began leafing through it, hoping to glean enough to persuade Lucy that she had read and adored every word. Though the plot was excessively difficult to puzzle out, she could, in fact, glean enough to ascertain that the story was absurd. Shortly after her arrival in Jamaica, Iris was ransomed from the pirates by a wealthy planter, who—as the price of his rescue—forced her to wed him . . .

So maybe it wasn't so absurd, Cecily conceded. Maybe Iris's situation was little more absurd than that of a girl compelled to marry a cousin she scarcely knew. And maybe, like Iris and her planter, she and Stephen would somehow come to live happily after.

❧ 6 ❧

Cecily stopped on the footpath in front of Aunt Esther's house, gazing at the stone facade and remembering her only prior visit. In their younger, happier days, Sir Frederick and Lady Osborne had spent every spring in town, but Cecily—despite her weeping and pleading and occasional tantrums—had been left behind. London during the Season was no suitable place for a child, Aunt Esther would say firmly, and Cecily would watch despondently as she and Uncle Frederick packed their splendid city clothes and drove merrily away, abandoning her to the rigorous mercies of Miss McNab, her fearsome Scottish governess.

Cecily was beginning to doubt she would *ever* see London when, on her twelfth birthday, Uncle Frederick and Aunt Esther announced a marvelous surprise. While Cecily must again remain in Derbyshire during the actual Season, she was to come to town as soon as the Seasonal festivities had ended and enjoy the wonders of the city for two full weeks. Cecily spent the rest of the spring in a fair frenzy of anticipation, and by the time she and Miss McNab set out in the post chaise, she was almost ill with excitement.

Even at twelve, Cecily had come to realize that reality rarely fulfills expectations, and as the coach neared the fringes of town, she steeled herself for inevitable disappointment. However, for the first time in her life—and, insofar as she could recall, the last—her visit to London was everything she had dreamed and more. Uncle Frederick and Aunt Esther took her to Westminster Abbey and St. Paul's Cathedral and Hampton Court and the Tower of London, where she was able to view the crown jewels. They took her to the opera and Covent Garden and Drury Lane, to Astley's Circus and Madame Tussaud's and a peep show in Coventry Street. Aunt Esther took her to the magnificent shops in Bond Street and Piccadilly and bought her an elegant French bonnet with a plume of ostrich feathers at the crown. When the two weeks were over, Cecily was utterly exhausted, but even as they drove back to Derbyshire, she elicited Aunt Esther's promise that she could return to the city at the end of the next Season.

But Aunt Esther had not remained in London till the end of the following Season; she had fled back to Derbyshire before the first of June, declaring she could not bear another moment in Uncle Frederick's company. By the Season after that, the Osbornes were so at odds that they elected not to go to town at all, and though they had separately visited the city from time to time in the ensuing years, they had never traveled together again.

So she had not returned to London after all, Cecily thought now, and she wondered if the house in South Audley Street had changed in the nine years since last she'd seen it or if she was simply viewing it with the critical eye of an adult. Even as a child, she'd been distressed to discover that townhouses actually *touched* one another; she had somehow assumed that city homes were nothing more than miniature country homes, surrounded by miniature parks and gardens. But she soon grew accustomed to the crowding, and by the end of her stay, she regarded the houses as small, perfect jewels, strung together to form one great glittering necklace.

Cecily counted it natural that the houses should now appear smaller than she recollected; children invariably perceived things to be larger than they truly were. But apart from their size, the neighboring homes were much as she remembered them, and she could only conclude that the Osborne jewel in the necklace had, indeed, tarnished. The stone front of the house was nearer gray than white; there were great patches of rust on the iron fence bordering the footpath; and one of the pilasters was chipped at the top, leaving a raw, gaping wound in place of the Ionic spirals which adorned its fellow columns. Cecily sighed, ascended the front steps—which, she observed, were desperately in need of sweeping—and rang the bell. She was left to wait so long that she began to suspect the bell was inoperable, but at length, the door creaked open.

"Yes?"

If Cecily had entertained any lingering doubts about Aunt Esther's reduced circumstances, they would have been resolved at once, for the woman standing on the other side of the threshold was surely the most wretched specimen of a servant she had ever encountered. In fact, Cecily would not have known her to be a woman had she not been wearing a dress: she was at least six feet in height, nearly as broad as she was tall, and her wild gray hair was cut considerably shorter than Stephen's. Added to which, she positively reeked of spirits, and Cecily waved one hand in front of her nose in a vain effort to dispel the overpowering fumes wafting toward her.

"Yes?" the woman repeated impatiently.

"I . . . I've come to see Lady Osborne," Cecily stammered. "I am her niece. Miss . . . ah . . . Lady . . ." But it wouldn't do at all to announce her marriage in this cowardly fashion. "Just tell her Cecily is here," she finished lamely.

"Umm." The housekeeper—or so Cecily presumed her to be—glanced around the vestibule, as though attempting to recollect what rooms adjoined it.

"Perhaps I could wait in the parlor," Cecily suggested, recalling that it was situated just to the left of the entry hall.

"Yes, the parlor. Yes, that would be fine." Without a further word, the housekeeper turned her back to the door, made her unsteady way across the foyer, and began lumbering up the stairs. "Lady Osborne!" she shrieked. "Your niece is here!" She rounded the landing and plodded out of sight, but her voice continued to reverberate through the vestibule. "Your niece!" For such a monstrous large woman, she had a remarkably shrill voice. "Your niece, Cynthia!"

Good God. Cecily closed the front door, judging it fortunate she was not a clever thief in disguise, and walked from the entry hall to the parlor, where she could not but notice additional symptoms of decay. The draperies, which she remembered as a vivid Chinese red, had faded to a

sickly pinkish hue, and the rod at one window was bent to
such a degree that the discolored curtains were sagging
tiredly on the Axminster carpet. The rug—like the front
steps—sorely wanted cleaning, as did the once-resplendent
Adam sofas and chairs. No, she decided upon closer inspection, a mere cleaning of the furniture would not suffice because in several cases, the upholstery had deteriorated
so far that the stuffing beneath was popping through the
holes and rents in the fabric.

Cecily sighed again and shook her head. She knew
nothing of Sir Frederick's financial situation; perhaps he
was sending Aunt Esther all he could afford. But as she
reflected on her own brief marriage, she recognized that it
would be prodigious easy for Uncle Frederick to deprive
his estranged wife of all but the minimum essentials of
existence. He need not "permit" her to hire a proper staff
or repair the house or recover the furniture—

"Cecily!"

She whirled around, but she caught only the merest
flash of a blue gown as Lady Osborne hurtled across the
room and seized her in a fervent embrace. To keep her
balance if nothing else, Cecily threw her own arms round
her aunt, and they teetered back and forth a moment in
silence.

"Cecily," Aunt Esther repeated at length. "My dear,
dear child. I have missed you dreadfully."

Cecily had not realized until that instant how very much
she had missed Aunt Esther, and she gulped down a
sudden great lump in her throat. "I . . . I have missed you
too," she managed to sniffle.

"But let me have a look at you." Lady Osborne un-
clasped her arms and stood away a bit. "How very handsome you've become! I always fancied you'd be a beauty,
but I do believe you're even lovelier than I envisioned."

Cecily wryly suspected that Aunt Esther was a trifle
prejudiced in her niece's favor, but she blushed with pleasure nonetheless and examined Lady Osborne in turn.
Aunt Esther was one of the few people Cecily knew who
was shorter than herself, barely five feet tall; and though
she had gained perhaps half a stone in the four years since
their previous meeting, she was far from being—as Sir

Frederick had conjectured—"most enormously fat." Her blond hair had been amply streaked with gray when Cecily last saw her, and she observed that the streaks were now reversed: Lady Osborne's hair was largely silver, threaded only here and there with gold. Apart from her hair, Aunt Esther did not seem to have aged at all; indeed, the new plumpness of her face had erased many of the lines Cecily recalled. And if her eyes had begun to fade, it would be impossible to tell, for Lady Osborne's eyes had always been remarkably pale—a blue-gray so light that they often appeared altogether colorless.

"You also look very well," Cecily said sincerely.

"Well?" Aunt Esther sniffed. "It is kind of you to say so, dear, but I'm sure I can't possibly look well in this . . . this rag."

She waved one hand the length of her blue dress, which was unmistakably one of Miss Lane's creations, and Cecily noted that the lace at the square neck was yellow and starting to fray. She glanced down and further observed several small holes in the skirt and one unsightly lump of thread where a larger hole had been awkwardly darned.

"As I am certain you can see for yourself," Lady Osborne continued bitterly, "*he* has not allowed me a single farthing for clothing." Cecily repressed another sigh. "Nor is it only clothing I must do without. No, he sends me so little money I can scarcely keep food upon the table. The house is falling quite apart, and I am mortified by the state of the furnishings, but does he provide me *one groat* for repairs?"

This was obviously a rhetorical question, and Cecily bit her lip and said nothing.

"No, he does not. And my servant? You have met Mrs. Fawcett. I am entirely persuaded she has been in Bedlam or Newgate at one time or another—possibly both—but she is the best I can afford with what *he* gives me. his clutchfistedness does not surprise me, of course, because he is the greatest nipcheese it has ever been my misfortune to know."

Aunt Esther paused for breath, and Cecily leaped into the breach. "Umm," she muttered. "Be that as it may, Aunt Esther, we must discuss my come-out—"

"Your come-out," Lady Osborne interposed. "That *was* a surprise. Why he should decide after all these years to sponsor your debut, I cannot imagine. You will be relieved to learn that he relented so far as to agree that I could refurbish the saloon a bit. We shall keep the parlor door closed"—she gestured vaguely toward the vestibule—"and engage some decent servants for the evening, and perhaps no one will notice the abject poverty in which I live."

Cecily cleared her throat. "That is all very well, Aunt Esther. However, there is a slight . . . ah . . . problem about my come-out—"

"I was so surprised," Lady Osborne went on, "that I should not be in the least surprised to discover that he is using your own money to finance your debut."

Inasmuch as Cecily's "own money" consisted of the five pounds per month Uncle Frederick granted her for incidentals—of which she had succeeded in saving the grandiose sum of three-and-ten—she judged this statement a trifle histrionic even for Aunt Esther. "Umm," she grunted noncommittally. "Whatever the case—"

"How is he?" Aunt Esther interjected. "I daresay he has grown most enormously fat."

Cecily choked back a laugh, a laugh so insane as to render *her* a candidate for Bedlam. "He has gained a stone or two," she sputtered aloud, "but on the whole, he is quite well."

"Yes, he would be." Lady Osborne emitted another sniff. "I doubt he has entertained a single second of remorse for his shameful behavior. I doubt he spares me a moment's thought except when he must send me a check. And that—God knows—is monstrous seldom."

"Umm," Cecily muttered again. "Well, at any rate, we must discuss—"

"I suppose he has lost all his hair," Aunt Esther said. In view of her refusal to mention "him" by name, she seemed prodigious concerned for his condition. "Which, I fancy, would be a blessing. When I left, his hair was turning orange."

"His hair *is* orange," Cecily snapped, "but he still has an abundant quantity." She regretted the need for sharpness, but she had to quell Lady Osborne's perverse interest in her estranged husband. "Uncle Frederick is very well indeed, and we must now discuss my come-out."

"Pray do forgive me, dear." Aunt Esther reached forward and patted her shoulder. "Naturally you're anxious, and I should have put your mind at ease straightaway. Let us sit down, and I shall tell you of the arrangements I've made."

Having captured her aunt's undivided attention at last, Cecily was inclined to blurt out her news without delay. However, upon reflection, she decided it would, in fact, be best if Lady Osborne were sitting when she learned of the abrupt union between her niece and nephew; and she trailed Aunt Esther to the nearest couch. Though Lady Osborne merely perched on the edge of the sofa, a clump of stuffing reared protestingly up through a tear in the upholstery beside her, and Cecily gingerly lowered herself to the opposite end of the couch.

"As I was saying, dear," Aunt Esther continued, "I have made all the arrangements for your come-out ball. The saloon furniture is being repaired even as we speak—"

"But I can't have a come-out," Cecily interrupted. "As I've been trying to explain for some minutes now, I . . ."

Lady Osborne's pale eyes had narrowed in puzzlement, and Cecily groped for the words least likely to trigger an apoplectic seizure. But there seemed no subtle way to deliver her shocking announcement, and she drew a deep breath.

"The truth of the matter is, Aunt Esther, that I am . . . am married." Her ladyship's eyes widened to great saucers. "Married to . . . to Stephen," Cecily stumbled on. "We were wed in Sheffield Friday afternoon." She belatedly recollected that she was supposed to fabricate a credible excuse for her precipitate marriage, but nothing came immediately to mind, and she sought to stall for time. "I daresay you are wondering why we wed so suddenly—"

"But I am not wondering at all!" Aunt Esther said.

"You . . . you aren't?"

"No, I can well perceive the motivation on both sides. Though you may not recall it, you had a great girlhood _tendre_ for Stephen, and I daresay it blazed up again the instant you saw him. And when he observed how handsome you'd become, he no doubt feared to expose you to the eager young bucks in town. Yes, he must surely have realized that a splendid catch such as yourself would be engaged before the Season was half over.''

Cecily was at a loss to conceive how she could possibly be termed a "splendid catch," but she was so relieved to be spared the necessity of inventing an alternate explanation that she elected not to comment. "You aren't overset then?" she said instead.

"Overset?" Lady Osborne echoed. "To the contrary, I am delighted. I've always been immensely fond of Stephen, and I'm excessively pleased he didn't fall into Priscilla Shawcross's clutches.''

"Ah, yes, Lady Shawcross." Cecily impulsively decided to pretend she knew more than she did. "I collect they had some sort of understanding.''

"Well, you collect wrong then." Aunt Esther's latest sniff was the very essence of disdain. "Priscilla followed him about like an adoring puppy, but what did she have to offer?'' Another rhetorical question. "I can barely tolerate the woman, but I must own to some sympathy for her predicament. Sir Simon was not a wealthy man to start, and he exhausted what little fortune he had before he died, leaving her virtually penniless. And what man will take a poor wife when he can have a rich one?''

A priggish man, Cecily thought, a man impelled by duty to snatch his skitter-brained cousin from the brink of Ruin. "And you are not overset about the ball?" she asked aloud. "About having to cancel it, I mean?''

"We can't cancel the assembly." Lady Osborne shook her head. "The invitations were delivered days ago, and I have engaged a caterer and a florist and an orchestra. No, we cannot cancel the ball.''

"But how can we proceed with it?" Cecily protested. "There is no longer a Miss Osborne to be brought out.''

"Fortunately, the invitations do not state the purpose of the assembly. The reason being," Aunt Esther added darkly, "that printers charge for each word printed, and I was well aware that *he* would complain interminably about every farthing I spent. So we shall convert your come-out ball to a wedding reception, and no one will be the wiser.''

Cecily was initially inclined to concur in this proposal, to resurrect at least this one small portion of her dream. However, it soon occurred to her that a wedding ball might well generate speculation about her and Stephen's hasty marriage, and she feared he would be very overset indeed if she exposed them to the risk of scandal. She was at the point of suggesting they treat the assembly as nothing more than a routine social gathering when she was struck by the glimmer of an idea.

"Perhaps we could convert the ball to a come-out for someone else," she said. "Lucy Chandler."

"Lucy!" Lady Osborne gasped. "Have you not yet met her? The poor girl could only find the experience most wretchedly humiliating. She is so homely I doubt a single man would stand up with her even at her own come-out."

"She appears homely," Cecily admitted, "but I suspect there's a good deal of beauty lurking beneath the surface. Just waiting to be exposed. If her hair were properly styled, and her clothes fit—''

"If Lucy has beauty to be exposed, it will require considerable digging," Aunt Esther interposed dryly. "And as the assembly is only eight days hence, there is no time to waste."

"But you are consenting to bring her out?" Cecily pressed. "You are nearly her relative after all."

"Yes, I nearly am," Lady Osborne snapped. "As a consequence of *his* disgraceful insult to Dorothea's memory."

Dorothea was Lady Osborne's late "dear sister," and Cecily gritted her teeth, passionately wishing she had not reminded her aunt of the elder Lord Trowbridge's ancient transgression. But Aunt Esther was nodding, albeit grudgingly, and Cecily drew a small sigh of relief.

"Yes, as the assembly is already planned, I shall bring Lucy out. But I must stress that there truly is no time to waste. Madame Boudreau, my mantua-maker, has reserved tomorrow morning for you and myself. I refer to her as my mantua-maker though I have not, of course, been able to avail myself of her services for some years. Since, as I stated earlier, *he* has not allowed me a farthing for cloth-ing.'' Cecily once more gritted her teeth. ''At any rate, if Lucy wants a debut, she must accompany us to Madame Boudreau's tomorrow. I certainly shan't bring her out in one of *her* old gowns.''

Cecily was beginning to find Lady Osborne's myriad pronouns exceedingly annoying, and she judged it best to depart at once, before her patience disintegrated altogether and an ill-chosen remark undid her victory. She stood up, and Aunt Esther rose as well.

''Shall we come for you tomorrow morning then?'' Cecily inquired politely.

''You will have to come for me because I've no car-riage. One of my horses died last summer, and naturally *he* has refused to replace it.''

Cecily ground her fingernails into her palms, but eager as she was to escape, she suddenly remembered another of Stephen's orders. ''Er . . . about your mantua-maker,'' she said. ''Madame Boudreau, is it? I trust she is not exorbitantly expensive.''

''Just above the average, I should guess. Why do you ask?''

''Stephen desired me to . . . I believe the phrase he used was 'order sensibly.' He doesn't wish me to expend an excessive sum on my clothes.''

''Humph,'' Aunt Esther snorted. ''You may do as you choose, of course, but I advise you most strenuously to nip his clutchfistedness in the bud. I bitterly lament that I did not defy *him* early on.''

Uncle Frederick, Cecily translated.

''And I had far less ground to stand on than you do,'' Lady Osborne continued. ''My father wasn't wealthy ei-ther, and what little dowry money there was went to *him* when he wed Dorothea.''

The elder Lord Trowbridge, Cecily translated.

''So I came to *him*''—Sir Frederick, Cecily translated, her head starting to ache—''with almost nothing. Whereas you came to Stephen with a splendid fortune, and you certainly shouldn't permit him to dictate your every expenditure.''

''Splendid fortune?'' Cecily echoed blankly.

"You do not count twenty thousand pounds a fortune?"

"Twenty . . . thousand . . . pounds?" Cecily's lips were so stiff she could hardly force the words through.

"More or less. Twenty thousand pounds was the sum your father entrusted to him—"

"Stop it, Aunt Esther!" Cecily screeched. "You are driving me mad with your he's and him's! Am I to collect that my father left me twenty thousand pounds? Left it in trust with Uncle Frederick?"

"Precisely. And *he* . . ." Cecily cast her a withering glare, and Lady Osborne gnawed her own lip a moment. "Frederick," she said at last, and her pale eyes grew oddly soft. "Frederick," she repeated, as though the name tasted good on her tongue. "Frederick was authorized to invest the money as he saw fit, and the bequest plus interest was to pass to you on your twenty-first birthday. So the present sum might be considerably more than twenty thousand pounds or somewhat less, depending on the wisdom of Frederick's investments . . ." She stopped, and her brows knit in a frown. "But surely Frederick told you of your inheritance?"

"No," Cecily said weakly. "No, Uncle Frederick never even hinted . . ." Her voice trailed off as well.

"Well, I cannot profess to be surprised." Aunt Esther's eyes hardened again. "In my experience, misers are invariably reluctant to discuss money, and *he*—as I believe I previously mentioned—is the greatest miser I have ever known."

Cecily was almost too stunned to register her aunt's reversion to the pronoun, much less tender another objection.

"Be that as it may," Lady Osborne reiterated, "you need scarcely seek Stephen's consent for every groat you spend. Although, of course, now you're wed, your money is legally his. But if I were you, I should feel that the income from my legacy was mine to use as I wished. I should take my thousand pounds a year and fritter it quite away if I pleased."

A thousand pounds a year. Dazed as she was, Cecily comprehended the enormity of this figure, and a terrible, tantalizing question penetrated her shock. "Did . . . did Stephen know of my inheritance?" she whispered.

"Oh, I am sure he did," Aunt Esther replied. "Your uncle and I kept it a secret from you only because we didn't wish your head to be swelled while you were still a child. We planned to inform you of your legacy when you turned eighteen so you would be armored against fortune hunters when you went up to London for your come-out. Obviously," she concluded with yet another sniff, "when *he* refused to sponsor your debut at the proper time, he elected not to advise you of your inheritance either."

"But someone did tell Stephen," Cecily said dully.

"Umm." Lady Osborne frowned again. "Now I think on it, I am not absolutely certain after all. I don't recall discussing the situation with him myself. On the other hand, I don't recall *not* discussing it. And what *he* might have discussed, I couldn't possibly say."

Cecily's nascent headache had become an exquisite exercise in torture—two white-hot nails cunningly driven into either temple—and she nodded as best she could and backed unsteadily toward the parlor door. "Very well, Aunt Esther," she mumbled. "I shall come by for you tomorrow morning with or without Lucy. At what time should I arrive?"

"Our appointment is at ten. However, as I indicated earlier, it has been so many years since I had occasion to travel to Leicester Square that I've no notion how long the drive might take."

After some debate, they agreed that Lady Osborne was to be fetched at a quarter before ten, and Cecily managed another nod and staggered into the vestibule. To her utter lack of astonishment, Mrs. Fawcett was nowhere in sight, and she let herself out the front door and stumbled down the steps. She tried to hurry along the footpath, but she was so dizzy that she was compelled to stop from time to time and lean against the nearest iron fence.

Twenty thousand pounds! The figure pounded in her already-throbbing head like a great drum. She had twenty thousand pounds. No, she amended, *Stephen* now had twenty thousand pounds. And if he knew that, knew of her fortune, his "honorable course" became something else entirely. If he knew, he must fairly have danced with joy when Dennis accepted a mere five hundred pounds to give her up. What was five hundred pounds when one stood to gain twenty thousand? Stephen would recover his investment in half a year . . .

Cecily reached the house in Brook Street at last and slipped through the front door as quietly as she could, wanting time to ponder the situation before she was obliged to speak with Stephen. Perhaps—if she reconstructed every word he had said to her the day of their wedding—she could determine whether he'd known of her inheritance or not. She crept toward the staircase, scarcely daring to breathe, but Stephen's voice lashed out to stop her.

"Is that you, Cecily?"

The voice emanated from the library, and before she could pretend she hadn't heard it and flee on up the stairs, Stephen himself loomed up in the entry.

"Ah, it *is* you. I'm eager to learn the outcome of your conversation with Aunt Esther. Will you come in?"

Cecily would much have preferred to decline this invitation—or command as the case might be—but even as she hesitated, Evans emerged from the dining room, granting her a dubious nod as he strode toward the staircase. The vestibule was hardly a suitable place for private discussion, she owned, and she stepped reluctantly past Stephen and into the library.

Like the rest of the house, the library was handsomely furnished, but Cecily's eyes flew past the sofas and chairs to the kidney-shaped Sheraton writing table situated next to the fireplace. It was clear that Stephen had been working at the desk: there were several open ledgers on the surface, and the chair was pulled haphazardly away from the table, as though he had bounded up at the first sound from the front door. So what had he been working on? Cecily wondered. Had he been deciding how to invest the twenty thousand pounds which had so fortunately fallen into his hands? Calculating what luxuries he could afford with additional income of a thousand a year?

"Will you sit down?" Stephen indicated the shield-back chair just inside the entry.

Cecily desperately needed to sit, for she had grown most fearfully dizzy again. But she wished to abbreviate the conversation as far as possible, and she shook her head and discreetly clutched the back of the chair for support.

"About Aunt Esther then." Stephen's tone was the one she had grown to despise, the voice of frigid courtesy. *Is your sole satisfactory?* "I trust you were able to fabricate a credible explanation of our marriage."

She could readily lie, Cecily thought; she could borrow parts of Lucy's comments and parts of Lady Osborne's and create an eminently believable whole. But, perversely, his very reserve had shattered her own intention to deliberate the matter before she spoke. She had to know, and she had to know now.

"As it happened, I was not required to fabricate an explanation." She took considerable pride in the awareness that her tone was quite as frosty as his had been. "No, as soon as I told Aunt Esther of our marriage, she was kind enough to supply *me* an explanation."

"Indeed?" She was watching him very closely, and she detected an unmistakable spot of color on either cheekbone. "And what might that have been?"

"Aunt Esther's theory is that you wed me for my fortune." This was not entirely true, Cecily admitted, but it was sufficiently close to the truth that she didn't feel compelled to add it to the long list of falsehoods she had uttered in recent days. "That you fell over head and ears in love with twenty thousand pounds."

"Ah, the money."

He nodded, and Cecily entertained a notion that he was peculiarly relieved. Like a child who knew all too well that his latest prank would ultimately come to light, he need no longer dread the inevitable moment of discovery.

"You don't deny it then," she said. "You don't deny that you knew of my inheritance."

"Your inheritance."

His demeanor had turned to one of prodigious discomfort, and Cecily was again reminded of a little boy. The first rush of relief having evaporated, he would now seek to justify his horrid behavior, shift the blame to someone else.

"Frederick did . . . ah . . . allude to an inheritance," Stephen went on. "However . . ."

But evidently he could manufacture no satisfactory "however" to acquit himself of this particular crime, and in a blinding flash, Cecily perceived the other half of his sin.

"You knew of my inheritance," she repeated, "and you further knew I *didn't* know. Had I known, I should have told Dennis, and he would certainly have mentioned my fortune when he demanded his . . . his bribe. He would never have settled for five hundred pounds if he believed himself at the point of wedding twenty thousand."

Her eyes raked his face again, but he said nothing.

"So another man *would* have had me, wouldn't he?" she hissed. "Indeed, I daresay there are a hundred men, a thousand men—a thousand *respectable* men—who would have overlooked my elopement for twenty thousand pounds."

"There are not a thousand respectable men in the British Empire, Cecily," Stephen said wryly.

"I'm sure you wouldn't think so," she snapped, "but you are begging my point. Which I quite understand because I should dissemble as well were I in your position. My point is that you tricked me into wedding you before I could come to London and talk to Aunt Esther and learn of my inheritance. And as a result of your deception, you now have twenty thousand pounds, and I have nothing."

"I'm excessively sorry for your opinion that you've been left with nothing," he said stiffly. "The fact is that I did not wed you for your fortune. However, as I doubt you are much interested in facts, I shan't belabor the subject."

"That is an excellent idea." Cecily negotiated a glacial smile, a smile so cold she fancied she felt slivers of ice at the corners of her mouth. "I've no desire to belabor the subject either. I shall only reiterate that in my view, you are in possession of twenty thousand pounds that rightfully belong to me, and I won't allow you to go on playing the martyr—acting as though you've rescued me from a fate worse than death—and ordering me about like a servant . . ."

She ran out of breath and gulped a new supply of air into her lungs.

"Aunt Esther and I are going to her mantua-maker tomorrow morning," she concluded. "And if I wish, I shall . . . shall . . ." She recollected the image she had conjured up the night before. "If I wish, I shall order a dress encrusted neck-to-ankle with diamonds."

"You wouldn't look at all well in a gown of diamonds," Stephen said. "Emeralds maybe."

Was he jesting? No, he couldn't possibly be jesting, and Cecily clenched her hands and drew herself up. "Perhaps I *shall* order a gown of emeralds," she informed him with great dignity. "At any rate, I shall need a carriage at half past nine, and I trust you'll see I have one."

She spun around and stalked out of the library, and she could have sworn she heard a chuckle behind her. But that was impossible too, of course; Stephen never laughed. She raced up the stairs, the day's events filling her head from one aching temple to the other. Indeed, her brain was so very crowded that she sensed some critical thought lurking just at the fringes of her consciousness, unable to gain entry. Try as she might, she could not make room for it; she had only a nagging inkling that there was a hole somewhere, a missing link in the chain that led from Stephen's knowledge of her fortune to his noble offer to "save" her from the consequences of her elopement.

When Cecily reached her bedchamber, she stretched out on the counterpane and stared at the ceiling for a long time. But the more she attempted to entice the thought from its lair, the farther it retreated into the darkness, and eventually she gave up. It would come to her, she decided. Sooner or later, the missing link would come to her.

7

Late in the afternoon, Eliza came to advise Cecily that his lordship would be dining at his club that evening.

"He trusts you will have no objection if your own dinner is brought to your room," the abigail added.

He was ordering her about again, if indirectly, and Cecily wondered his reaction if she sent Eliza speeding back with word that Lady Trowbridge demanded to be served in the dining room. But she had created enough havoc for one day, she judged, and she managed a polite nod. "Yes, that will be fine," she muttered.

"Very good. Then I shall bring your dinner at half past six."

Eliza bobbed a curtsy and backed into the corridor, and Cecily remembered the project she had discussed with Aunt Esther.

"And Miss Chandler?" she said. "Does she dine in her room as well when his lordship is from home?"

"Yes, ma'am, she does."

"Then will you ask her if we might eat together?"

"Yes, ma'am, I shall." Eliza stepped on into the hall, then turned back. "Er . . . I do hope you thought to eat in here, ma'am. It's very hard to find a place for even *one* tray in Miss Chandler's bedchamber."

"I'm sure it is," Cecily agreed dryly. In fact, she could only assume that Lucy customarily dined on her bed, which—according to Cecily's recollection—was the sole item of furniture not heaped half to the ceiling with debris. "Yes, invite Miss Chandler to join me here, Eliza, and bring our trays at half past six."

In the event, Lucy appeared some five minutes before the trays, and as she stumbled across the threshold, Cecily was compelled to own to some hesitation about the wisdom of a come-out. Evidently, she reflected grimly, her sister-in-law had taken extraordinary pains with her so-called toilette the night before, for, if possible, she looked rather worse this evening than she had then. Her gown was certainly older and longer and looser than the one she had previously worn, and—though it was difficult to tell—Cecily suspected she had put neither comb nor brush to her hair in the intervening four and twenty hours. Added to which, Lucy's spectacles were so smudged as to render it excessively doubtful that she could see through them at all, her fingers were stained with ink, and there was also a great spot of ink on her right cheek. But as Aunt Esther had pointed out, Lucy's transformation would require considerable digging, and Cecily essayed a bright smile and squared her shoulders with determination.

"I'm so glad you suggested we eat together, Cecily!" Lucy's face lit up with delight, and Cecily observed that she did have a lovely smile and excellent teeth. "That is the worst part of coming to town for the Season: I do sometimes weary of dining alone."

"Stephen is often from home then," Cecily said idly.

"Oh, nearly every night. If there is no social engagement on his calendar—which, of course, there usually is during the height of the Season—he goes to White's. His club. As he did tonight. Though I was somewhat surprised he went *tonight*—"

Lucy was interrupted by a clatter in the corridor, and Cecily beckoned Eliza through the open door. The abigail was followed by another maid Cecily had not previously encountered, and she directed them to set the trays on the dressing table and the washstand, whose surfaces she had cleared before Lucy's arrival. Inasmuch as Lucy was her guest, Cecily granted her the use of the dressing table and lowered herself into the desk chair, which she had drawn before the washstand. She unfolded her napkin and laid it in her lap, trying to overlook the circumstance that her knees were most uncomfortably jammed against the rosewood front of the washstand.

"But I shouldn't care for it if I were you," Lucy said, swirling her spoon through her mulligatawny.

"Care for what?" Cecily had quite lost the thread of the conversation.

"That Stephen went to White's tonight. I was reminded of Hestia and Prince William."

Hestia was clearly one of Lucy's heroines, and Cecily was beginning to surmise that all her heroes were princes. She must review the biographical data about Iris's planter, she counseled herself; he was probably a scion of royalty in disguise. "In what way?" she asked aloud.

"Though William was passionately in love with Hestia when they married, it took her some time to reform his behavior. Six hundred and ninety-one pages to be precise."

"Reform?" Cecily choked on her soup and coughed

frantically into her napkin, lest she strangle quite to death. "Reform *Stephen*?" she gasped at last.

"Not in *that* sense," Lucy said. "William . . . Well, I shall be frank about it: I modeled William after Stephen. Both are somewhat too inclined to tipple and gamble with their male friends. Apart from that, they are . . . are . . ."

Her voice trailed off, as if she had already said too much, and Cecily hesitated. Much as Lucy professed to like her new sister-in-law, her primary loyalty must inevitably remain with Stephen; she could not be expected to take Cecily's part in any dispute between them. But there was no dispute at issue here, Cecily reasoned, and Lucy might be able to shed some light on her brother's mysterious behavior.

"Stephen and William are a both a trifle priggish?" she prompted.

"You've noticed then." Lucy's nod was one of great relief. "About Stephen, I mean; you haven't yet met William. I shall give you that book when you've finished the one you're reading. How far have you got, by the by?"

"To the point where . . . where . . ." Cecily desperately racked her brain, but she could not recall the planter's name. "To the point where *he*"—she chose to borrow from Aunt Esther—"has gone down to the wharf to meet the pirate ship. But let us return to Stephen," she continued hastily. "Did he change, or was that my imagination? I was only a child at the time."

"I was scarcely more than a child myself." Lucy flashed a wry grin, and Cecily observed that her cheeks—or what could be seen of them through the veil of hair—dimpled very prettily when she smiled. "I am not so much older than you, Cecily, but I recall very well when Stephen changed. It was just after Walter died."

Walter was Stephen's elder brother, whom Cecily had never known, and it belatedly occurred to her that Lucy must have felt his passing very hard. "I'm sorry," she murmured. "I daresay you were immensely grieved by Walter's death."

"I wasn't grieved in the least," Lucy rejoined crisply. "Indeed, no one in this household was grieved. Not a single person, from the smallest footboy to Stephen himself.''

Cecily's mouth dropped open with shock, and before she could rehinge her jaws, Lucy flew on.

"Did Stephen not tell you? Well, perhaps he has had no chance. Walter didn't exactly 'die,' you see; that is a euphemism we have always employed to describe his demise. The truth is he was killed in a brawl at a gin shop in Covent Garden. And no one who knew him was in the least surprised by the circumstances of his passing, for he had devoted the whole of his adult life to the pursuit of debauchery.''

"And that is what caused Stephen to be so very proper!" Cecily said. "His brother's monstrous bad example.''

"I think not.'' Lucy shook her head, and her filthy spectacles slipped a little further down her nose. "They never got on, but Stephen was remarkably tolerant of Walter's rakeshame conduct. Indeed, he used to jest with me about it, insofar as a grown man can joke about such matters with a girl of twelve or thirteen. With *any* female, so far as that's concerned. No, it was only after Walter's death that Stephen got . . . got . . .''

"Got priggish,'' Cecily supplied. "And if it wasn't grief—and you say it wasn't—how do you account for it?''

"My opinion is that Stephen would have preferred to remain in the army. He seemed very happy there, and though he was too modest to discuss his accomplishments in any detail, I believe he was a splendid officer. I think he bitterly resented the necessity to resign his commission when Walter was killed, and I think he resents it to this day. I say that because whenever he talks about the army, there is a certain . . . a certain look in his eyes.''

Which still didn't explain Stephen's excessive propriety, Cecily thought. Years of longing for his abbreviated military career might render him restless or generally out of spirits, but she could perceive no possible connection between the loss of his commission and his sudden, permanent conversion into an odious prig. Well, he wasn't always odious, she conceded, and perhaps there was even hope for his priggishness. He hadn't seemed priggish at all on their wedding night, when his mouth was fastened to hers and his hands were moving over her body. Not until the wretched moment he had discovered her barefoot—

"Do you fancy I am right?"

Lucy shattered Cecily's reverie, and she realized, with a familiar flood of mortification, that her cheeks were blazing. She busied herself with her mutton before Lucy could adjust her grimy spectacles sufficiently to notice what must surely be a horrifying blush.

"You . . . you may very well be right," she stammered. "But we have talked enough of Stephen. I wished to speak with you about another matter. Were you aware that Aunt Esther was planning a ball for my come-out?"

"Oh, yes."

Lucy bobbed her head again, and Cecily briefly feared her glasses would slide altogether off and tumble into her plate. But she shoved them up at last—though only to the middle of her nose—and went on.

"Yes, Stephen mentioned that you had gone to visit Lady Osborne this morning to advise her to cancel her plans for the assembly. I hope she wasn't unduly disappointed."

"As it happened, there was no cause for disappointment because plans for the ball have proceeded too far to allow a cancellation. So . . ."

Cecily stopped, casting about for the right, careful words in which to couch her proposal. But—as had been the case when she was obliged to inform Lady Osborne of her marriage—there seemed no subtle way to broach the subject, and she drew a deep breath.

"So, after some discussion, Aunt Esther and I agreed that the assembly should be a come-out for *you*."

Cecily sat back in her chair, discreetly massaging her wounded knees, and awaited Lucy's reaction. Which, to her considerable surprise, took the form of a merry peal of laughter.

"A debut for *me*?" Lucy sputtered at length. "Good God, Cecily; I am four and twenty."

"There was a girl in Uncle Frederick's day who did not come out till she was four and twenty." Cecily could see no harm in aging the heroine of Sir Frederick's story by a mere year. "And she ultimately wed a *duke*."

"I'm not certain I should be at all happy wed to a duke." Lucy was suddenly serious.

"Then you needn't marry one." Cecily sat forward again and propped her elbows on the washstand, trying not to wince as her knees slammed back against the front. "You needn't marry *anyone*, Lucy; not unless you truly want to." Brave words indeed from a woman who had herself been forced into wedlock a scant three days since. "But would you not prefer . . ."

She stopped once more to grope for the proper words. "You told me only a few minutes ago that you're lonely here in town. Would you not prefer to have your own circle of friends? Your own social calendar? Yes, even your own *partis*; you could readily reject them if you chose."

"*Partis*?" This time Lucy's laugh was brittle round the edges. "Who would court me? You can't possibly understand, Cecily, because you are very handsome. Whereas I'm prodigious plain—"

"But you aren't!" Cecily protested, praying that "considerable digging" would, in fact, expose the beauty she'd envisioned. "If you had proper clothes, and your hair was . . . er . . . trimmed a bit . . . Oh, do give it a chance, Lucy. At least consent to go with Aunt Esther and me to her mantua-maker. Madame Boudreau has reserved all of tomorrow morning just for us."

"And that is precisely the problem," Lucy said. "Tomorrow morning would be only the beginning. There would be fittings after that and an appointment with the *coiffeur* and the preparations for the ball. And then, from courtesy if nothing else, I should no doubt be invited to other people's assemblies and parties. In short, I should be occupied the whole of the Season, and in all that time, I'd have no opportunity to work."

Cecily perceived at once that this was Lucy's principal objection to a come-out and one that must be addressed with great delicacy. "Have you ever paused to consider why your work is so important to you?" she said gently.

"Is it not because your books enable you to escape into a world of dreams?"

The eyes behind the spectacles narrowed, but Lucy said nothing.

"And if that is the case," Cecily went on, "do you not realize that you've no notion what you're escaping *from*? You say you wouldn't wish to wed a duke, but you can't possibly know that because you've never met a duke. Indeed, you have no conception of reality at all, for you've always hidden from the world as it really is. And is that not rather . . . rather cowardly?"

Lucy dropped her eyes and gazed at her hands, offering no clue to her emotions. Cecily could not guess whether she was chastened or vexed, tending toward agreement or opposition, and she plunged ahead.

"Give it a chance, Lucy," she pleaded again. "Make yourself look as well as you can and allow Aunt Esther to bring you out, and I shall ask nothing more. If you decide when the Season is over that you're truly happier in your world of dreams, I shall accept your decision with never another word. Will you do it?"

"Will you help me?" Lucy whispered.

"Of course I shall help you. I'll be with you every second."

"Then . . . then I shall do it."

"Excellent!" Cecily leaped to her feet, repressing a moan as her knees scraped the front of the washstand. "We must leave tomorrow morning at half past nine . . ." She suddenly recollected a circumstance she had not previously considered, and she bit her lip. "I do trust Stephen will not object," she said nervously. "To paying for your wardrobe, I mean."

"Stephen will not have to pay for my clothes." Lucy shook her head and rose as well. "My father left me a substantial legacy. As yours did you."

"Stephen told you of my inheritance?" Cecily said sharply. Lucy nodded. "When . . . when was that?"

"The first time your come-out was discussed, which must have been the year you turned eighteen. I remarked that your situation put me in mind of Aphrodite, who was also an impoverished orphan. Fortunately, she won the heart of Prince Arthur—''

"But Stephen?" Cecily interrupted impatiently. "What did he say?"

"He said your situation was not in the least like Aphrodite's because your father had left you quite well-fixed."

"Did he speak of it again?" Cecily pressed. "Has he mentioned my legacy recently?"

"Not that I recall." Lucy once more shook her head. "At any rate, since Stephen needn't pay for my clothes, I should like my come-out to be a surprise for him. Though he's never pinched at me to make my debut, I believe he's always hoped I would, and I . . . Well, I should simply like it to be a surprise. Will you keep the secret?"

Cecily agreed to this condition, and Lucy departed shortly thereafter, promising to be ready at half past nine the next morning. Cecily closed the door behind her and reviewed the final part of their conversation, but she shortly recognized that Lucy had only clouded the issue of her fortune. Stephen had remembered her inheritance three years since— that much was certain—but was his failure to refer to it again an indication that it had slipped his mind? Slipped his mind sufficiently, at least, that he honestly hadn't considered the ramifications of her money when he spoke with Dennis? When he offered for her hand?

Cecily sighed, for there was no way to be sure. And, consequently, no point in continuing to tease herself with speculation. No, she would put her legacy entirely out of her thoughts and concentrate on Lucy's come-out.

By half past ten the following morning—though she would not have thought such a thing to be possible—Cecily was beginning to entertain considerable nostalgia for Miss Lane's modest establishment in Buxton. To begin with, Madame Boudreau's shop was positively forbidding in its splendor: one could scarcely walk from the front to the rear without brushing against a tall cheval glass or tripping over an elegant gilt chair. Safely seated in one of the chairs, the client was further intimidated by the sheer size of Madame's stylebook, which contained dozens of magazine clippings in addition to the mantua-maker's own drawings. To make matters worse, the styles soon came to look alike; it became increasingly difficult to spot the extra rouleau or the slender bit of lace trim that distinguished this particular gown from the last. It was especially hard to differentiate between the evening dresses because they all featured corsages cut shockingly low in the front. Cecily had an uneasy suspicion that Stephen would not much approve such a bold display of bare flesh, and she repressed an inclination to ask Madame Boudreau if she didn't perhaps have some patterns dating from 1810 or so, with high, square necks.

"These won't do at all, Madame Boudreau." Aunt Esther shook her head, and Cecily drew a small sigh of relief. "For Miss Chandler, that is. She is making her come-out this year, and she will require something far more modest. Surely you have a stylebook expressly designed for your younger clientele."

"But I am not young, Lady Osborne." Lucy had been studying the clippings and drawings with far more interest than Cecily had dared to hope for, and she now glanced up and gave Aunt Esther her lovely dimpled smile. "I am nearly five and twenty. And in the unlikely event you've failed to notice, I am well above five and a half feet in height. I don't believe I should look at all well in a demure little gown of white muslin, do you?"

"I . . . ah . . ."

From the moment Jordan had assisted her into the barouche that morning, Aunt Esther had been studying Lucy— sometimes surreptitiously, more often with an undisguised stare. At the outset, or so Cecily fancied, her pale eyes had been bitter with the recollection that this was the daughter of the hated *her* who had so precipitately supplanted her "dear sister" in the late Lord Trowbridge's affections. But her gaze had subsequently turned to one of frank appraisal, and evidently she had at last reached a judgment, for she answered Lucy's smile with a slight smile of her own.

"I daresay you're right, dear. And if you've no objection, I should really prefer you to call me Aunt Esther. We are nearly relatives after all."

Cecily gulped down a triumphant giggle, and during the

ensuing hour, the three of them each chose some dozen garments from Madame Boudreau's enormous stylebook. Cecily remained excessively nervous about the evening gowns, but inasmuch as neither Lucy nor Lady Osborne appeared a trifle daunted by their daring design, she swallowed her doubts and selected several dresses cut so low she feared she would spill right out of them. Had she anything to spill, she amended; she could not but note that Madame carefully remeasured her bosom before recording the figure in her order book.

It required another two hours to bear Madame Boudreau's measurements to the linendraper across the street, purchase the fabrics for their garments, and deliver the materials back to Madame, who advised them that—after fittings on Thursday and again on Saturday—their ball gowns and dresses would be finished Tuesday afternoon. Cecily cast a wary glance at Lucy as the mantua-maker described this hectic schedule, but her sister-in-law was nodding with astonishing enthusiasm. Nor did she betray any sign of impatience when Aunt Esther insisted they must now launch their quest for headdresses and shoes and the numerous other accessories required to complete their wardrobes.

Their shopping was not finished until almost five o'clock, at which juncture Lady Osborne pronounced herself well-satisfied with their endeavor. Except for the circumstance that their gowns would not be ready till Tuesday.

"That is the completion date I initially specified," she admitted, "as that is the day of our assembly. However, I have since been invited to Lady Crandon's ball, which is to be held the night after next." She scowled with vexation that the honor of conducting the first major assembly of the Season had been so rudely snatched away. "Well, we shall simply decline to attend; we certainly shan't appear at Lady Crandon's in rags." Aunt Esther's eyes darted from her own dress to Cecily's, then lingered for a long, appalled moment on Lucy's, which was in rather worse condition than the gowns of the scullery maids at Osborne Hall. "I assure you we shall miss very little, for Lady Crandon's parties are invariably dull in the extreme."

Cecily had forgotten Lady Osborne's annoying habit of issuing commands in an oblique fashion that nevertheless permitted no debate: *we* shall decline to attend; *we* shall miss very little. In the present instance, however, she was compelled to concur in Aunt Esther's opinion, and she stifled a sigh of irritation and bobbed her head in agreement.

"That leaves only the matter of the *coiffeur*," Lady Osborne said as the barouche clattered to a stop in South Audley Street. "I fancy it would be best to have our hair styled on the day of the assembly. I shall desire Monsieur Claude to come to my house first and then send him to you—"

"No, that won't do," Lucy interposed. "I failed to tell you, Aunt Esther, that I wish my come-out to be a secret from Stephen; he's to know nothing of it till the night of the ball. So if you've no objection, I shall keep my clothes here and have my hair done here, and when he arrives for the assembly, he will be *completely* surprised."

Lady Osborne declared this a splendid idea, and Jordan was directed to bear Lucy's parcels into the house along with Aunt Esther's own. When the carriage was emptied of all but Cecily's packages, Lucy announced she would walk back to Brook Street and enter by the rear door, lest Stephen realize she had accompanied Cecily to Leicester Square and perceive what she was at.

"And you are not to mention this to Lord Trowbridge," she cautioned the coachman sternly. "Not this nor any of my future excursions."

Jordan glanced suspiciously at Cecily, as though wondering what new mischief the former Miss Osborne might be plotting, but he nodded, remounted the box, and clucked the horses to a start. Cecily gave Lucy a bright smile and a cheerful wave, but as the barouche rolled toward Brook Street, she felt another flutter of uneasiness. Lucy's unexpected enthusiasm for her come-out had lent the project a frightful new dimension: what if, despite all their efforts, she could not be transformed after all? Lucy would never forgive her—Cecily would never forgive herself—if the debut proved a wretched failure. And Stephen? Cecily could scarcely bear to contemplate his fury if her meddling led to Lucy's public humiliation. "Fury" was not really an adequate word, she amended, but she feared there *was* no adequate word to describe the magnitude of his potential rage.

Cecily's head had begun to ache again by the time the carriage halted in Brook Street, and she grimly reflected that marriage seemed prodigious detrimental to her health. She could not recollect half a dozen headaches in the whole of her life before yesterday, and now, evidently, they were to be a daily occurrence. She raced up the steps and through the front door, hoping that once she removed her bonnet—

"Cecily?"

The scrape of Stephen's chair immediately followed the sound of his voice, and she clenched her hands and whirled around.

"I do wish you would not . . . not lurk about," she snapped as he appeared in the library entry. "It seems I cannot pass through the vestibule without courting the risk of an ambush."

"Would you prefer to converse in one of our bedchambers?" he asked coolly. She felt the onset of a familiar, maddening blush. "No, I thought not. Therefore—"

He was interrupted by an uncertain tap of footfalls on the front steps, and Jordan shortly staggered into the foyer, Cecily's parcels precariously balanced in his arms. As he had also elected to carry one small package—her ivory fan, Cecily believed—by clutching the string around it between his teeth, he was able only to grunt a greeting to his master before he toiled on across the entry hall and up the main staircase.

"I collect your shopping excursion was a great success," Stephen said dryly. "When am I to see your gown of emeralds?"

"Please spare me your mockery, Stephen. I'm in no humor for it, not today. I am altogether exhausted, and I have a dreadful headache."

"Are you feverish as well?"

Before she could deduce his intention, he strode to her side and laid the back of one hand against her cheek. She was quite certain she had not been feverish until that instant, but her face now seemed fearfully warm beneath his hand, and her knees grew peculiarly weak.

"No, you are not," he said gruffly. "Perhaps you'd feel better without your hat."

He began untying her bonnet ribbons, his long fingers astonishingly gentle, and Cecily found it exceedingly difficult to breathe. His eyes remained on her face, causing him to fumble a bit with the ribbons, and Cecily thought they darkened even as she watched. Though that, she owned distantly, could be merely the reflection of his coat, the moss-green frock coat he had worn the night he came to Osborne Hall. He finished with the ribbons at last and stared at her a moment more, and then, without warning, his lean jaws tightened and he dropped his eyes.

"There." He spun abruptly round. "Remove your hat and come into the library if you will. I've matters of importance to discuss with you."

He had utterly shattered the spell between them—if, indeed, there had been one—and reverted to the frosty husband who ordered her peremptorily about. Cecily fairly jerked her bonnet off and stalked after him, enraged to discover that her knees were still weak. She could bear all the other aspects of her marriage, she thought, could accept Stephen's priggishness and his coldness and even his deceit. It was only this she found intolerable: the terrible physical power he wielded. She felt it as keenly as a wound, a wound he had inflicted on their wedding night and left to fester—

"The first matter is this." Stephen was standing at the writing table, and he waved a heavy ivory envelope. "I discovered it just this morning as I was sorting through the mail that arrived in my absence. An invitation to Aunt Esther's ball."

"Yes," Cecily muttered. "Yes, I neglected to advise you yesterday that the assembly could not be canceled. However, as you must have read for yourself, the invitation makes no reference to my come-out."

"I did observe that." He inclined his head, and his hair gleamed gold in a shaft of sunlight streaming through the window. "I wished to be sure neither you nor Aunt Esther had it in mind to make the ball a wedding reception. For reasons I trust are obvious, I've no desire to draw attention to our marriage."

"No, it will not be a wedding reception," Cecily said.
"Excellent."

Stephen dropped the envelope on the desk and walked across the room. Cecily was determined not to let him weave his spell again, and she prepared to back away, but he stopped well before he reached her and cleared his throat.

"The other matter is somewhat more . . . more delicate," he said. "A guest will be arriving tomorrow to spend the Season with us. Lady Priscilla Shawcross."

His eyes searched her face, eyes now a pale green-gold, and Cecily impulsively decided to say nothing.

"Priscilla is Lucy's aunt," Stephen went on. "Her mother's younger sister."

"Ah, yes," Cecily said innocently. "You did mention that Lucy had an aunt."

"So I did. However, I believe I failed to mention that . . ." He emitted another cough, toyed with his neckcloth a moment, drew a deep breath. "What I am attempting to say is that you may hear certain . . . certain *on-dits* about Priscilla and myself, and I wanted to assure you that such rumors contain not a shred of truth. My relationship with Priscilla has always been one of perfect propriety."

What devil seized her tongue Cecily could not have said, but she was suddenly, perversely driven to lash out at him. "I quite believe that," she hissed, "for you are surely the most proper man I have ever encountered. Indeed, I daresay there is not another man in all the world who would wed his cousin merely to save her from scandal. If, in fact, that *was* your sole motive. And even if it was not—even if you were eager to lay your hands on my fortune—I doubt there is another man in the world who would take a wife and then decline to exercise his marital privileges . . ."

She stopped and bit her lip, but it was, of course, too late. Stephen's eyes had narrowed to the merest slits, slits so pale as to be nearer yellow than green.

"You gave me unmistakably to understand that the exercise of my marital privileges would require nothing less than an assault." His voice was soft, dangerously soft, so soft she could scarcely hear him. "And I gave you to understand—or so I thought—that I shall never take you by force. So if it is *marital privileges* you want, Cecily, you will have to come to me. If I have never forced myself on a woman, neither have I ever begged one's favors.''

He whirled about again, and Cecily fled blindly in the opposite direction, fled into the vestibule and up the staircase. As she raced around the first landing, there was a great crash in the library below, and she could not but wonder if she had heard the sound of her marriage splintering into a million irretrievable fragments.

℀ 8 ℀

At some point in her childhood—so long ago she could no longer remember when or why—Cecily had developed the habit of prioritizing her problems by their degree of immediacy rather than their ultimate importance. Whether this practice was good or bad she had never paused to consider, for, like most habits, she had found it impossible to break. So it was that by the following morning, she had pushed the critical matter of her disintegrating marriage to the back of her mind and begun to consider, instead, the minor but imminent complication of Lady Shawcross's arrival.

One factor to be determined was the general nature of her response to this former rival for Stephen's affections. If, indeed, Cecily amended grimly, Lady Shawcross was a *former* rival; that remained to be seen. In any event, after some debate, she decided it would be best to pretend that she had not, in fact, heard any *on-dits* of a relationship between her husband and their visitor. She would welcome Lady Shawcross into her home as if she were nothing more than Lucy's aunt, distantly related by marriage to herself and Stephen both.

That—the actual welcome—was the most urgent problem to be resolved. Aunt Esther employed one of two alternate procedures when houseguests were expected, choosing her method according to her degree of regard for the visiting party. If Lady Osborne was sincerely fond of the arriving guest or guests—Stephen, for instance—she would fairly hang out her bedchamber window until she spotted the carriage rolling up the drive, at which juncture she would race down the stairs and out of the house and throw the coach door open herself as soon as the vehicle came to a halt. This, Cecily wryly judged, would not be a suitable way for her to greet Lady Shawcross.

Aunt Esther's second procedure, the one she adopted when she didn't particularly care for her visitors (or could barely tolerate them), was considerably more restrained. Under this method, the butler admitted the guests, showed them to the drawing room, and went upstairs to advise Lady Osborne of their arrival. Sooner or later—the elapsed time now being dependent on Aunt Esther's level of hostility—she would make her way to the saloon, greet her visitors, and desire one of the servants to show them to their rooms. The specific servant selected for this task, as well as the accommodations themselves, were also influenced by Lady Osborne's opinion of the guests. Cecily well recollected an occasion when the most junior of the chambermaids had been appointed to escort a family of four up the stairs, after which climb the entire group had been packed into the very smallest of the guest bedchambers. She could not remember the precise sin which had prompted this horrifying treatment, but she did recall that the family had abbreviated their stay from four nights to one and had never again darkened the door of Osborne Hall.

But Aunt Esther's second technique wouldn't do either, Cecily decided, for it reckoned without the necessity of informing Lady Shawcross of Stephen's abrupt marriage. This was an unsavory task *someone* had to perform, and Cecily certainly didn't wish it to be her. And if she arranged to greet her ladyship in the saloon immediately after her arrival, she might well be confronted with just that circumstance.

Good day, Lady Shawcross; I am Lady Trowbridge. Oh,

you were not aware there was *a Lady Trowbridge* . . . No, it wouldn't do at all.

There was, of course, the distinct possibility that Stephen was planning to greet Lady Shawcross himself and advise her of the startling change in his marital status. Granted the opportunity, Cecily would have inquired his intentions on this head. However, she had not been granted such an opportunity because her husband had gone to White's again the night before.

Cecily ground her fingernails into her palms, then drew a deep, steadying breath. Lacking knowledge of Stephen's plans, her safest course by far was to avoid greeting Lady Shawcross at all. At best, she would interrupt a difficult conversation between Stephen and his erstwhile admirer; at worst, she would be compelled to announce the news of their marriage herself. No, it was surely preferable to meet her ladyship at dinner, after her initial shock had subsided. Cecily would sail graciously into the dining room as though nothing whatever were amiss . . .

As the day progressed, Cecily remained firm in her determination not to acknowledge Lady Shawcross's arrival, but she found herself peering with increasing frequency out her bedchamber window, attempting to calculate the precise time her ladyship could be expected to appear. Since Lucy had mentioned only that Lady Shawcross would be coming from Hampshire, the calculation was dreadfully imprecise. If her ladyship was traveling from the coast—Bournemouth, say—the journey was likely to require twelve hours or more. On the other hand, if she had left from the eastern part of the county, near Farnborough or Aldershot, she could readily reach London in half a day. Nor did Cecily have any notion of Lady Shawcross's personal habits. If she was inclined to rise early, she might be in Brook Street before noon; if she preferred to sleep till midday, her arrival could be delayed until well after midnight.

At three o'clock—utterly exhausted by her constant dashes to the window—Cecily drew her desk chair as close to the marble sill as she could, sat down, tweaked the draperies discreetly apart, and undertook an uninterrupted surveillance of the street below. Her vigil was rewarded approxi-

mately half an hour later by the sight of a post chaise
trotting along Brook Street from the direction of Grosvenor
Square. When the coach halted in front of the house,
Cecily wriggled to the very edge of the chair and propped
her elbows on the sill in order to obtain a better view.

Cecily's first observation was that if Lady Shawcross
was, indeed, penniless, she disguised her poverty prodigious well. Not only had she eschewed public transport in
favor of a post chaise, she had hired a chaise-and-four
rather than a chaise-and-pair. Furthermore, the roof of the
coach was so heaped with luggage that Cecily was at a loss
to comprehend why it had not caved in long since or—at
the very least—why her ladyship's multitudinous trunks
and cases had not fallen off and been scattered the length
and breadth of Hampshire. Nor, it shortly proved, was all
of Lady Shawcross's baggage perilously secured to the top
of the carriage. As Cecily watched, the two postilions
dismounted and opened either door of the coach, and the
one on the near side of the carriage began withdrawing still
more cases from the interior of the vehicle.

Perversely fascinated by this immense array of luggage,
Cecily undertook to count the pieces, and just as she
reached an even dozen Lady Shawcross herself appeared
on the scene. Cecily leaped out of her chair so hastily that
it toppled over behind her, but even from her improved
perspective, she could discern very little. Lucy had remarked that her ladyship was tall, and this did appear to be
the case, for she fairly towered over the smaller of the
postboys and was not much, if any, shorter than the other.
Though her excessive height might be an illusion, Cecily
owned, because Lady Shawcross was wearing a black
crepe bonnet so high that its elaborate crown must surely
add nearly half a foot to her natural stature.

Unfortunately, the ruffled brim of her ladyship's hat,
which protruded several inches beyond the standing collar
of her carriage dress, also served to hide her face and hair,
and Cecily's eyes drifted downward. But Lady Shawcross's
dress, which was black as well and looked to be of
bombazine, was cut very full and had sleeves extending
almost to the knuckles, rendering even the most cursory
evaluation of her form extremely difficult. It was only

possible to ascertain that Lady Shawcross was not inordi-
nately heavy and that—based on the clippings and drawings in Madame Boudreau's stylebook—her ensemble was
in the very height of fashion. Indeed, Cecily judged it
quite likely that her ladyship had not worn her carriage
dress until this very day.

After some discussion with the postilions, Lady Shawcross
hurried across the footpath and soon escaped Cecily's
limited field of vision. She watched a few seconds more as
the postboys bore the first pieces of her ladyship's volumi-
nous baggage toward the house, then sighed and left the
window, plucking up the desk chair and returning it to its
proper place as she passed the writing table. Her long
hours of speculation and observation had gone virtually for
naught, she reflected dismally. She had succeeded only in
learning that Lady Shawcross possessed an enormous wardrobe, much of which was probably new, and for the first
time, she shared Aunt Esther's regret that their own splendid new attire would not be finished for a week.

But the bitter reality was that her new clothes were *not*
yet ready, and Cecily embarked on a painstaking analysis
of the garments she actually had. At length, she concluded
that her primrose gown remained by far the best of the lot,
and she cast about for some means to cloud Stephen's
memory of its unhappy association with their wedding.
Her eyes darted round the room as she puzzled through
this dilemma, and eventually she registered the numerous
boxes Jordan had delivered to her bedchamber the day
before. She dug through them until she located the yellow
Kent toque which perfectly matched the most daring of the
evening dresses she had ordered.

The headdress did not exactly match her ancient primrose gown, she conceded, and it was far too formal for a
quiet family dinner. But when she donned the toque and
the dress together, she thought the effect vastly preferable
to greeting Lady Shawcross in "rags"; and she spent the
last hour before dinner carefully tugging her curls out from
beneath the headdress and arranging them about her face.

Cecily's greatest remaining fear was that Stephen and
Lucy would be late for dinner, leaving her to confront
Lady Shawcross alone, so she was immensely relieved

when she approached the dining room to hear the sound of voices within. A voice, she amended, and as she did not recognize it, she assumed it was that of her ladyship, who was apparently relating a lengthy anecdote to her companions. Cecily stopped at the edge of the archway and peered cautiously into the room.

Lucy and Lady Shawcross occupied adjacent places on the far side of the table, and Cecily's eyes flew at once to the latter. Inasmuch as her ladyship was seated, it was possible to determine the dimensions of her form only from the waist upward, and these dimensions were generous in the extreme. Indeed, Cecily feared that if Lady Shawcross were to draw herself up too quickly, she *would* spill out of her dress, which was cut so very low in the front that it bordered on the indecent. However, there seemed little likelihood of any such untoward incident, for her ladyship's forearms were crossed in front of her on the table, and she was leaning so far forward that her ample bosom had come to rest atop her silverware.

Cecily glanced up and saw, with a stab of dismay, that Lady Shawcross looked precisely the way she herself had always wished to look. Her hair, which was uncovered except for a narrow band, was blond, the color of wheat; and her eyes were so dark a blue as to verge on violet. Cecily initially took some dim comfort in the observation that her ladyship's complexion was almost too fair—lacking any trace of color even at the cheekbones—but her budding satisfaction died with the further observation that Lady Shawcross had the perfect heart-shaped face, the aquiline nose, the tiny mouth of the models in *Ackermann's Repository*. As if to heap insult on injury, her ladyship smiled at the conclusion of her story, and Cecily noticed that her teeth were quite flawless.

"But this must be Cecily." Lady Shawcross flashed another smile. "There; lurking at the door. Do come in, my dear. I promise not to bite you."

Cecily flushed with mortification and stepped on into the room, and Evans hurried forward to assist her into her chair. When she was seated, she glanced again across the table and saw that her ladyship had somehow straightened without falling out of her gown. Her shoulders now rested against the back of her chair—exposing an astonishing expanse of smooth bare flesh—and her violet eyes were narrowed in undisguised appraisal.

"This is Lady Shawcross," Stephen said gratuitously. "Lucy's Aunt Priscilla."

"Must you, Stephen?" her ladyship protested prettily. "You create the impression that I'm a doddering old woman. When, in truth, I'm but four years older than Lucy."

"Six years older than I," Lucy corrected.

"Six years then," Lady Shawcross snapped.

Cecily was pleased to note that her irritated scowl produced a sunburst of tiny lines around either eye. "I'm very happy to meet you," she murmured aloud.

"She is adorable, Stephen!" Lady Shawcross transferred her eyes to the head of the table and clapped her hands with delight. "I well understand why you were so enchanted." She might have been remarking on a stray puppy the viscount had glimpsed beside the road and impulsively elected to adopt. "And I am wild about your gown, dear." Her eyes returned to Cecily. "Wherever did you have it made? *My* mantua-maker certainly had no such style to offer."

"I . . . it was made in Derbyshire," Cecily mumbled.

"And *on dit* there is no sense of fashion in the Midlands." Lady Shawcross clicked her tongue against her perfect teeth and shook her blond curls in disbelief. "Speaking of fashion"—the eyes darted back to Stephen—"you will never guess what Lady Worden has done. She has bought herself a *high-flier phaeton*, and you know as well as I that she cannot be a day under seventy years of age. Be that as it may, she races about the town as if the devil himself were behind her and has reduced the local populace to a state of abject terror. Lady Ramsey is fairly beside herself with envy, of course, and has begun to mutter that she may purchase a phaeton as well. And I should wager my last groat that *she* is nearer eighty than seventy . . ."

Lady Shawcross continued in this vein—spinning tale upon witty tale of her and Stephen's Hampshire neighbors—until Cecily's mind could no longer absorb the fusillade of unfamiliar names. Which, she grimly suspected, was precisely the point of the exercise: her ladyship wished to remind Stephen, as well as Cecily herself, that the new Lady Trowbridge was a rank intruder. But her endless commentary did have the advantage of sparing Cecily the requirement to make any conversation whatever, and long before the lemon tart was served, she had ceased altogether to listen.

"Is that correct, Cecily?"

Stephen's voice jarred her from her reverie, and when she looked up, she found everyone gazing expectantly at her.

"I . . . I'm afraid I wasn't attending," she stammered.

"We were discussing Lady Crandon's ball," Lady Shawcross said. "The assembly tomorrow night. When I mentioned it to Lucy earlier in the day, she indicated that you have decided not to go."

"No," Cecily murmured.

"Then I trust you will not object if I borrow Stephen for the evening. Lady Crandon's balls are excessively dull, and I should hate to go alone."

It was on the tip of Cecily's tongue to agree to this excursion, but she suddenly discovered that she objected very much indeed to Lady Shawcross's casual appropriation of her husband. "I fear you misunderstood," she blurted out. "I intended to convey that, no, I have not decided not to go to the ball."

Her sentence contained so many negatives that it made scant sense even to her, and, not surprisingly, Lady Shawcross frowned in puzzlement.

"What I mean," Cecily continued doggedly, "is that I told Lucy I was *considering* not attending the assembly." She cast a piercing stare across the table, silently begging her sister-in-law not to contradict her, and perceived a slight twitch at the corners of Lucy's mouth. "And now that I *have* considered it, I have decided I shall go after all."

"How wonderful," Lady Shawcross cooed. "I shouldn't have wanted you to miss the very first ball of the Season."

She sketched a pleasant smile, but her eyes were as hard and cold as two glittering sapphires, and Cecily narrowly repressed a little smirk of triumph.

*   *   *

By half past eight the following evening, Cecily's triumph had turned to bitter regret for the cockleheaded foolishness of her decision to attend Lady Crandon's assembly. Just what had she fancied she would wear? she wondered, studying her reflection in the mirror above the dressing table. Had she expected to open the mahogany wardrobe and find it magically stuffed with her new clothes? In fact, she had returned to Madame Boudreau's for her initial fittings only this morning, and she honestly believed that one of her new gowns—even held together with pins—might be preferable to the primrose. Which, of course, was what she had been compelled to wear, and she suspected Lady Shawcross would take keen delight in watching her rival parade about in a wretched old dress. Particularly inasmuch as it was the same wretched old dress she had worn *last* night.

Cecily sighed and adjusted the garland of white satin roses in her hair. At least her accessories were new, she thought with a brief flood of optimism. She had purchased the headdress after her fitting, and she was wearing her new white kid gloves and her new white satin slippers . . . But it really didn't signify, she admitted, for no amount of garnishment could disguise the essential hideousness of the primrose gown. She toyed briefly with the notion of summoning Eliza back and dispatching her downstairs with the news that Lady Trowbridge was gravely ill and would have to forgo the ball after all. But Lady Shawcross would see through that ruse in an instant, Cecily feared; and she squared her shoulders, snatched up her ivory fan, and strode determinedly into the corridor.

Lady Shawcross wore a garland of satin roses in her hair as well, Cecily saw when she reached the vestibule, but that was surely the only similarity between their ensembles. Her ladyship's gown, which was—if possible—cut even lower than the one she had worn the night before, was a splendid confection of pale blue net over satin, with a great flounce of blond lace around the bottom of the skirt. Cecily initially thought that if she were Lady Shawcross, she would favor a darker shade of blue, one more nearly matching her eyes. However, she soon realized that the small knots of sapphire ribbon adorning her ladyship's sleeves complemented the violet eyes far more dramatically than would an entire dress, and she was certain Lady Shawcross herself was well aware of this effect.

"Don't you look lovely!" her ladyship said kindly. "I do adore your gown. But I believe I told you so last night."

"Are we ready then?" Stephen said impatiently. "The carriage is waiting."

So immersed had she been in her inspection of Lady Shawcross that Cecily had scarcely glanced at Stephen, and she now observed that he looked excessively handsome. She had never before seen him in evening attire, and she perceived at once that his breeches and clinging silk stockings and wasp-waisted coat enhanced his lean figure wonderfully well. Indeed, she reflected despondently, Stephen and Lady Shawcross made a remarkably handsome pair: they were both tall and slender, and her blond hair seemed to emphasize the golden streaks in his. As if she had read Cecily's thoughts, her ladyship seized Stephen's arm and propelled him out the front door, leaving Cecily to trail in their wake.

Cecily had entertained a fervent hope that Lady Crandon's assembly would be so very crowded that she would be quite lost in the throng, but this proved not to be the case. Whether word of her ladyship's prodigious dull parties had spread among the *ton* or whether it was still too early in the Season to attract a large number of guests, Cecily was insufficiently experienced to say. She only registered the dismal fact that there were fewer than two dozen people in the ballroom when they arrived—all evidently so bored that they were eagerly watching the entry to see who might come to share or alleviate their common suffering. In short, Cecily was well and miserably aware that every eye in the room was upon her as Stephen presented her to their hostess.

"Your wife?" the Countess of Crandon boomed. She was an extremely elderly woman, smaller even than Aunt Esther, and Cecily was at a loss to conceive how she could summon forth such a monstrous loud voice. "I did not recollect that you were married, Lord Trowbridge."

"Oh, he wasn't," Lady Shawcross assured her. "Not until very recently. But I daresay you'll agree that however suddenly he took a bride, he chose most wisely."

Her ladyship's tone once more conjured up the image of a homeless little dog, and Cecily was genuinely relieved when neither she nor Lady Crandon patted her approvingly on the head.

"Perhaps you will serve as a good example for my nephew," Lady Crandon said. "Were you attending, Philip?" She tugged the sleeve of the man beside her, who, in fact, had not been attending the conversation but gazing into the ballroom. "Lord and Lady Trowbridge have but recently wed."

"Indeed?" He smiled at Stephen and Cecily in turn, and from the corner of her eye, Cecily could see Lady Shawcross's glower of vexation. "Pray do accept my best wishes."

"Permit me to present my nephew," Lady Crandon belatedly added. "The Earl of Ashford, my brother's heir. I fancy you are acquainted with my brother, Lord Trowbridge. The Marquis of Rotherham."

"So I am." Stephen nodded. "Is he here this evening?"

"I fear not." Lady Crandon sighed. "He arrived in town only today, and his journey left him quite exhausted. Far too tired to attend a lively assembly straightaway. Or so he claims; I sometimes suspect Charles of deliberately contriving to avoid my parties."

Cecily glanced from her ladyship to Lord Ashford and found the latter affecting such innocence that she was hard put to stifle a giggle. The earl was several years younger than Stephen, she estimated, and not nearly so handsome as her husband: a stubborn cowlick awkwardly separated his dark brown hair at the right rear portion of his head, and his face was so lean that it seemed to consist less of flesh than of sharp, protruding bones. But it was a pleasant face nonetheless, and the fine brown eyes were twinkling with mischief.

"I assure you that you're mistaken, Aunt Anne," he

said solemnly. "Papa quite *adores* your parties, and he would certainly be here if he could."

"Umm," Lady Crandon muttered. "Be that as it may, Philip's father and I are equally eager to see him properly married, and I do trust you'll prove an inspiration, Lady Trowbridge."

Cecily briefly wondered why their hostess had elected to address these remarks to herself alone, but when she gazed about, she observed that Stephen and Lady Shawcross had drifted on into the ballroom. Her ladyship's fingers were firmly fastened round Stephen's elbow, and they were chatting with a couple not far beyond the entry—

"Do you not agree, Lady Trowbridge?"

Cecily spun her head at the sound of her name and realized, with a stab of panic, that she had absolutely no notion what it was Lady Crandon had asked her to agree to.

"Aunt Anne gives me far too much credit."

Lord Ashford might have been reading her mind as well, and far more sympathetically than Lady Shawcross had, for he flashed an easy grin. His mouth was rather too large for his face, Cecily noted, and his teeth too large for his mouth, but his merry brown eyes somehow compensated for every other deficiency. He reminded her of someone, but in her confusion, she could not say whom.

"Aunt Anne is determined to paint me as an utter wastrel," the earl went on. "She delights in telling everyone I meet that I've spent the past eight years—every moment since I came down from Cambridge—wending my rakeshame way around the world. The truth is, Lady Trowbridge, that I've *not* been around the world; I altogether missed the Orient."

"Well, you visited some of those disgusting islands in the East," Lady Crandon said defensively. "Where the women go about half unclad. To say nothing of Australia—"

"Furthermore," Lord Ashford interjected smoothly, "my tour involved a good deal more than sinful adventure. I devoted a substantial portion of my time to the inspection of my father's foreign holdings. He has properties on every continent but Asia and on many of the more . . . ah . . . . nondisgusting islands as well."

"Philip makes excuses." Lady Crandon drew another martyred sigh but affectionately tapped her nephew's shoulder with her fan. "But the *real* truth is, Lady Trowbridge, that he has sown his wild oats throughout the civilized world—and much of that yet uncivilized—and been abroad long past the time he should have settled himself down. I trust you will make it a point to introduce him to every suitable girl you know."

Lord Ashford was now being discussed as though *he* were an orphaned puppy, and Cecily cast him a look of commiseration. But he was smiling again—perhaps he had never stopped smiling—and she realized it was Lucy he resembled. Not physically, of course; Lord Ashford was a man, Lucy a woman, and their features were in no way similar. But they shared the same dry, self-deprecating wit, the same ready grin, the same interest in distant, romantic places. The fact that Lord Ashford had actually seen these places while Lucy was only dreaming of them seemed a further point of connection between them: Lucy would surely be enthralled as the earl narrated the details of his extensive travels.

"Indeed I shall," Cecily responded aloud. "Fortunately, I can promise that every suitable girl I know will be at my aunt's ball next Tuesday." Lady Crandon flushed with displeasure, and Cecily hastily transferred her attention back to Lord Ashford. "Lady Osborne's assembly," she elaborated in a low voice. "I hope to see you there."

"I have enjoyed meeting you, Lady Trowbridge."

The earl's bow was as noncommittal as his words, and—whether for good or ill—the butler at last announced another arriving party. Lady Crandon tugged her nephew's sleeve again, this time most commandingly; and with a final, apologetic smile, Lord Ashford turned to the entry, leaving Cecily to step on into the ballroom alone.

And alone she would remain, Cecily judged, grimly surveying the dance floor from her vantage point at the perimeter of the room. She had been vaguely aware, toward the end of her conversation with Lady Crandon and Lord Ashford, that the orchestra had finished tuning their instruments and struck up a waltz, and she now observed that Stephen and Lady Shawcross were whirling around the floor. Well, they were whirling as best they could, she amended: the orchestra was so very bad that none of the dancing couples seemed able to follow the dubious rhythm of the music. Most—like Stephen and Lady Shawcross— were maintaining a brave facade, but even as Cecily watched, one pair collided with a great thud and began heatedly to debate just who had made the fatal misstep. They were still arguing, with mounting animosity, when Cecily crept to the refreshment parlor.

Apart from any other criterion, Lady Crandon's refreshments amply justified her reputation as the worst hostess in Britain. Everything was lukewarm, from the flat champagne to the dessert jellies, which had melted to such a degree that they might more accurately be termed soups. Fortunately, Cecily had a lifelong affinity for cheese, which suffered relatively little from the depredations of a hostile environment; and she fairly stuffed herself with the Stilton, Cheddar, and Double Gloucester her ladyship had provided, washing down the whole with a glass of tepid champagne. Then, despite the fact that a young man of approximately sixteen had clearly fallen in love with her and was frantically attempting to engage her in conversation, she excused herself from the refreshment parlor and repaired to the ladies' withdrawing room. With any luck, she reasoned, collapsing onto the bench in front of the long mirror, she could remain here, undisturbed, until it was time to leave the ball—

"Ah, at last I discover you alone, Lady Trowbridge."

Even had Cecily not recognized the voice, she would have identified the heavy scent Lady Shawcross wore, and she started and peered into the glass. Her ladyship's reflection closed the door and crossed the room, and Cecily instinctively moved toward the nearer end of the bench so as to provide more space. But Lady Shawcross shook her head and remained standing at Cecily's back.

"No, I fancy our discussion will be a brief one. There is but one small thing I wish to tell you."

Cecily sensed the commencement of what Aunt Esther had always termed a "scene," and her stomach knotted with apprehension. "And what . . . what is that?" she stammered.

"That I am not in the least wounded by Stephen's decision to marry you."

These were so far from the words Cecily had expected to hear that her shoulders sagged with relief. "It is very kind of you to say so, Lady Shawcross—"

"I am not wounded because I well understand that his decision was in no way influenced by personal preference." Cecily saw, too late, the cold glitter of the violet eyes in the mirror. "Stephen wed you for your money, solely for your money, and you would do well not to delude yourself on that head. But then you can't possibly have done so—can you?—for you know the date of your marriage as well as I."

"The date," Cecily echoed noncommittally.

"Stephen has been talking of you for years." To Cecily's mingled satisfaction and alarm, her ladyship's pale face had flushed with fury. "Chattering of his rich little cousin who stood to inherit a fortune on her twenty-first birthday. Well, he wasted no time, did he? No, he hurried to Derbyshire two scant days before the event and wed you virtually the *instant* you turned one and twenty."

"But . . ."

But Cecily could not refute her ladyship's charge without revealing the true circumstances of her marriage, and those circumstances were suddenly very clouded indeed. Was it possible that Stephen *had* plotted from the outset to marry her? He wouldn't have planned such a precipitate wedding, of course; he would have thought to woo her during the journey to London and announce their engagement shortly after they arrived. At Aunt Esther's ball perhaps. And if that was the case, he would have regarded her elopement, once he'd succeeded in stopping it, as a veritable gift from heaven—

"So do not imagine that I was overset," Lady Shawcross continued bitterly. She was evidently unaware that her cheeks had turned quite scarlet with rage. "Knowing of your inheritance, I did not suppose for an instant that Stephen would marry me. Unlike you, I have never had a farthing in the world to call my own."

Much as she detested "scenes," Cecily could not hold her tongue a moment more. "Then you must be most fearfully in debt," she said coolly, "for you surely possess the finest wardrobe I have ever seen."

"Thanks only to your husband's generosity."

Cecily was so stunned that before she could consider her reaction, her mouth dropped open.

"You didn't know?"

Lady Shawcross's flush receded, and her tiny lips curved into a pleasant smile, and Cecily would have wagered her own last farthing that her ladyship was well aware she did not know of Stephen's "generosity."

"Oh, yes." Lady Shawcross's voice was now as smooth and sweet as honey. "Yes, Stephen wrote me—early in March, I believe it was—and kindly suggested that since my mourning was finished, I should come to London for the Season and be reintroduced into society. He thoughtfully enclosed a check to cover my expenses. I should guess—wouldn't you, Lady Trowbridge?—that early March was approximately when he determined to go to Derbyshire and marry his rich little cousin. I should guess that his generosity was in the way of a payment to salve his conscience. But I have taken enough of your time; I promised dear Stephen I should be away only five minutes."

With a final smile, Lady Shawcross walked across the withdrawing room and opened the door, her passage so silent that Cecily briefly fancied she had dreamed their encounter. But, though her vision was literally blurred with shock, she caught a last glimpse of the elegant blue gown just as her ladyship closed the door, and she could not but reflect that Lady Shawcross's numerous trunks were fairly spilling over with Lady Trowbridge's lost fortune.

❧ 9 ❧

"Cecily!" Aunt Esther stamped her tiny foot with irritation. "Wherever is your mind, child? I daresay we've all been a trifle preoccupied with the assembly, but you are so distracted it has grown quite impossible to converse with you."

Lady Osborne had always been inclined to sweeping criticisms of her niece's behavior, but in the present instance, Cecily was grimly compelled to own her right. She *had* been most fearfully distracted since the night of Lady Crandon's assembly, so much so that she hardly recollected their second fittings and the final preparations for Lucy's come-out. Indeed, the preceding four days had passed in a blur, and she could not but wonder if she had erred in electing not to confront Stephen straightaway.

That had been her intention after she recovered from the shock of Lady Shawcross's revelation: to stalk out of the withdrawing room and challenge Stephen with the incontrovertible proof of his deception. However, she shortly realized that a public quarrel would embarrass her far more than him, to say nothing of positively delighting Lady Shawcross, and by the time the assembly was over, she had decided that the best course was temporarily to keep her silence. Sooner or later, probably sooner, Stephen would be the one to initiate a confrontation—would issue a particularly haughty command or tender some especially unpleasant remark—and Cecily would then unsheathe the weapon Lady Shawcross had supplied her and catch him entirely unawares.

"I asked," Aunt Esther continued somewhat more patiently, "whether you approve the placement of the potted

palms. Do you not believe the one on the left side of the
hearth should be moved to the front window?''

Inasmuch as the florist's men had already departed and
the palm was certainly too heavy for her and Lady Osborne to manage alone, Cecily judged her opinion of
prodigious little consequence. Nor, to say the truth, did
she care a deuce *where* the palms were placed. Though she
had held her tongue for four long days, she had been
unable to put the magnitude of Stephen's betrayal out of
her mind. He had plotted for weeks to lay his hands on her
fortune, had spent a goodly portion of it to placate his
former *parti* even before they were wed—

"Cecily!" Aunt Esther stamped her foot again.

"The palm looks very well where it is," she muttered.

"Lady Osborne!" Mrs. Fawcett's shrill voice penetrated
the saloon. "Monsewer Claude is through with Miss Chandler! He's ready for the next one!"

"That woman!" Aunt Esther hissed. "I plan to give her
a bottle of brandy this evening and instruct her not to leave
her room. But come, let us see if Monsieur Claude has
been able to do anything with Lucy's hair."

They crossed to the drawing-room entry, and Cecily
observed that the recovered furniture, which had been
positioned round the walls, looked quite resplendent. She
wondered if the check Stephen had sent Lady Shawcross
had been sufficiently generous to allow her ladyship to
reupholster *her* furniture. She trudged into Aunt Esther's
bedchamber, glanced dispiritedly up, and sucked in her
breath.

Had she not known it was Lucy Chandler seated in
front of the dressing table, Cecily would have been persuaded that Mrs. Fawcett had admitted an elegant stranger
to Lady Osborne's private quarters. In fact, she peered
briefly down at Lucy's ancient dress to confirm that this
was her sister-in-law, and when she looked back up, she
saw the eyes of her mirrored reflection widen with astonishment. Though Monsieur Claude had cut Lucy's hair
excessively short in the front, he had left the back long and
dressed it in several braids piled high on Lucy's crown.
The arrangement, held in place by a circlet of white bows,
dramatically enhanced Lucy's sparkling emerald eyes while

the short curls around her face exposed splendid cheekbones and a delicately curving jawline. For a moment,
Cecily could only gape, but at length, she shook her head
in disbelief.

"You don't like it?" Lucy whispered.

"I love it! You look magnificent, Lucy. Truly stunning."

Lucy drew a small sigh of relief, then reached for her
spectacles and set them on her nose. The effect was so
grotesque that Cecily was hard put to stifle a giggle.

"How . . . how well can you see without your glasses?"
she said carefully, not wishing to wound her sister-in-law's
feelings.

"Oh, I can see you perfectly." Lucy snatched the spectacles off again as if to prove her point. "I need them only
for close work—reading or writing or sewing."

"Well, you won't be reading or writing or sewing this
evening," Aunt Esther said crisply, "so I suggest you
leave them off."

"Enough of spectacles," Monsieur Claude snapped. "I
am having five more appointments today. I do you next."
He stabbed one finger at Cecily, tugged Lucy none too
ceremoniously out of the chair, and gestured Cecily to take
her place. "Your hair I don't leave so long," he went on
when she was seated.

"I fear you misunderstood, Monsieur," Cecily said politely. "I want my hair only to be dressed. Dressed and
trimmed a bit perhaps, but certainly not cut—"

"It must be cut." He peremptorily waved her to silence.
"Is terrible the way it is."

On this tactful note, he began wielding his scissors with
an enthusiasm verging on frenzy, and Cecily dropped her
eyes and watched with horror as great locks of auburn hair
fell to the threadbare carpet beneath her feet. By the time
Monsieur grandly announced that he was *fini*, Cecily supposed she must be altogether bald, but when she dared to
peek into the glass, she discovered that he had wrought a
minor miracle. He had cut and styled her hair in the
French fashion—a profusion of soft curls ending at her
jawline—and if her face still wasn't perfectly heart-shaped,
neither did it appear so dreadfully square. She even fancied her nose seemed a trifle longer and her mouth a bit

smaller, and for the first time in days, she began to anticipate the assembly with at least a modicum of excitement.

Perhaps, she thought as Monsieur Claude jerked her up from the chair and beckoned Aunt Esther across the room, perhaps tonight she would look nearly as well as Lady Shawcross. And maybe Stephen would be so *bouleversé* that he would forget he had wed her only for her fortune.

"Good God!"

Stephen's eyes darted from Cecily's new coiffure to the toes of her satin slippers, then stole back up again and lingered on the daring corsage of her gown. Cecily repressed an inclination to tug the bodice upward because she had attempted this maneuver at least fifty times already with no success whatever. She had realized, of course, that the corsage of the dress—which was of deep yellow satin trimmed with white lace—formed a very low V in the front, but it hadn't seemed half so shocking in the privacy of Madame Boudreau's fitting room as it did now. Could she really wear such a garment in *public*? she'd wondered after abandoning her fruitless efforts to stretch the bodice an inch or two. Had it not been half past eight by then, she would have tried on the rest of her new gowns, though she doubted she would have found one much more modest than the yellow. As it was, she had carefully arranged her mother's pearls around her neck—covering at least a little of the alarming expanse of bare flesh—and comforted herself with the reminder that her dress, however bold, was still not as daring as Lady Shawcross's gowns.

"Well," her ladyship said coolly. As if with deliberate malice, she had chosen to wear a dramatic black dress with a high, square neck and long sleeves. "The caterpillar emerges from her cocoon, and we behold a butterfly."

"Umm," Stephen muttered.

His eyes had returned to Cecily's face, and she fancied they were very dark. But that might be merely in contrast to his skin, she owned, for his face was exceedingly pale. Pale with anger? she wondered anxiously. She couldn't guess and really didn't want to know, and before Lady Shawcross could once more sail out the door ahead of her,

Cecily hurried across the vestibule and led the way to the barouche.

As Cecily had expected, Aunt Esther was awaiting them in her own vestibule, wringing her hands in anguish. With the assembly scheduled to begin in ten scant minutes, *everything* had gone wrong, Lady Osborne bitterly reported. Of the eight footmen she had engaged for the evening, only six had appeared, and one of them was so jug-bitten he could barely stand erect. Speaking of rumpots, Mrs. Fawcett had vanished some hours since and would probably invade the saloon at the very height of the festivities and create a horrid scene. Though how there were to *be* any festivities Aunt Esther really couldn't say because the caterer had prepared only half as many lobster patties as instructed. Furthermore, there was some sort of substitution in the orchestra; Lady Osborne wasn't certain of the details, but she *was* sure they would be unable to play a single decent note . . .

Cecily sighed and glanced into the dining room—where, insofar as she could see, the caterer had laid out a perfectly splendid feast—then propelled her aunt up the stairs to the saloon. Here, too, matters seemed to be under perfect control, the floor and the chandeliers equally gleaming and the orchestra tuning their instruments in a most professional manner.

"You look very handsome this evening, Aunt Esther," Stephen said.

Cecily suspected that he wished, as she did, to divert Lady Osborne's attention from her numerous imaginary problems. But whatever his motive, his compliment was valid: Aunt Esther's gown of pale blue crepe over sarcenet and her own new coiffure became her prodigious well.

"Why . . . why thank you, Stephen."

Evidently taken aback by this interjection of a bright note into her dark litany of disasters, Lady Osborne lapsed into silence, and at that moment, Lucy entered the drawing room.

"Good God!"

This time Stephen's eyes widened with incredulity, and though Cecily had fancied herself prepared for Lucy's transformation, she could not quell a gasp of amazement.

She had seen Lucy's hair earlier in the day and her dress during the course of their fittings, but she had not seen the two together and had not—in her most optimistic imaginings—envisioned the effect. Lucy was . . . Well, she was beautiful; no other word could adequately describe her. The emerald satin corsage of her gown, which had been cut from the same pattern as Cecily's dress, rendered her long neck positively swanlike and revealed nicely-rounded arms and a shapely bosom. But Lucy's upper body didn't much signify, for one tended to look immediately downward and note the endless fall of apple-green lace below the bodice, ending, at last, in a tier of satin rouleaus around the bottom of the skirt. No one this night would say that Lucy Chandler was excessively tall, Cecily thought; the universal opinion would be that every other woman in Britain was excessively short.

"Are you surprised?"

Lucy had reached Stephen's side, and she took his arm and beamed up at him. Her green eyes were sparkling, Cecily observed, and her cheeks were flushed with excitement.

"I . . . I am stunned," he choked.

"Oh, I knew you would be thrilled!" Lucy dropped his arm and clapped her hands. "I told Cecily so. Though it was all her idea, you understand; she assured me I wasn't too old for a come-out."

"Did she indeed?"

Stephen transferred his own eyes to Cecily, eyes now more yellow than green, and she dismally collected that he *was* angry. Why this should be, she could not conceive, and before she could speculate any further, a little man bounded into the saloon.

"They are here, Lady Osborne!" His voice was shrill with panic. "It lacks five minutes to nine, but the first guests are *here*."

"Then direct the footmen to show them up the stairs," Aunt Esther snapped. "And when they reach the entry, announce each guest by name."

"Yes, ma'am."

He scurried away, and Lady Osborne wrung her hands again. "Mrs. Whitcomb's butler," she moaned. "I borrowed Polson for the evening, quite forgetting that Mrs. Whitcomb has never entertained more than four guests at a time in the whole of her life. He will get all the names wrong—''

"Sir Peter and Lady Kelham," Polson announced in a ringing voice the chief steward at Carlton House might well have envied: and the assembly was underway.

Cecily had intended to remain at the entry only a moment or two, only until Aunt Esther and Lucy's initial nervousness subsided. But the guests surged into the drawing room so quickly that she soon found herself part of the official receiving line: Lady Osborne greeted each arriving party and presented them to her "dear niece, Miss Lucy Chandler," who subsequently introduced them to Cecily. Cecily did not in the least regret her chance promotion to assistant hostess, for she was most eager to draw Lucy and Lord Ashford to one another's immediate attention. If Lord Ashford came, she amended apprehensively, when some forty-five minutes had elapsed and the stream of arrivals began to thin. And what if he did come and proved too short for Lucy? Cecily vaguely recollected that he was far taller than she, but the great majority of the adult world was taller than she—

"The Marquis of Rotherham," Polson intoned. "The Countess of Crandon. The Earl of Ashford."

Cecily whirled toward the entry, hoping to present the earl to Lucy herself, but this proved impossible when his father and aunt preceded him down the line. Cecily observed that the marquis was approximately his sister's age and conjectured that Lord Ashford, like Lucy, was the child of a second marriage. When Lord Rotherham gallantly addressed her as "Lady Snowcroft," she further surmised that he was monstrous hard of hearing.

It appeared Lady Crandon suffered no such handicap because she at once embarked on a whispered description of the shocking affront to her dignity which had occurred the morning before. She had been innocently shopping in Bond Street, her ladyship reported (properly accompanied by a footman, of course), when—she dropped her voice still further—when a young man approached her and made an *indecent advance*.

"Very young," Lady Crandon insisted. "Not a bit above sixty. And he asked me—not my footman, mind you; he boldly inquired of *me*—where Hoby the bootmaker was located."

In normal circumstances, Cecily would have been wildly amused by her ladyship's narrative. As it was, however, she could see from the corner of her eye that Lord Ashford had moved from Aunt Esther to Lucy, and Lady Crandon's chatter reduced their conversation to an indecipherable buzz in Cecily's ears. Inwardly squirming with impatience, she was unable either to attend her ladyship's discourse or hear the one adjacent, and she heaved an audible sigh of relief when Lady Crandon finished her tale at last and led her brother on into the saloon. Cecily then turned toward Lucy and the earl and found them gazing at each other with such fascination that she was compelled to emit a polite cough in order to capture their attention.

"Ah, Lady Trowbridge." Lord Ashford—with considerable reluctance, Cecily thought—transferred his merry brown eyes to her. "I collect you were being regaled with Aunt Anne's account of the recent horrifying assault upon her person." He flashed his easy grin. "I'm sure the poor fellow was suitably chastened when he discovered she'd sent him toward Oxford Street rather than Piccadilly."

Cecily had failed to register the denouement of her ladyship's story, and she laughed aloud. "And I collect you met my sister-in-law while I was occupied," she rejoined casually.

"So I did." He looked back at Lucy, who had never ceased to look at him. "Indeed, I told Miss Chandler that I cannot but judge it rather unfair that the two loveliest women in London are members of the same family."

Cecily was certain he'd told Lucy no such thing, that his original compliment had included no reference whatever to Lady Trowbridge. They continued to stare at one another, and Cecily noted with satisfaction that he was much taller than Lucy; Lucy scarcely reached his chin.

"Has Lord Ashford spoken of his travels?" she asked nervously. Though they seemed quite content to remain immersed in their mutual inspection, she was beginning to find the silence oppressive. "He has been nearly round the world, Lucy, and I fancy he'll be delighted to learn that you share his interest in distant places.''

"Really?" The earl did, in fact, seem delighted. "Have you traveled extensively as well, Miss Chandler?"

"No, I've hardly traveled at all, but I've written several books set in foreign lands."

Good God. Cecily had intended—but unfortunately forgotten—to advise Lucy not to mention her numerous unpublished novels. Lord Ashford would think such a pastime eccentric at best and more probably count it a symptom of dubious sanity. She parted her lips, preparing to explain that Lucy had merely penned a few romantic poems about blue seas and palm trees, but before the first word could emerge, the earl's own mouth dropped open.

"You write *books*?" he said, his voice hushed with awe.

"Not very good books, I fear," Lucy said cheerfully. "Not sufficiently good to be printed, at any rate."

"Perhaps that's due to the subject matter," Lord Ashford suggested. "I have thought, Miss Chandler—immodestly, I confess—that my own experiences might make for an interesting book. But as I can scarcely compose a literate letter, I had quite abandoned the idea till now. It now occurs to me that you and I might write such a book together: I supplying the material, you performing the actual writing . . ."

His voice expired in another grin, and Cecily was persuaded that he'd conceived the grand notion of recording his experiences no more than fifteen seconds since. But Lucy knew that, Cecily saw, for her cheeks had dimpled with an answering grin. Furthermore, Lord Ashford knew that Lucy knew: his smile broadened, and his brown eyes fairly flashed with deviltry.

"It's an interesting proposition, Lord Ashford." Lucy lowered her own eyes at the last critical second, and Cecily was astonished by her instinctive sense of coquetry. "Perhaps we can discuss it in greater detail later."

"Oh, be assured we shall. Having survived just such an ordeal myself a few evenings ago, I understand that you must remain in this miserable receiving line a few minutes more. But when you're dismissed, I shall be waiting to claim your hand for the first set.''

He bowed away, his eyes still fixed on Lucy, and nearly collided with Stephen, who was striding toward the entry. Cecily briefly fancied he had come to escort her into the saloon, but he walked on past with the barest of nods and disappeared into the corridor.

As the earl had predicted, the receiving line did not long survive his departure. Cecily was compelled to chat with a perfectly insufferable admiral, who confided that he had been "more or less solely responsible" for Napoleon's defeat, and then with a minor Prussian diplomat who had apparently mastered two words of English.

"I am delighted to meet you, Baron von Reichmann," she murmured.

"Excellent ball," he responded.

"Are you alone this evening?" A discreet glance over his shoulder had already confirmed that he was.

"Excellent ball," he said happily.

"I'm told your country is beautiful, and I hope to visit it one day."

He bobbed his head with great enthusiasm. "Excellent ball," he agreed.

"I do feel you should know," Cecily could not resist whispering, "that I am the illegitimate daughter of the Prince Regent. With the aid of a hundred thousand armed men, I intend to seize control of the government tomorrow morning."

"Excellent ball," the baron assured her, and with a click of his heels, he retreated into the drawing room.

"Well, I believe that is it," Aunt Esther said when the baron had vanished into the crowd. "Everyone of any consequence is here. Except for Lady Jersey, and I did not honestly expect her to come. Though she, of course, will expect us to come to Almack's tomorrow evening."

"Then let us surprise her," Lucy said gaily. "Since she shunned our ball, let us decline to go to Almack's."

"*Decline to go to Almack's*?" Lady Osborne echoed. Lucy might have proposed they abandon the Church and join some peculiar religious cult. "One does not decline to go to Almack's, dear; one offers up thanks to have been granted vouchers of admission. But that is tomorrow, and tonight is tonight. Go dance and enjoy yourselves, and I shall check on the refreshments. I suspect the caterer has already exhausted his inadequate supply of lobster patties."

Cecily peered into the saloon, confirmed that Lord Ashford was, indeed, waiting for Lucy, and shook her head. "No, permit me to check on the refreshments," she said, and before Aunt Esther could pose an objection, she hurried out of the drawing room and down the stairs.

As Cecily had anticipated, the caterer's "inadequate" array of refreshments had scarcely been touched, for it was far too early in the evening for anyone to have grown hungry. She had consequently expected to find Stephen in the dining room merely nursing a glass of champagne, and she frowned in puzzlement when a quick survey from the archway revealed the room deserted. Well, it wasn't quite deserted—an elderly dowager was eagerly wolfing down Lady Osborne's precious lobster patties—and with a pleasant nod, Cecily retreated into the vestibule. Wherever Stephen had gone, she reasoned, he would have to pass through the entry hall in order to return to the saloon; and she positioned herself at the bottom of the staircase, hoping that if any additional guests arrived, they would mistake her for a particularly colorful and lifelike statue.

The long-case clock in the foyer was no longer functioning, but when Cecily calculated that some ten minutes had passed, she began to fear the worst—that Stephen, overcome by his inexplicable vexation, had left the assembly and walked back to Brook Street. No, she soon amended, this wasn't the worst possibility: the *absolute* worst would be if Stephen and Lady Shawcross had left the ball together. She gritted her teeth, then remembered glimpsing her ladyship's jet head ornament when Baron von Reichman stepped into the saloon. Which had been well after Stephen's haughty exit.

Cecily drew a tremulous breath, but her relief was short-lived. If Stephen had left the assembly, she couldn't return to the drawing room and meet Lady Shawcross's knowing, mocking violet eyes. Cecily's own eyes stole to the front door, and she momentarily toyed with the notion of walking back to Brook Street herself. But the night-dark streets of London abounded in disorderly revelers, to say nothing of actual criminals, and at length, she shook her head and crossed the vestibule to the parlor. As Aunt Esther had vowed it would be, the door was closed, and with a wary glance over her shoulder, Cecily eased it open and sidled across the threshold. She pushed the door carefully to behind her, turned around, and beheld Stephen regarding her with cool curiosity from the near end of the threadbare couch.

"Stephen!" she yelped. "What . . . whatever are you doing here?"

"I am drinking a glass of brandy." He plucked if off the sofa table and held it aloft in confirmation. "May I pour you one?"

He inclined his gold-and-chestnut head toward the liquor cabinet but, Cecily noticed, made no move to rise.

"No, thank you." She had never had any clear idea what she intended to say when she located him, and—once persuaded he was gone—she had forgotten whatever vague intentions might have been whirling in her mind. "I was merely seeking a short rest from the ball, and now I've had it, I shall go back." Her right arm crept behind her ribs, and her hand began to search for the doorknob.

"Rest?" Stephen laughed, but the sound was without merriment. "I should think, to the contrary, that you'd wish to savor every moment of the lively controversy you've inspired."

"Controversy?" Cecily could only suppose he was referring to some *on-dit* of her elopement, and her questing fingers froze.

"Yes. Everyone is debating with great intensity whether Lady Trowbridge or Miss Chandler is the handsomest woman in England. Fortunately, no one has been sufficiently indelicate to solicit my opinion, for I should be quite at loss to say."

"Are you equally at loss to say why you're angry?" Cecily demanded. "I can but surmise that you preferred us as we were, traipsing about in our ragged old gowns and situated squarely under your thumb."

"I'm not certain I am angry." His voice was curiously flat. "Nor, if I am, that I've any right to be so. No, let us rather say that I am . . . am shocked. I was unready to see my wife and sister looking like . . . like . . ."

"Like cyprians?" Cecily supplied acidly.

"That is much too strong a word, Cecily."

"Indeed it is," she snapped, now so angry herself that she was not in the least mollified by the mildness of his tone. "I judge the current fashions somewhat bold myself, but Lucy and I look no more shocking than any other young woman in town. In fact, if I may point it out, our attire is considerably more modest than that Lady Shawcross normally favors."

"Priscilla is neither my wife nor my sister."

It was, perversely, his very calm that drove Cecily over the brink, drove forth the words she had bottled up so long. "No, but she has a good deal in common with your wife, does she not?" she hissed. "Specifically, the circumstance that her clothes were paid for by the same man."

In her various imaginings of this confrontation—and there had been at least a dozen—Cecily fancied she had anticipated every one of Stephen's conceivable reactions. She had prepared herself for outright denial, for rage that Lady Shawcross had betrayed him, for a string of lame excuses. The one response she had not expected was utter composure.

"I daresay any honorable man in my position would have acted as I did," he said levelly. "I am Priscilla's only male relative, and I feel it my responsibility to see her properly settled. Surely you don't resent my fulfillment of a family duty."

"Oh, I resent it very bitterly indeed." Cecily had long since ceased to grope for the doorknob, and she now clenched her hands at her sides. "Don't prate to me of honor, Stephen, or of family duty either. The truth is that you were stricken with guilt—I shall give you that much credit—when you decided to abandon Lady Shawcross and wed your wealthy cousin. So, yes, I resent most bitterly that you used *my* fortune to ease your conscience."

Stephen gazed a moment into his glass, as though it contained the tea leaves of a Gypsy fortune-teller, then set it back on the sofa table and shook his head. "I can only reiterate my earlier assurance that I did not wed you for your . . . your fortune.''

"I did not believe your earlier assurance," Cecily said frostily. "And if you reiterate it a million times, I still will not believe it. Did you suppose I was deaf and blind? Did you fancy I should never learn that you've talked about my money for years? Lucy knew of my inheritance; Lady Shawcross knew; everyone knew but me."

"If I did speak of your inheritance, it was only in passing—"

"And how I wish I had known!" Cecily flew on. "Had I known, I should have questioned your noble offer to save me from the consequences of my elopement. Or so I choose to believe; I cannot be sure. Because—and again I grant you credit, Stephen—you employed the perfect tactic in Sheffield. So perfect that you might have talked me round even if I had been aware of my legacy. Yes, you're so impossibly priggish that I might have been persuaded honor *was* your principal motive.''

To Cecily's mortification, her eyes had filled with tears, and she spun around and began once more to grope for the doorknob. But her vision was so clouded she could scarcely see the door, much less the knob, and as she fumbled, she heard the creak of springs behind her. She found the knob at last, but before she could pull the door open, Stephen's fingers fastened on her shoulders.

"Don't go, Cecily. Please; not yet. Give me a moment to tell you something.''

"If you intend to reiterate again that you did not marry me for my money—"

"I assure you I do not, for I'm thoroughly sick of discussing your money.''

His voice was edged with bitterness, but his hands on her shoulders were astonishingly gentle, and she permitted him to turn her back round to face him. His eyes were gentle as well, she noted distantly, and dark with some emotion she couldn't read. He dropped his arms, and her skin, where he had touched her, suddenly seemed very cold.

"I want to tell you about Mrs. Tidwell," he said abruptly.

"Mrs. Tidwell?" Cecily repeated. She could not recollect having met her. "Is she here this evening?"

"Happily, she is not. I understand that Mrs. Tidwell remarried long ago and now resides in Canada."

Remarried? Cecily was beginning to entertain an impression that she had arrived late at Drury Lane and missed the entire first act of the play.

"I was acquainted with Mrs. Tidwell some years since," Stephen went on. "When she was the wife of General Tidwell, my commanding officer in Gibraltar. The general was well above fifty—closer to sixty, I should guess—but Mrs. Tidwell was only ten or twelve years older than I. And she soon made it unmistakably clear that she would welcome my . . . ah . . . companionship."

"But you'd have nothing to do with a married woman," Cecily said wryly.

"I'd have nothing to do with that *particular* married woman. In those days, I didn't care a damn for convention, but I was well aware on which side my bread was buttered. I didn't judge Mrs. Tidwell sufficiently irresistible to gamble my whole career for her favors."

He lapsed into silence, and Cecily wondered again if she had missed something. If this was the end of the play, she had altogether failed to grasp the point.

"The Tidwells often entertained us officers," Stephen continued at last, "so I sensed nothing amiss when I was invited to dine at their home one evening. I was somewhat surprised to be admitted by Mrs. Tidwell's personal maid and advised that we were to eat upstairs rather than in the dining room, but even then I had no notion what she was at. I did not grow alarmed till the abigail showed me to Mrs. Tidwell's bedchamber, and by that time, it was too late. Before I could offer an objection, the maid disappeared, and Mrs. Tidwell emerged from her dressing room. She was wearing only a negligee, and at the risk of seeming to stoop to vulgarity, I must report that it left very little to the imagination."

"What . . . what did you do?" Cecily asked.

"I shall never know what I *would* have done because I was granted no opportunity to act. Since I could ill afford to offend the wife of my commanding officer, I should probably have attempted to persuade her that—though I found her prodigious appealing—a liaison would be dangerous to us both. But as I indicated, I had no chance. The corridor door flew open, and General Tidwell strode into the room, his own dinner engagement having been unexpectedly canceled.''

"Good God!'' Cecily said.

"Precisely.'' Stephen flashed a crooked, mirthless grin. "At that juncture, Mrs. Tidwell demonstrated a thespian talent quite unrivaled by any actress I have ever seen upon the stage. I had forced my way into her bedchamber just a few seconds since, she claimed, obviously catching her in a shocking state of dishabille; and she thanked God her husband had intervened before I could force myself on her as well.''

"And he believed her, of course.''

"He believed her''—Stephen nodded—''and ordered me confined to quarters while he pondered my fate. He was keenly inclined to haul me before a court-martial, he said, but as such a proceeding would prove dreadfully embarrassing to his dear wife, he might merely discharge me from the army in disgrace.''

"And that is what happened?'' If so, Cecily reflected, the secret had been splendidly kept. "You were cashiered?''

"No, I was not, for the very next day I received word that Walter had been killed. I pointed out to General Tidwell that since I had now inherited my brother's title, I should have to leave the army in any event, and he agreed to let me go in peace. I suspect that in the interim, he had done a bit of poking about and discovered that a court-martial might prove very embarrassing to his wife indeed. Be that as it may, I resigned my commission and returned to England, and General Tidwell himself was killed in battle a year or so later. And Mrs. Tidwell, as I believe I mentioned, subsequently remarried and left the country.''

"Well, at least the story had a happy ending,'' Cecily said philosophically.

"So I thought until very recently. Until you, Cecily, began to complain of my . .'' He sketched another crooked smile. "I fancy 'impossible priggishness' will do as well as any of the several terms you've used.''

She opened her mouth—whether to defend herself or apologize she wasn't certain—but he laid one finger over her lips.

"No, allow me to finish. You're quite right to say that I've been obsessed with propriety these past nine years; I was beginning to recognize that just as you came in. I realized, even before you pointed it out, that it was absurd of me to be overset by your and Lucy's gowns. But I *was* overset, and I further realized that since my experience with Mrs. Tidwell, I've sought to avoid scandal to the exclusion of virtually everything else."

Cecily knit her brows in confusion, and he removed his finger from her mouth. "But there was no scandal," she protested.

"No," he conceded, "but that was the result of sheer good fortune. Had fate not twisted precisely as it did, my reputation could have been destroyed, my livelihood lost . . ." He shuddered. "Despite the many years that have passed, despite General Tidwell's death and Mrs. Tidwell's removal to Canada, I still fear that some rumor of the incident might emerge. It's for that reason I've never told anyone what occurred. Not until tonight; not until I told you."

"And why did you tell me?" Cecily said.

"Because—having finally puzzled it out for myself—I wished you to understand why I behave as I do. Not necessarily to excuse my conduct; merely to comprehend it. I have tried for hours to remember the exact thoughts I entertained as I sailed home from Gibraltar, but since I cannot, I surmise my brain was fearfully scrambled. Some hidden portion of my mind must have resolved that I should never again permit myself to be maneuvered into a compromising situation. Neither myself nor anyone connected to me."

"So that truly is why you wed me." Cecily was talking as much to herself as to him. "You honestly thought to save me from the scandal of my elopement."

"Your elopement undoubtedly influenced *when* I wed you. As to the why . . ." He stopped, then almost imperceptibly shook his head. "Well, perhaps Lucy's opinion contained a degree of truth. I was quite overwhelmed when I encountered you at Osborne Hall, and I daresay your elopement merely expedited the inevitable.''

He stopped again, his eyes now so dark that they were nearer black than green. "In short," he said hoarsely. "I must own to some deceit when I mentioned the raging debate in the saloon. Had I been called upon to express my view, I should have been compelled to say that Lady Trowbridge is the handsomest woman in Britain. And I believed so long before tonight, Cecily. I believed so when you were still traipsing about in your ragged old gowns.''

His right forefinger touched the hollow of her throat, trailed lightly downward, and inscribed a line across her chest, as though he were tracing the square neck of her ancient primrose dress. His finger traveled back up her collarbone, coming to rest on her bare shoulder, and Cecily now had the impression that they were trapped in a portrait, eternally frozen in paint, doomed to join the display above the sideboard in Brook Street. He had said she would have to come to him, and that she was not yet prepared to do. But she was equally unready to brush the warm finger off her shoulder and tear her eyes from his, so she simply stood there—stood perhaps half a foot in front of the door, her heart pounding deafeningly in her ears, her ribs so tight around her lungs that she could scarcely breathe. One of them must eventually relent, she thought frantically, must either advance or retreat; and though she believed she watched him very carefully, she was never able to say who was the first to move. She found herself in his arms, and she neither knew nor cared how she had come to be there.

He did not hold her as he had on their wedding night; he took her mouth at once, and she would have had it no other way. She had not realized until that moment how desperately she craved his touch, and she sensed in him the same hunger, the same wild longing born of weeks of deprivation. He groaned and pulled her closer, lifting her feet from the floor, and transferred his lips to her neck and then her shoulder—lips so warm she thought he must surely leave little burns on her skin. He set her back on the floor, and as his mouth found hers again, he pressed her against the door, pressed his body the whole length of hers until she fancied she could feel every bone, every muscle. He raised his head and stared down at her, his eyes blazing like dark coals in his face; and before he could once more bend his head, Cecily heard the sharp click of the doorknob.

"Stephen?" Lady Shawcross said.

He sprang away, hastily adjusting his coat and neck-cloth, and—freed of his weight—the door opened with such force that Cecily nearly lost her balance. She stumbled three or four paces forward and caught herself up just as her ladyship stepped across the threshold.

"Forgive me for disturbing you, but I've begun to feel a trifle unwell." Lady Shawcross spoke directly and exclusively to Stephen. "I daresay it's the champagne; my digestion invariably rebels when I consume inferior champagne. At any rate, I was in hopes you might walk me home. I should desire Jordan to drive me, but then he would have to return for the rest of you . . ." Her voice trailed apologetically off, and she winced and bit her lip, as though she were suffering an excruciating spasm of pain.

Stephen glanced at Cecily, but he had been neatly trapped; he could hardly decline to render assistance to a woman allegedly in distress. He nodded and, with a final adjustment of his neckcloth, followed her ladyship into the vestibule. The front door closed behind them, and Cecily grimly awarded a point to Lady Shawcross.

❧ 10 ❧

To Cecily's amazement, it took Stephen under five minutes to walk to Brook Street and return to Aunt Esther's. He strode directly from the front door to the parlor, where Cecily had waited for him, and seized her in an embrace even more passionate than the one Lady

Shawcross had interrupted. As his kisses grew increasingly feverish, Cecily chanced to glance down and observed that she was wearing a negligee—a mere scrap of lace which left absolutely nothing to the imagination. She initially supposed that Stephen had brought it with him from Brook Street, but upon reflection, she realized she had never owned such a revealing garment. She then remembered that Mrs. Tidwell had arrived in town a few hours since and collected that Stephen had borrowed her negligee. Not that it signified, for his warm hands readily penetrated the thin shield of the fabric . . .

Cecily's eyes flew open, the dream so vivid that her cheeks were quite ablaze. Indeed, she entertained a brief hope that it hadn't entirely been a dream, but she shortly recalled the actual sequence of events following Stephen's departure from the assembly.

The truth was that after carefully adjusting her own clothes, Cecily had gone back to the saloon to await Stephen's return, and he had failed to appear. Four and twenty hours before, she would have been mortified by his abandonment, but having witnessed Lady Shawcross's performance for herself, Cecily could well imagine that Stephen had been trapped anew when they reached Brook Street. Her ladyship had no doubt murmured—with another wince of pain—that a glass or two of brandy might settle her delicate stomach. Or that a few hands of cards might enable her to fall asleep despite her torment. Or . . . Well, the possibilities were endless. In the event, Lady Shawcross had probably employed a combination of tactics to keep Stephen by her side for several hours, until it was too late for him to undertake the walk back to Aunt Esther's.

The whole truth was, Cecily conceded, that after their conversation, after that magical interlude in the parlor, she was prepared to forgive Stephen almost anything. She wriggled to a sitting position, propped a pillow behind her back, and glanced at the door connecting to his bedchamber, her face warming again. Though it had been nearly four when the barouche clattered into Brook Street and deposited her and Lucy on the footpath, Cecily had remained perched on the edge of her bed, immersed in a study of the connecting door, for many minutes following their arrival.

Stephen had said she would have to come to him; she remembered his furious admonition all too well. But surely, she thought, surely the situation had changed. He had been as stirred by their searing kisses as she—of that she was certain—and once it became clear he would not return to the ball, she had assumed he was eagerly awaiting her own return to Brook Street.

So perhaps he hadn't heard her. Cecily removed her slippers and slammed them one at a time against the bedpost, hoping Stephen would assume they had merely fallen to the floor. When this ploy elicited no response, she emitted a series of great coughs, ultimately irritating her throat to such an extent that she truly did begin to choke. But still there was no reaction, no suggestion of activity in the adjoining bedchamber, and at length, Cecily reminded herself that he had left the assembly fully five hours since. He must be dead asleep by now, and with a sigh, she stood, removed the rest of her attire, crawled beneath the bedclothes, and eventually drifted to sleep herself.

"Cecily?"

A low voice jarred her from her reverie, a voice so muffled that she started and once more peered at the connecting door. But the subsequent light tap of knuckles on wood unmistakably came from the direction of the corridor; and even as Cecily concluded that only one other person in the household would use her Christian name, the door creaked open, and Lucy peered cautiously into the room.

"You are awake!"

Lucy stepped across the threshold, closed the door behind her, and hurried across the Brussels carpet. She was wearing one of her new walking dresses—a peach-colored creation of jaconet muslin over sarcenet—and carried a leghorn hat in her hand.

"You are going out," Cecily said gratuitously as Lucy sank on the bed beside her.

"No, I have *been* out. Do you not recollect my telling

you last night? Telling you that Philip had asked me to drive with him in Hyde Park this morning?''

Philip? Now Lucy brought it up, Cecily did vaguely recollect her previous mention of an excursion, but she was quite certain Lucy had referred to her prospective companion as ''Lord Ashford'' rather than ''Philip.'' Evidently, she surmised optimistically, the courtship was proceeding apace.

''Though it isn't considered fashionable to go to the park in the morning, Philip much prefers it then,'' Lucy added. ''He judges it far too crowded in the afternoon.''

Her tone made it clear that anyone not sharing Philip's opinion was altogether lacking in sense, and Cecily bit back a smile. ''Well, I am glad you enjoyed yourself,'' she rejoined aloud.

''I did not merely *enjoy* myself, Cecily.'' Lucy lowered her sparkling emerald eyes and began to draw the brim of her hat nervously through her fingers. ''That is what I wished to speak to you about. Is it possible . . .'' She dropped her voice, as if dozens of people were milling about the bedchamber. ''Is it possible I've fallen in love with Philip after only a few hours' acquaintance?''

Though her memory of Lucy's book was by now excessively dim, Cecily seemed to recall that Iris had fallen in love with her planter the instant she glimpsed ''the golden halo of his hair'' towering above the rest of the throng on the dock. She started to point this out, but Lucy was so very serious that she decided it would be cruel to joke her. She cast about for a gentler response, but before she could find one, Lucy flew on.

''I wished to ask you in particular because I fancy you must have felt as I do when you met Stephen. Met him again, I should have said. Is that the way it was, Cecily? Did you know immediately that Stephen was the man you'd dreamed of all your life? That you could spend the rest of your days with no other man but him?''

Cecily wryly wondered Lucy's reaction if she chose this moment to reveal the true circumstances of her precipitate marriage. But that she couldn't do, of course, and she once more groped for the proper words.

''You must not compare yourself and Lord Ashford to

Stephen and me," she said at last. "Nor to any other couple in the world—the real world or the world of your imaginings. You can only listen to your own heart, Lucy, and follow where it leads you."

Lucy was silent a moment, but at length, she raised her eyes and nodded. "Yes, that is excellent counsel," she agreed. "I shall go where my heart leads me, and tonight it will surely lead me to Almack's, for that's where Philip will be." She flashed her dimpled smile and sprang up from the bed. "Will you help me decide what to wear, Cecily? Since all my heroines were wretchedly poor, the one thing I never did imagine was that a splendid new wardrobe could actually be a *problem*."

"Yes, I shall help you," Cecily said. "I shall come to your room as soon as I've dressed and had breakfast. What time is it, by the by?"

"Well, it was noon when Philip and I returned from the park—"

"Noon!" Cecily could not remember having slept so late since the slothful days of her adolescence, and she threw the bedclothes aside and scrambled to her feet. "I shall certainly hurry then."

"Yes, if you hurry, you might still catch Stephen and your uncle in the breakfast parlor."

Lucy walked back across the room and opened the door, and Cecily belatedly registered her words.

"My uncle?" she gasped. "Uncle Frederick is *here*?"

Lucy spun around, clapping one hand contritely over her mouth. "Oh, dear," she moaned. "I intended to tell you straightaway, but I was so eager to seek your advice about Philip that I quite forgot. Yes, Sir Frederick was just emerging from his chaise when Philip and I reached the house. We all came inside together and encountered Evans in the vestibule, and Evans suggested that Sir Frederick join Stephen in the breakfast parlor. I knew you'd want to see him at once—Sir Frederick, that is—and I did plan to tell you . . ." Her voice expired in another little moan.

"Do not tease yourself about it," Cecily said soothingly. "I doubt Uncle Frederick will evaporate while I dress. Go on now, and I shall come later to discuss what you should wear to Almack's.''

Lucy nodded again, stepped on into the corridor, shut the door, and Cecily sped to the dressing table. Why had Uncle Frederick come to London? she wondered, attempting to coax her hair into at least a remote semblance of the coiffure Monsieur Claude had created. Had he decided, upon his return from Liverpool, that her come-out could not be entrusted to Aunt Esther after all? That he must supervise the proceedings himself? If so, he had arrived a day too late, but perhaps he had never known the precise date of the assembly. And—whatever the motive for his journey—how had he reacted when he learned of her sudden marriage? Sir Frederick was fond enough of Stephen, but if he'd truly aspired to wed his niece to a duke . . .

Electing not to ring for Eliza, Cecily went to the wardrobe, donned her new morning dress of white jaconet, and hurried into the hall. The long-case clock at the top of the stairs was just chiming one as she passed it, but when she reached the breakfast parlor, she found it empty except for Evans, who was clearing two used place settings from the table.

"Good morning, Lady Trowbridge." The butler had gradually ceased to regard his new mistress with overt suspicion, and he now managed a tiny smile. "I regret to say that the hot food is gone; I had not planned for a guest at breakfast. Shall I desire Mrs. Vaughan to prepare more?"

"Please." Cecily inclined her head. "And while she does so, I shall greet my uncle. If you can tell me where he is."

"Indeed I can, ma'am. Sir Frederick and his lordship repaired to the library immediately they finished their breakfast. I collect they had a matter of some importance to discuss."

Cecily made her way back through the dining room and across the vestibule. The library door was closed, but as she lifted her hand to knock, Stephen's voice came clearly to her ears.

"That is it then." His tone, even filtered through the door, was unmistakably one of finality. "The whole twelve thousand pounds."

"Yes." Uncle Frederick's voice. "It turned out precisely as we . . ."

Evidently Sir Frederick was situated farther from the
door than Stephen, for his next words were indistinguish-
able. Precisely as we "planned"? Cecily silently supplied,
her flesh beginning to crawl with a terrible suspicion.

"Actually, I should say it turned out far better," Stephen said.

"You are right, of course. One cannot but . . ." Another indecipherable murmur. ". . . had her come-out . . ."
Buzz, buzz. ". . . conceived a *tendre* for someone else."

Sketchy though these snatches of conversation were,
they were ample to confirm Cecily's suspicion, and she
stood, her hand still upraised, as though she had been
turned to stone. As, indeed, she felt she had, for it was
clear not only that Stephen had wed her for her money but
that he had conspired with Uncle Frederick to bring the
marriage about. Clear that they had agreed to divide her
fortune between them. A fortune which, over the years,
had grown from twenty thousand pounds to twenty-four;
the twelve thousand Stephen had mentioned was obviously
Sir Frederick's share.

One aspect of their shameful bargain remained unclear:
the specific role Uncle Frederick had been assigned to
play. What task had he pledged to perform in exchange for
half his niece's legacy? He had consented to finance her
debut, of course, and delivered her into Stephen's hands
for the journey to town. But these efforts were insufficient
to earn him a twelve-thousand-pound commission, and
Cecily could only surmise that he had come to London to
abet the marriage in some other way. Perhaps Sir Frederick had been appointed to drive her into Stephen's arms in
the event his nephew's courtship was not progressing satis-
factorily. Or to voice subtle slurs about any other suitor
she might have come to fancy; he himself had expressed
the fear that she might conceive a *tendre* for someone else.
Or—were the situation to reach such a dire pass—maybe
Uncle Frederick would have forbidden her marriage to an
"unsuitable *parti*" until such time as she could be persuaded of Stephen's charms.

But matters had, indeed, turned out far better than the

conspirators could have dreamed. Cecily had been safely wed to Stephen even before they arrived in town, and he and Sir Frederick were left with only the pleasant chore of dividing her money—

"Cecily!"

She had not heard the end of the discussion, had not detected the sound of footsteps in the library; and when Uncle Frederick threw the door open, she nearly tumbled across the threshold.

"My dear child! I was just setting out to search for you."

He seized her in a warm embrace, then thrust her away, and she wondered if he realized that she had remained frozen in his arms. Apparently not, for he was beaming down at her, his hands still resting on her shoulders.

"You look splendid, my dear, simply splendid; one can see at once that marriage quite agrees with you. Naturally, I was somewhat shocked when Stephen informed me of your union, but now I've grown accustomed to the notion, I couldn't be more delighted."

"Yes, I daresay you are delighted."

Her voice was as cold as her body, encrusted in ice, but he evidently failed to register her tone as well. He patted her shoulder, then wearily raked his fingers through his outlandish orange hair.

"If you'll excuse me, I should like to go upstairs and rest. I traveled straight through from Liverpool, and I now discover I'm not so young as I fancied when I undertook such a grueling journey."

He sketched a sheepish smile and melted Cecily's heart not a whit.

"However, though I'm aching in every limb, Stephen tells me I must go to Almack's this evening. I've always despised the place, but one does not decline to go to Almack's."

He was echoing Aunt Esther's words exactly, and in other circumstances, Cecily would have been hard put to quell a laugh. As it was, she watched in stony silence as he walked to the stairs and began to climb them, and when he had disappeared around the landing, she slipped into the library. Stephen was seated at the writing table, scratching at his ledger, no doubt entering the recent deduction of twelve thousand pounds from his assets. She slammed the door closed, and he started and spun his head, then leaped to his feet and strode across the room.

"Cecily!"

His voice was cheerful, his face suffused in a brilliant smile, and she could not but own that he was a magnificent actor. Much more talented than Mrs. Tidwell. If, in fact, there had ever been a Mrs. Tidwell; it was entirely possible Stephen had fabricated his woeful story to divert her attention from the embarrassing subject of her money. He reached her side, stopped just before his Hessians could tread on her slippers, and Cecily willed herself not to succumb to his lethal physical power.

"I heard you chatting with Frederick," he said, "and when the conversation ceased, I assumed you'd accompanied him upstairs. There's no doubt the poor man needs his rest; he has been upon the road in excess of four and twenty hours."

Did he sound a trifle discomfited? Cecily wondered. She thought so, prayed so, and she ground her teeth together lest she speak too soon.

"You are looking very handsome this morning," Stephen went on. "Although—having resigned myself to the current scandalous dictates of fashion—I'd rather come to fancy the sort of gown you wore last night."

He extended one forefinger, as if to trace the high scalloped neckline of her morning dress, and Cecily furiously batted it away. "Don't touch me," she hissed. "Do not even think to touch me."

"You *are* vexed then." He dropped his hand and sighed. "I feared you would be, and I can but beg your indulgence. I intended to come back to the ball, but Priscilla seemed so very ill that—"

"Priscilla," Cecily interjected. "I had forgotten Lady Shawcross. It seems to me, Stephen, that you struck a rather bad bargain."

"Bargain?" he echoed quizzically.

"You needn't pretend any longer," Cecily snapped. "I overheard your discussion with Uncle Frederick, and I know quite well what the two of you have been at. That is why I say it appears you made a bad bargain. Having paid Uncle Frederick half my inheritance for his assistance and spent another thousand pounds or so on Lady Shawcross, you are left with relatively little, are you not? Surely you could have courted and wed a woman with a fortune of but *ten* thousand pounds and spared yourself such trouble.''

''What the deuce . . .'' His voice trailed off, and he essayed a wonderfully convincing frown of confusion. ''What is it you believe you overheard?''

''I overheard you giving Uncle Frederick twelve thousand pounds, after which the two of you agreed that things had worked out far better than you planned. He was most relieved that my come-out had been avoided, allowing me no opportunity to conceive a *tendre* for someone else. As well he should be, of course, because he need now do nothing to earn his fee.''

''Good God!'' Stephen massaged his forehead a moment, then reluctantly nodded. ''Yes, I can see how you might have construed it so,'' he said. ''But you are altogether wrong, Cecily. You didn't hear all that was said.''

''Then tell me the rest of it,'' she challenged.

He hesitated, shook his head. ''That I cannot do.''

''No?'' She emitted a bitter laugh. ''Then I can only collect that you exhausted your fertile imagination last night. Spinning tales designed to persuade me of your so-called honor.''

''Spinning tales?'' he repeated sharply. ''Are you implying that I invented Mrs. Tidwell?''

''It doesn't much signify whether you did or not. Whether you concocted the story from start to finish or conveniently chanced to remember it, your objective was the same. You sought to deceive me; deceive me *again*, I should have said. As you did when you pretended to . . . to find me handsome.''

To Cecily's dismay, her eyes had once more begun to fill, and she whirled around and reached for the doorknob. But she could not leave on this note, could not permit him the satisfaction of her abject surrender.

''My chief regret,'' she spat, ''is that I perceive no means of exacting retribution. But perhaps I shall think of something. Yes, if I put my brain to it, perhaps I shall discover myself as devious and imaginative as you are.''

She jerked the door open, rushed into the vestibule, and narrowly missed a collision with Evans.

''Ah, Lady Trowbridge,'' he said brightly. ''I was just coming to advise you that your breakfast is ready.''

''I am no longer hungry,'' Cecily choked, and—keenly aware of his curious eyes on her back—she fled up the stairs.

Cecily's bedchamber had been cleaned in her absence, and she sprawled upon the counterpane and stared sightlessly at the ceiling. She was determined not to cry, not to grant Stephen that satisfaction either, and she forced her mind away from him and dredged up happy memories of the life she had led before her disastrous marriage. She recalled the doll she had received for her eighth birthday, which—if not as magnificent as the one she'd so passionately wanted— had nonetheless been splendid indeed; and reviewed her long-ago trip to London in excruciating detail. Her thoughts then turned to Moonbeam and their daily rides around the grounds of Osborne Hall, and she anxiously wondered how the mare was faring. She had neglected to instruct Pickett to have the horse exercised regularly while she was away, but surely he possessed sufficient wit to initiate an exercise program himself.

When her welling tears had dried at last, and the great lump in her throat had decreased to a slight thickness, Cecily sat up in the bed and allowed her mind to return to Stephen. She was almost inclined to weep again when she recollected her final words, for she feared that—far from salvaging any pride—she had merely succeeded in making a dreadful cake of herself. Retribution indeed! Stephen and Uncle Frederick had her fortune firmly in their grasp; what punishment could she possibly inflict? None, of course, and Stephen well knew that. He would probably report her empty threat to Sir Frederick, and they would share a hearty laugh at her impotent rage.

But, as the saying went, it was useless to cry over spilt milk. She could not retract her foolish statement; she could only affect not to be overset by any amusement her husband and uncle might display. She would go to Almack's this evening and behave, insofar as she could, as if nothing were amiss . . .

Almack's. Cecily had forgotten her promise to help Lucy select a gown for the assembly, and she stood and plodded dispiritedly out of her room and down the corridor. Lucy's bedchamber door was ajar, and with a light tap, Cecily pushed it on open, stepped across the threshold, and stumbled to an astonished halt. The floor was free of litter, an Axminster carpet clearly visible where Cecily remembered a garden of books, and she briefly fancied she had blundered into the wrong bedchamber. But when she peered about, she found Lucy standing beside her writing table, removing books and papers from the surface and placing them in a trunk at her feet.

"Cecily!" Lucy glanced up and flashed her dimpled smile. "I collect you had a nice long chat with your uncle."

"A short chat actually," Cecily said grimly. "But most enlightening."

"Well, you should count yourself fortunate you didn't come earlier. Had you done so, I might have impressed you into service."

Lucy closed the lid of the trunk just as two footmen panted into the room bearing another trunk between them.

"How many more, Miss Chandler?" one of them asked wearily as they deposited the empty trunk beside the writing table and grasped the handles of the one Lucy had filled.

"Two or three, I should guess."

Their faces falling with this unwelcome intelligence, the footmen lifted the full trunk and staggered into the hall, and Lucy began to fill the empty one.

"Parker and Hobbs are rather vexed, I fear," she remarked cheerfully. "They've carried half a dozen boxes to the attic already and two trunks before that one." She inclined her head toward the door.

"I surmise that you have decided to terminate your . . . ah . . . career," Cecily said.

"I never had a career, Cecily." Lucy ceased her labors and looked levelly across the room. "As you pointed out, I simply chose to bury myself in a world of dreams. So let us say that I have decided to move from that world to the real one. I'm still not sure I should be happy wed to a duke, but I fancy I might be very happy indeed with a certain earl of our acquaintance.''

She grinned again, then nodded at the bed. When Cecily glanced in the indicated direction, she saw Lucy's white crepe dress laid out on the counterpane.

''I believe I shall wear that gown tonight,'' Lucy said. ''Unless you were planning to wear your white one. As I recall, they are much alike.''

Cecily had given no consideration to her attire, nor could she generate the remotest interest in the matter, and she shook her head. ''No, I'll wear something else,'' she murmured.

''I shall see you this evening then.'' Lucy resumed her packing of the trunk. ''I must own that I'm most curious to observe Aunt Esther's reaction to Sir Frederick.'' She paused and frowned. ''Do you think we should warn her he will be there?''

Cecily had not considered this either, and she knit her own brows a moment. She suspected that if Lady Osborne knew Uncle Frederick would be at Almack's, she would decline to go after all; would, in fact, contrive to avoid him throughout his stay in town. And as furious as Cecily was with her uncle, she could not but recollect the odd softness in Aunt Esther's eyes when she had spoken his name.

''No, I don't think we should warn her,'' she replied at last. ''I think her reaction might surprise Aunt Esther herself.''

❧ 11 ❧

"I must confess," Lady Osborne said grudgingly, "that he does not look so bad as I had fancied."

In fact, Cecily thought, peering across the main room of Almack's, Uncle Frederick looked remarkably well in his evening attire. Since he had gained little weight in his calves, his legs appeared thinner in breeches than in pantaloons; and his wasp-waisted coat made his rotund belly seem smaller than it was. Furthermore, he had obviously been barbered following his rest, for his hair—though it remained inevitably orange—was in astonishingly good order.

"But I could be mistaken," Aunt Esther added. "I have scarcely glanced at him, after all."

Cecily bit back a smile. The truth was that from the moment Lady Osborne had discovered her estranged husband was present, her eyes had never left him. As a result of this absorption, she had struck one unfortunate gentleman quite smartly on the chin while gesturing with her fan and committed the unpardonable sin of failing to acknowledge Countess Lieven's nod of greeting.

"I do not intend to *speak* to him, of course," Aunt Esther went on, "because I am most overset by his arrival. I've no doubt he came to town with the express intention of embarrassing me. I am sure Lady Jersey has already begun to gossip of a reconciliation, and *he* will take keen delight in ignoring me and holding me up to ridicule."

Inasmuch as Lady Jersey was arguably the most powerful woman in Britain, Cecily could not suppose she had the slightest interest in the marital difficulties of an obscure Derbyshire baronet and his wife. Nor did she see how Uncle Frederick could ignore Aunt Esther when she

was bent upon ignoring *him*. But she judged it unlikely
that logic would alter Lady Osborne's opinion, and she
elected not to respond.

"I wonder why he *did* come?" Aunt Esther said.

Cecily's amusement abruptly evaporated, and her fingers tightened round her own fan. She had debated for
hours whether or not to inform Lady Osborne of Sir Frederick and Stephen's scheme. She longed to confide in
someone, and Aunt Esther would certainly be a sympathetic listener. Would not be at all surprised to learn that
her husband's historic clutchfistedness had inspired him to
undertake such a shameful endeavor. If she did retain
some affection for Uncle Frederick—and Cecily was now
persuaded she did—the news of his latest transgression
would utterly destroy it, and any hope of a reconciliation
would vanish.

And what would be the advantage in that? Cecily asked
herself the same question she had posed a dozen times
before. Her fortune was irretrievably lost; Aunt Esther's
unhappiness would not serve to restore a single groat.
Indeed, Cecily had come to recognize the ironic possibility
that her stolen legacy might help to bring her aunt and
uncle together. Sir Frederick's miserliness had always been
a major point of conflict between them, and surely—with
twelve thousand additional pounds in his coffers—he would
mend his nipcheese ways.

"Perhaps he came to see you," she responded, the
debate resolved at last. "Perhaps he had it in mind to
effect a truce."

Lady Osborne's mouth opened, then snapped closed,
and Cecily decided to hold her tongue as well. It wouldn't
do to press the issue too far, and she gazed around the
room, affecting elaborate interest in the proceedings. Lucy
and Lord Ashford had stood up for the first two sets
and—since they could not properly dance again—were
now seated in a corner, engaged in lively conversation.
Fond as she was of her sister-in-law, Cecily could not
repress a stab of envy. It seemed increasingly likely that
Lucy would, in fact, be happy with her earl while Cecily
remained bound to a man who cared only for her money—

"Will you look at that!" Aunt Esther hissed.

Cecily transferred her eyes back to Uncle Frederick and saw that Lady Shawcross was now standing beside him. Her ladyship had recovered from her mysterious affliction as swiftly as she had contracted it and looked quite radiant in an excessively bold gown of midnight-blue satin.

"It is abundantly clear what she is at, is it not?" Lady Osborne continued furiously. "Do you note the . . . the *seductive* way she is gazing up at him?"

Cecily gulped down a laugh, for it was altogether impossible, from this distance, to discern Lady Shawcross's expression. Nor could her ladyship conceivably be gazing "up" at Sir Frederick, seductively or otherwise. She was at least as tall as he, perhaps a trifle taller, and the great ostrich plume on her head made it appear that she towered fully a foot above him.

"Yes, it is *abundantly* clear." Aunt Esther snapped her delicate ivory fan neatly in half. "Now she has lost Stephen, she thinks to ensnare *my husband* in her clutches."

Cecily parted her lips, preparing to point out the absurdity of this notion, but it suddenly occurred to her that jealousy might be the one emotion more powerful than Lady Osborne's bitterness.

"I believe you are right, Aunt Esther," she said solemnly. "I believe that is Lady Shawcross's intention precisely, and you must nip her effort in the bud. You must interrupt their conversation *immediately*."

"What . . . what would I say?" Lady Osborne sounded like a schoolgirl suffering the torments of her first *tendre*.

"You might start by saying, 'Good evening, Frederick,' " Cecily suggested.

Aunt Esther tentatively nodded and began to walk across the room. She now looked like a terrified adolescent approaching her chosen *parti*, and—as if she were the anxious mother—Cecily discovered that she couldn't bear to watch. She turned away; briefly encountered Baron von Reichmann, who remarked that tonight's assembly was an "excellent ball"; then hurried to the refreshment parlor.

Though she had skipped breakfast entirely and choked down only a few bites of her dinner, Cecily was not in the least hungry. And it was fortunate she was not, she soon observed, for the refreshments consisted of nothing but bread and butter, cake, lemonade, and tea. Cecily took a slice of cake and a glass of lemonade and perched on a chair just beside the door, hoping that anyone merely glancing into the room would fail to notice her. She was even less inclined to engage in idle chatter than she was to eat, and any desultory enthusiasm she might have felt for the latter activity evaporated when she found that the cake was stale.

On the whole, she owned, setting her plate on the floor, she was wretchedly disappointed in Almack's. The magnificent establishment she had envisioned had turned out to be exactly what it was: a gaming club converted to assembly rooms. The orchestra was no better than the one Aunt Esther had employed; the company, if somewhat larger, was much the same; the refreshments were dreadful . . . A party of three matrons sailed into the room, and Cecily hastily bent over to push her plate out of sight beneath her chair.

"Well, I can scarcely credit it," one of the women said.

From her contorted position, Cecily could see only their skirts, and she perceived that they had stopped between her and the table. Obviously they had retired from the dance floor to gossip rather than to partake of the limited refreshments.

"No, I cannot believe it," the same voice insisted. "I have always judged him a perfect gentleman."

"And you have always been a lamentable judge of character," a second voice snapped. "There is no question about it, Charlotte. Her husband discovered them together in her bedchamber."

"No, her husband did not merely *discover them together,*" the third woman put in triumphantly. "As I understand the situation, he caught them *in the act.* Caught them in the act, suffered an apoplectic seizure, and collapsed and died on the spot."

"He did not die then," the second voice corrected. "He was killed in battle some months later."

Until that moment, Cecily had listened to their conflicting *on-dits* with distant amusement, idly pitying the ill-starred "gentleman" who had been found in the wrong bedchamber at the wrong time. But at the mention of

battle, her heart seemed to stop beating, seemed to freeze
to her ribs; and she could not have sat up had she wished
to.

"Perhaps you're right." The first voice again. "However, I do question whether a court-martial was justified."

"I fancy it was," the second woman rejoined.

"But there was no trial!" the third voice said. "On that
head, *you* are wrong, Amanda. Before his death, her
husband ordered him cashiered."

Dear God. Cecily's gloves were clinging wetly to her
palms, and beads of perspiration had begun to form on her
brow as well. Dear God.

"How can that be, Helen?" The second woman emitted
a derisive sniff. "You're the one who's claiming her
husband died within minutes of discovering them together.
And if he was dead, he could hardly have issued such an
order, could he?"

"Well, maybe Colonel Bidwell *didn't* die at once,"
Helen conceded stiffly.

Colonel Bidwell. The name, though slightly distorted,
was sufficiently accurate to shatter Cecily's last, faint hope
that they might be discussing some other scandal after all.
Why? she wondered desperately. Why should the story
surface now? The incident had occurred nearly a decade
ago . . .

But speculation was fruitless; Stephen must be warned.
Perhaps the rumor had just begun to circulate, and he
could somehow put an end to it before it spread any
further. She set her glass on the floor, leaped to her feet,
and fled the refreshment parlor, ignoring the sudden gasps
behind her.

"Was that *Lady Trowbridge*? Good God, she must have
heard our every word . . ."

Cecily paused on the perimeter of the main room, her
eyes combing the crowd for Stephen, but even as she
peered about, she perceived the futility of any warning.
The knot of people nearest her had fallen silent upon her
approach—a breathless, watchful silence—and when she
stepped a bit ahead, they began to whisper frantically
among themselves. She spotted Stephen at last on the far
side of the room, and as she hurried toward him, the

reaction of every group she passed was the same: a deathly hush when they recognized her, an eager buzz when they counted her safely out of earshot. Everyone knew some version of the story by now, she reflected dismally, attempting to maintain a serene smile. With the possible exception of Lord Rotherham and Baron von Reichmann, who were incapable—respectively—of hearing and comprehending spoken English.

And, of course, Stephen knew as well. Long before she reached him, Cecily had realized that there was no chance he could have failed to hear the rumor, but his appearance came as a shock nonetheless. His face was dead white—or so she fancied until she noticed even paler lines of fury round his mouth—and his eyes glittered like cold jewels, like some strange mating of emerald and topaz.

"Stephen." She stumbled to a halt beside him, panting for breath. "I just heard—"

"Did you indeed?" he interposed frigidly. "Then you will not be surprised to learn that I plan to leave the assembly at once."

"No." Cecily shook her head without pausing to ponder his reaction. "No, that would be a mistake, Stephen. If you create the impression that you are . . . are slinking away, you can only serve to make matters worse."

"Worse?" He emitted a mirthless chuckle. "How could matters be any worse, Cecily? Tell me that if you can."

"There are half a dozen different tales being told, and they are filled with wild contradictions. Sooner or later, people will come to see that and begin to wonder if there's any truth in the story at all. And they will particularly wonder so if you stay and pretend that nothing is amiss. Whereas if you go, you will lend credence to the rumors—"

"And if I stay, they will continue to whisper behind their hands and point me out as though I were an exotic circus beast. No, thank you, Cecily; I do not choose to be the center of such attention. I am leaving, and Priscilla has determined to go as well."

He tossed his head, and Cecily belatedly observed that Lady Shawcross was standing at his other side. In addition to her bold gown and her ostrich plume, her ladyship was now wearing an expression compounded—in roughly equal parts—of concern, sympathy, and noble courage.

"Priscilla and I are leaving," Stephen reiterated. "I have sent for Jordan, and I shall desire him to return for Lucy and Frederick. You may go with us now or stay behind and drive back with the two of them."

Cecily much favored the latter option: surely the rumors would begin to fade if it appeared that Lady Trowbridge herself attached no importance to them. But before she could voice this decision aloud, it occurred to her to wonder what new *on-dits* might arise if Stephen departed with Lady Shawcross and left his wife alone at Almack's. It might well be bruited about that Viscount Trowbridge had substituted one form of adultery for another and was conducting an *affaire* with his sister's aunt.

"I . . . I shall go with you," she muttered.

Stephen led the way out, Lady Shawcross immediately behind him and Cecily trailing in her ladyship's wake. They had no difficulty passing through the crowd, Cecily noted; Stephen might have been a second Moses parting a sea of humanity rather than salt. Evidently he had sent for Jordan well before Cecily arrived on the scene because the barouche was waiting in front of the entry. Stephen muttered instructions to the coachman, Jordan assisted the women into the forward-facing seat, Stephen took the one across, and the carriage rattled to a start.

They clattered from King Street into St. James's and on up to Piccadilly in silence, but as they jogged into Bond Street, Lady Shawcross heaved a tiny sigh.

"If it is any comfort, Stephen," she said, "I do fancy Cecily is right in one respect."

Cecily had not supposed her ladyship would ever admit to such a thing, would take her part in any circumstances, and her mouth dropped open. Fortunately, it was dark inside the carriage, and neither of her companions seemed to notice.

"Yes," Lady Shawcross went on, "Cecily is right to say that little damage will ultimately be done. As she points out, the rumors are widely divergent, and people will soon start to doubt the substance of the story. And even if they do not, another *on-dit* will shortly come along to supplant this one. You know how gossip goes, Stephen.''

"Umm," he growled.

"So do not tease yourself about it," her ladyship added soothingly. "I shall be very surprised if the tale survives a week. Next Wednesday night, Almack's will be buzzing with some other baseless rumor, and you'll be quite forgotten."

"Umm."

"Though I do wonder . . ." Lady Shawcross paused. "I do wonder why anyone would choose to invent such an *old* scandal. That is the one point on which everyone seems to agree—that the incident took place nearly ten years since. If someone wished to blacken your name, why would he not fabricate a more recent event?"

"Why indeed?" Stephen said icily.

Cecily's eyes had been fastened on his shadowy form, and as the barouche rolled beneath a streetlamp, she saw that his eyes were also fastened on her—eyes still glittering like cold, hard, green-gold jewels. Dear God! She felt his suspicion as keenly as a knife slipped between her ribs, and her hands grew damp again. Dear God; he thought *she* was responsible, thought she had deliberately, maliciously betrayed his confidence.

The carriage halted in front of the house, and Stephen threw the door open, clambered out, and stalked across the footpath, up the steps, and through the front door. By the time Jordan had assisted Cecily and Lady Shawcross to the ground and escorted them into the vestibule, Stephen had disappeared; and Cecily was compelled to ascend the stairs with her ladyship, who punctuated their climb with words and phrases and little clucks of puzzlement.

"Why?" Cluck, cluck. "Such a strange story to emerge now." Cluck, cluck. "Gibraltar." Cluck, cluck. "So many years ago . . ."

At the second-floor landing, without a word of her own, Cecily abandoned Lady Shawcross and raced down the corridor to her bedchamber, leaving her ladyship to cluck her solitary way to her own room. She had instructed Eliza to turn down the bed but not to wait up—little dreaming she would be home before eleven—and she sank onto the blanket and stared at the connecting door.

There was no question Stephen was awake tonight: he was slamming drawers and doors as if he aspired to bring the house down, and Cecily detected the occasional muffled exclamation which could only be a curse. At length, she heard the splinter of glass as well, and she winced, wondering what it was he had broken. Was there a brandy decanter in his bedchamber, or had he knocked the washbowl to the floor? No, the washbowl would have broken with a dull thud rather than a tinkle. The pitcher maybe, or a lamp.

But the immediate casualty of his wrath didn't signify, Cecily admitted, for she was the true target. He had been punished beyond her wildest imaginings, and she should be crowing with delight at his assumption that she had exacted retribution after all. Yes, if she let it lie, Stephen would never cross her again. Their relationship would become one of perfect frosty courtesy . . .

And what would be the advantage in that? It was an echo of the question that had haunted her, though in different context, throughout the day. No, she amended, maybe the context wasn't so different after all. Just as she had come to recognize that her fortune was permanently lost, she now recognized that she and Stephen were permanently wed. Nothing could undo the words Mr. Henley had uttered, nothing short of an annulment or a divorce so scandalous as to be virtually unthinkable. She and Stephen were bound together for the remainder of their lives, which—in view of their excellent health—might be forty years or more.

Forty years. Endless years of hostility and suspicion or of . . . of something better. She had never escaped Stephen's physical spell, and despite her harsh words this morning—her accusation that he had merely pretended to find her handsome—she believed he was equally attracted to her. His mouth on her mouth, his body eagerly pressed against hers, could not have been altogether a lie; and she suspected that many reasonably happy marriages had been built on a far shakier foundation than that of mutual desire. He had said she must come to him, and if she could penetrate his rage in no other way . . .

Cecily stood and—her hands now trembling—removed her gloves and her toque and her slippers, her gown and her underclothing. Though she had purchased no lingerie since her marriage, her best nightdress chanced to be relatively new, and she dug it from one of the drawers in the chest and pulled it over her head. She then plucked her dressing gown from the foot of the bed and saw at once that it wouldn't do at all: it was so far from new that there were numerous small holes in the flannel and a few mere threads at the elbows, where the fabric had nearly worn away.

She sped to the dressing table, examined her image in the mirror above it, and decided that her nightgown—of opaque yellow satin—was far less revealing than Mrs. Tidwell's lace negligee. Though she doubted Mrs. Tidwell's negligee had risen and fallen in such alarming fashion, betraying every breath she drew . . . Before her courage could disintegrate entirely, Cecily strode across the room and rapped on the connecting door.

Stephen's bedchamber was quiet now, and when her knock elicited no immediate response, Cecily began to fancy he had gone downstairs while she undressed. But she eventually heard the sound of footfalls—steps so heavy they set the floor to shaking a bit—and a few seconds after that, the door flew open.

"Cecily," he said tonelessly. "What a surprise."

She had lacked the time to consider his precise response, but she had vaguely supposed it would take one of two forms: he would perceive at once what she was at and seize her forgivingly in his arms, or he would slam the door in her face. She had never imagined that he would simply look at her—gaze at her without a flicker of emotion—as though she were, indeed, an unexpected and rather unwelcome guest who must be politely greeted before she was politely dismissed.

When she could bear his scrutiny no longer, Cecily dropped her eyes and observed that he had started to undress as well. He had removed his coat, his waistcoat, and his neckcloth; and his shirt—which now hung outside the waistband of his smallclothes—was more than half unbuttoned. The hair on his chest was all one color, she saw, all dark blond . . . Her cheeks grew fearfully warm, and she hastily raised her eyes again.

"What is it you want, Cecily?" he asked coolly.

"I . . . I . . ." He had caught her woefully unprepared; she had not thought she would be required to explain. "I know you believe I was the one who initiated the *on-dit* about you and Mrs. Tidwell—"

"Now why should I believe that?" His voice was fairly dripping with sarcasm, but surely sarcasm was better than that awful, emotionless courtesy. "You are, it is true, the only person who knew of the incident before tonight. And I related it to you only four and twenty hours since. But how could I possibly leap to the absurd conclusion that you repeated the tale at Almack's? No, I am sure it was sheer coincidence. A mere trick of fate that, after nine years, the story suddenly surfaced one short day after you heard it."

"You *think* I was the only person who knew," Cecily protested desperately. "But if you look back—"

"One day after you heard it," he reiterated relentlessly. "And not even twelve hours after you vowed to exact retribution for my alleged theft of your alleged fortune. But I daresay that was a coincidence too, eh, Cecily?"

Her "alleged" fortune? His wrath had obviously driven him to duplicate his adjectives, and Cecily bit back a sharp retort.

"I did not come here to argue, Stephen," she said as levelly as she could. "I came to—"

"I know quite well why you came," he snapped. "There's but one reason you'd appear at my bedchamber door clad only in a nightgown."

His eyes raked her from head to toe, as they had so often in the past, but this time there was a difference. This time, when his eyes returned to her face, they were as pale and dead as they had been at the start of their journey.

"What I've yet to puzzle out," he said, "is the why of the why. I can but surmise that your vicious little mind somehow fancies we have reached a draw. You believe I stole your inheritance, you retaliated by dragging my name through the mud, and the game ended with no clear victory on either side. Is that how you see it, Cecily? Having neither won nor lost the first game, do you now think to begin another?''

"I . . ." Dear God, why hadn't she waited till tomorrow, waited to reason the whole thing through? "I . . ."

"Well, I won't play." He had reverted to his dreadful coldness. "You're exceedingly desirable, my dear, but I shan't sell my soul for a few nights in your bed. Instead, if you'll excuse me, I shall bid you good evening."

Stephen executed a flawless bow and calmly shut the door, as if he had at last got rid of his annoying visitor. Cecily stood motionless, her cheeks now burning with humiliation, until his retreating footfalls stopped and she heard the creak of bedsprings. He was not going to come back, she realized, and she turned and stalked to her own bed, fervently wishing she *had* been the one to circulate the tale of his encounter with Mrs. Tidwell.

12

Cecily's bedchamber was steeped in shadow when she woke, and she initially surmised that the sun had risen only a few minutes since. However, she soon heard the tattoo of rain against the window, and when she plodded across the room and peered between the draperies, she beheld a day as bleak as her mood: a relentless drizzle falling from a low, gray sky. She dropped the curtains, trudged to the dressing table, and was relieved to observe that she did not look half so bad as she felt. Her fitful tossing and turning had left her exhausted, left her aching in every muscle, but—apart from a slight smudge beneath either eye—there was no physical evidence of her restless sleep.

Nor did it signify, Cecily remembered with another flood of relief, because there was no social event to attend that evening. She had invited Aunt Esther to dine in Brook Street, but the invitation could readily be withdrawn—

"Cecily?"

Lucy's voice was low again, so low that it was nearly lost in the accompanying squeak of the corridor door. Did her sister-in-law not judge it odd that Stephen's new wife spent every night in her own bedchamber? Cecily wondered distantly. *Alone* in her own bedchamber? Apparently not, for Lucy now bounded over the threshold, slammed the door behind her, raced across the Brussels carpet, and collapsed on the bed.

"Thank God you are awake," she said breathlessly. She clawed a few stray tendrils of chestnut hair off her forehead; after eight and forty hours, Monsieur Claude's coiffure was beginning to fall apart.

"Surely you haven't been driving in Hyde Park this morning." Cecily sank into the dressing-table chair and waved vaguely toward the window.

"No, Philip and I had tea in the saloon." Lucy was still panting a bit. "He just left. That is what I must talk to you about, Cecily. Philip and me."

Good God. Cecily chided herself for her thoughtlessness. She had been so immersed in her own problems that she had altogether failed to consider Lord Ashford's reaction to the scandalous *on-dits* circulating round Almack's.

"Do not tease yourself about it, Lucy," she said as confidently as she could. "The rumors concerning Stephen and Mrs. Tidwell are unlikely to survive the week." She realized she was paraphrasing Lady Shawcross, but in the circumstances, she was compelled to own her ladyship right. "Naturally Lord Ashford is overset, but—"

"Overset?" Lucy interjected. "Oh, no, Philip isn't overset at all. In fact, he was rather disappointed when I assured him the story couldn't possibly be true. Philip has perpetrated more than his share of mischief, and I fancy he would have preferred his future brother-in-law to be a reformed rake as well."

"Then I suggest you go on as you have . . ." Cecily belatedly registered Lucy's words. "Brother-in-law!" she gasped. "Lord Ashford has proposed marriage?"

"*That* is what I wanted to talk to you about." Lucy

wriggled to the edge of the bed and flashed her dimpled
smile. "Philip and I agreed this morning that as neither of
us is growing any younger, we haven't the time for a
lengthy courtship. We plan to announce our engagement
this evening, and I knew you'd take our part if necessary.
Should someone remark that we're acting rashly, you can
point out how very happy you and Stephen are."

Cecily gulped down a hysterical laugh. "If you are
certain, Lucy—"

"I've never been so certain of anything in my life,"
Lucy interposed firmly. "Nor has Philip. And we could
not be more certain were we to delay our engagement for
twenty years. We were . . . well . . . we were meant for
each other, Cecily."

"Then I wish you every happiness." Cecily spoke around
a swelling lump in her throat.

"Thank you." Lucy's voice was a trifle unsteady as
well. "Now, if you've no objection, I shall discuss the
menu with Mrs. Vaughan myself. I fancy she is best with
mutton."

"Mrs. Vaughan?" Cecily echoed sharply. "You intend
to announce your engagement *here*?"

"Did you not understand that?" Lucy countered question with question. "I remembered that you'd invited Aunt
Esther to dinner, and since Sir Frederick and Aunt Priscilla
would be present in any event, I perceived no harm in
asking Philip and his father and Lady Crandon to join us.
Do you mind?"

To say the truth, Cecily minded most strenuously; indeed, the very notion of a dinner party set her temples to
throbbing. But Lucy would be wretchedly disappointed
and embarrassed if she were compelled to rescind the
invitations she had issued, and Cecily managed a bright
smile of her own. "No, I don't mind."

Lucy bobbed her head and sprang off the bed, but
before she could move toward the door, Cecily recalled the
last, confused thoughts she had entertained before falling
into her troubled sleep.

"Wait a moment, Lucy." Lucy sank obediently back
onto the bed. "I wish to ask you something else."

"If you plan to inquire again whether I'm sure of my love for Philip—"

"No, it's nothing to do with Lord Ashford. Well, indirectly it is," she amended. "You said you assured him that the *on-dits* about Stephen and Mrs. Tidwell couldn't possibly be true. I consequently collect that Stephen never mentioned her to you. Did not mention Mrs. Tidwell, I mean."

"The name I heard was Kidder . . ." Lucy stopped, her brows knitting in a frown. "What an odd question, Cecily. I might almost infer that there *is* some truth in the story."

Cecily hesitated. Stephen's furious conviction to the contrary, she had not betrayed him, and she did not wish to do so now. But she desperately needed Lucy's assistance, and if she could not trust Lucy, there was no one in the world she could.

"The wife of Stephen's commanding officer in Gibraltar was a Mrs. Tidwell," she said carefully. "And there was a . . . an incident involving her and Stephen and her husband." Lucy's green eyes widened with shock. "But the details of the event have been grossly exaggerated, of course," Cecily added hastily.

"Then I shan't trouble myself to revive Philip's hopes." Lucy sketched another winsome grin.

"Are you certain, Lucy?" Cecily pressed. "Absolutely sure that Stephen didn't tell you the story? He might have referred to it only casually, only in passing."

"I am absolutely sure." Lucy nodded again. "And"—a little stiffly—"I am rather distressed by your implication that I should have repeated the story had I known it."

"Not deliberately!" Cecily protested. "I did not suppose that for an instant. I merely thought you might have related the tale to Philip while some third party was on the listen."

"Well, I did not." Lucy's tone was still a trifle wounded.

"But it had to have been a person *like* you." Cecily was speaking largely to herself, reviewing aloud the theory she'd formulated the night before. "Stephen must have told someone of Mrs. Tidwell years ago—so long ago he no longer remembers the occasion. Someone who, for whatever reason, has been segregrated from society till now . . . Uncle Frederick!''

She yelped her conclusion so triumphantly, so loudly, that Lucy started and nearly toppled off the bed.

"Uncle Frederick," Cecily repeated, lowering her voice. "That is the only explanation. They used to hunt together, and they'd have more than a few glasses of brandy after they returned from shooting. At some juncture, Stephen must have got sufficiently foxed to tell his story, and Uncle Frederick carelessly spilled it out last night . . ."

"But why should I try to guess what happened?" Cecily leaped out of her chair, raced to the bed, and snatched up her tattered dressing gown. "I shall go to Uncle Frederick's bedchamber at once and ask him."

"That is an excellent idea," Lucy said dryly. "Except for the circumstance that Sir Frederick isn't here."

"He has left the house already?"

Cecily dropped her dressing gown back on the bed and glared accusingly at the window. The dark day had persuaded her that it was still early morning, but she now conjectured it was closer to noon. Uncle Frederick shared one trait with Dennis Drummond: neither man rose much before eleven unless routed from bed by the exigencies of travel or some genuinely dire emergency.

Dennis. Why, after all this time, should she suddenly think of Dennis?

"Left?" Lucy shook her head. "No, Sir Frederick did not *come back* to the house. I couldn't locate him when the assembly was over, and I assumed he'd been taken up in someone else's carriage. But his bedchamber is situated directly across the hall from mine, and his door was open when I returned. And it was still open fifteen minutes ago, and the bed hasn't been disturbed."

"Then . . . then—"

"Sir Frederick spent the night with Aunt Esther! Isn't it wonderful?" Lucy jumped up from the bed again and clapped her hands with joy. "So perhaps the dinner party should be as much in celebration of their reunion as of our engagement. But there won't be any party if I don't confer with Mrs. Vaughan, will there?"

Lucy sped across the room and into the corridor, and Cecily gazed despondently after her. She was delighted by Lucy and Lord Ashford's impending engagement, thrilled to learn of her aunt and uncle's reconciliation, proud that she'd been instrumental in bringing both couples together. But she could not repress the bitter thought that while she was busily arranging the futures of those around her, her own life had fallen quite apart. Uncle Frederick had been her last hope of proving her innocence to Stephen, and he was . . .

He was less than a mile away. Good God. Cecily rushed to the wardrobe and yanked out her apple-green walking dress. Not that she planned to walk to South Audley Street, for the rain was still beating a steady torrent against the window. But if she hurried downstairs and ordered out the carriage, she could be at Aunt Esther's within the hour. In fact, this procedure was really better than a private conference with Uncle Frederick, Cecily decided, her natural optimism rapidly overcoming her despair. Sir Frederick had a convenient habit of "forgetting" his mistakes, but Cecily knew—from years of horrifying experience—that Lady Osborne's memory was virtually perfect. Aunt Esther forgot nothing but names, and these slipped her mind only when she willed them to.

Cecily tied the ribbons of her leghorn hat, tugged on her gloves, and raced out of her bedchamber and down the hall. The hands of the long-case clock at the top of the stairs read half past ten, and she estimated that she could readily be back in Brook Street before noon. Yes, she calculated, pounding down the staircase, it would take no more than a quarter of an hour to hitch the barouche and another fifteen minutes to drive to South Audley Street. Sir Frederick would no doubt be rising just as she arrived, and their discussion should require no more than half an hour. So she would actually return at a quarter before twelve, and by noon, she would have related Uncle Frederick's sheepish confession to Stephen. And by five minutes past noon . . .

Her vision of what might happen next had grown quite explicit by the time she reached the vestibule and found Evans diligently straightening the mirror above the pier table. Fortunately—or so she prayed—her hot blush had subsided a bit before the butler detected her presence and spun around.

"Ah, Lady Trowbridge." His smile was a trifle warmer than the one he'd tendered yesterday; evidently he was not privy to his master's personal concerns. "Will you be wanting breakfast this morning?"

"Only a cup of coffee while I wait," Cecily replied. "I'm quite anxious to see my aunt, and I should like you to order out the carriage at once."

"I trust you are referring to the barouche, ma'am."

Evans was frowning over his shoulder—evidently the oval mirror was not situated precisely to his liking—and Cecily bit back an impatient retort.

"Yes, the barouche," she said politely.

"Well, I am sorry to say it is not available."

The butler extended one forefinger and carefully shifted the bottom of the mirror perhaps one one-hundredth of an inch to the left. Apparently satisfied with the result of this endeavor, he transferred his full attention back to Cecily.

"Not available," he repeated. "Mr. Stephen normally uses his curricle for errands about the town, but on a day like this . . ." He spread his hands, and as if to verify his half-stated opinion, a great rumble of thunder shook the house. "His lordship naturally took the barouche, but I do expect him back at any time. He planned only a brief visit to Guthrie. His tailor."

His tailor. New clothes. New clothes purchased with her stolen legacy. She had turned the tables on herself, Cecily reflected, grinding her fingernails into her palms. In her eagerness to salvage some scrap of happiness, she had persuaded herself that Stephen had a legitimate grievance. That she was somehow bound to explain a wrong she hadn't committed. Meanwhile, he was merrily spending the fruits of the wrong he *had* committed . . .

"It doesn't signify, Evans," she said stiffly. "I shall wait and speak with my aunt this evening."

"But you are dressed to go out," he protested, "and I'm sure Mr. Stephen will return very shortly—" The doorbell pealed, and he triumphantly bobbed his head. "What did I tell you! There he is now. He has instructed me to leave the door unlocked during the day, but I invariably forget, and *he* invariably forgets his key. But let me hurry out and desire Jordan not to unhitch the carriage.''

Evans strode energetically across the entry hall, and Cecily—perceiving that any further objection would be futile—turned and began to creep back up the staircase. She no longer wanted the carriage, and she wanted even less to confront Stephen. It was enough that she was paying his tailor; she needn't view the parcels. And she would pretend not to notice when he wore his new attire—

''Lady Trowbridge?'' Evans's voice caught her up as she started to round the first-floor landing. ''You have a caller, ma'am.''

Cecily stopped, her hand riveted to the banister. The caller could only be some London matron bent upon extracting the details of Stephen's liaison with Mrs. Tidwell. It might even be Charlotte or Amanda or Helen, claiming a desire to apologize for the gossip Cecily had overheard in the refreshment parlor. Her inclination was to flee on up the stairs, but she shortly realized that escape was out of the question. The caller, whoever she was, had already observed that Lady Trowbridge was awake and dressed, and her refusal to receive guests would be interpreted as confirmation of her husband's misconduct.

Cecily assumed a bright smile, turned around, and peered into the vestibule. The caller was obscured by the shadow of the door, but as Cecily started down the staircase, she stepped into the gloomy light of the foyer. He, not she, Cecily saw, and she stopped again, frozen with shock, when she recognized the figure of Dennis Drummond.

''Good morning, Cecily.''

She had the impression that she had been standing on the stairs for long minutes, perhaps hours, quite unable to move. But only a few seconds could have passed, she soon perceived, for Dennis was just removing his beaver hat.

''Dennis?'' she gasped.

She entertained a desperate hope that she was experiencing a particularly vivid dream, but her hope was dashed when a postilion panted through the front door and deposited a valise on the floor of the vestibule. Dennis withdrew a purse from his coat pocket, and as he began fumbling through its contents, Cecily somehow managed to place one foot before the other and descend the remainder of the staircase. By the time she reached the entry hall, Dennis had paid the postboy, and the latter—evidently displeased with the size of his tip—stalked out the front door and slammed it resoundingly in his wake.

"Dennis?" Cecily repeated dumbly.

He looked far better than she recollected. Dennis normally wore a shirt open at the neck and a disreputable pair of riding breeches; and his one "good" ensemble—which he donned for his infrequent appearances at the parish church in Buxton—was a collection of ill-matched, ill-fitting garments so old they had long since faded and lost their shape. But his attire today would surely inspire the envy of the foremost dandy in London: elegantly-tailored blue pantaloons, a slightly lighter coat, a splendid ivory waistcoat, a pale-blue neckcloth tied in a complicated Oriental.

But he could well afford new clothes, Cecily reminded herself. Like Stephen, Dennis had rigged himself out at her expense, and she clenched her hands again.

"This is very awkward, Dennis," she snapped. "I regret the necessity to speak so harshly, but you cannot be surprised to learn that your visit isn't welcome."

"Visit?" His brown eyes widened, and he shook his sandy head. "I certainly did not intend to stay here, Cecily; I shall remove to a hotel as quickly as possible." He gestured vaguely toward his valise. "And *I* regret any brief embarrassment I may cause you. The fact is I learned a few days since—from Sir Robert Norcott, who got it from his sister—that you had wed Lord Trowbridge. And at that juncture, conscience impelled me to come to town and assure myself that you were well."

He did not sound like himself either, Cecily reflected distantly. The Dennis Drummond she remembered was not half so courteous, not nearly so well-spoken.

"And I am most relieved to find you are," Dennis went on. "Indeed, if you will pardon my boldness in saying so, you are lovelier than ever I've seen you."

"Thank you," Cecily murmured. Relieved? Why should he be relieved? Why, when it came to that, had he been sufficiently concerned for her welfare to travel all the way to London? If appearances were any indication, he had quite enjoyed her five hundred pounds—

"But I shall take no more of your time." Dennis heaved a deep sigh. "Now I'm persuaded he's treating you well, I shall go on." He plucked up his valise. "Though, if you've no objection, I shall advise you of my direction when I know it. In the event you should . . . should require my assistance."

His words were growing increasingly curious, ever more puzzling. Nor was she the only one to think so, Cecily observed: Evans's keen blue eyes were darting back and forth between them, and his lips were parted with fascination.

"Wait a moment, Dennis," she said impulsively. "You won't find a hackney coach in Brook Street, and I shouldn't want you to walk up to Oxford in the rain. Stay and we'll have tea. Will you see to it, Evans? We shall be in the library."

The butler nodded—albeit with considerable reluctance—and as he trudged away, Dennis set his case back on the floor and trailed Cecily into the library.

"What a handsome room!" Dennis sank into the shield-back chair and gazed approvingly about. "Yes, Cecily, it's clear he's treating you well, and my confidence on that head more than justifies my long, grueling journey. I had expected to arrive last evening, but the rain delayed us at Watford."

"That is what I wished to ask you about." Cecily was too nervous to sit; she remained standing just inside the door, her shoulders braced against the wall.

"About my journey? I left Buxton on Tuesday and spent that night in Rothwell—"

"No, not about your journey," Cecily interposed impatiently. "I wished to ask why it was you feared Stephen might be . . . might be mistreating me."

"Pray do forgive me." Dennis drew another sigh. "I now own that my alarm was foolish, but in view of his lordship's threats . . ." His voice trailed apologetically off.

"Threats?" Cecily echoed. Her brain was fairly whirling with confusion now. "Stephen threatened *me*?"

"Oh, no; good God, no. I was referring to his threats against my father and myself . . ." Dennis stopped again. "But surely you know what happened in Sheffield."

"I thought I knew," Cecily rejoined grimly. "I was under the impression that you demanded a thousand pounds to give me up and hold your tongue about our elopement. Demanded a thousand but accepted five hundred."

"*Demanded.*" Dennis repeated the word as though it were the foulest of curses. "So that's the story he told you. Well, I left myself open to such a fabrication, of course." He sorrowfully shook his head. "Much as it pains me to confess it, I did, in fact, accept five hundred pounds in compensation. I can only beg you to understand that I was terrified by his threats."

"Yes, let us return to the threats," Cecily said, her blood beginning to chill in her veins. "What exactly did Stephen threaten?"

"He vowed to ruin us; no more and no less than that. He swore that if I married you, he'd arrange to have the King and Dragon closed down within the week. He and Sir Frederick would arrange it together, I should have said. And after that, they would launch an attack on our other enterprises, and we'd shortly be left with nothing."

There it was, Cecily thought. There, at last, was the missing link, and she marveled that she'd been too cockleheaded to deduce the truth for herself. How could she have believed that Dennis had so readily played into Stephen's hands? So conveniently proposed to return to Buxton and create no further mischief? The instant she learned of her fortune, she should have drawn the obvious conclusion: that Stephen had somehow forced Dennis to abort their elopement and keep his silence.

"What was I to do?" Dennis continued rhetorically. "My father and I are insignificant country merchants. How could we hope to withstand the combined powers of a baronet and a viscount? I saw at once that I must abandon any notion of wedding you, and when your cousin offered five hundred pounds to ease my loss . . . Well, as I said before, I can but beg you to understand the circumstances that prompted my shameful acceptance of his bribe."

Yes, Cecily reflected, she understood all too well. Indeed, in light of Dennis's revelation, she now comprehended the full magnitude of Stephen's cleverness, his glibness, his ruthlessness. She wanted to convey these thoughts to Dennis, but she was so enraged that she had literally begun to tremble, and she did not trust herself to speak. As she strove to quell her wrath, she detected the clatter of a tray in the vestibule, and she glanced eagerly toward the doorway; perhaps a cup of tea would soothe her. But the rattle suddenly stopped, and Cecily heard the creak of the front door, followed by a low murmur of conversation. Dear God, she inwardly moaned. Dear God, do not let it be—

"Drummond!" Stephen hissed.

He had loomed up in the library doorway, not a foot from where Cecily now sagged against the wall. He, too, was wearing a beaver hat, and he jerked it off and struck it upon his leg, spattering Cecily with little droplets of water.

"I could scarcely credit Evans's intelligence," Stephen continued furiously. "Could hardly believe you would dare invade my own home. But I daresay you've exhausted the first five hundred pounds and come to ask for more. Is that it, Drummond?"

"I . . ." Dennis struggled to his feet. "I . . ."

"Do not trouble yourself to respond, Dennis." Cecily drew herself up and turned to face Stephen. "You're too late," she said frigidly. "Your appointment with your tailor took a trifle too long. Dennis has already had an opportunity to tell me what *really* happened in Sheffield."

"Please don't feel compelled to take my part, Cecily." Dennis galloped forward and joined them at the door. "My very last desire was to foment a quarrel between you." His eyes shifted remorsefully from her to Stephen and back. "My only wish was to ascertain that you are well, and I shall now go on to a hotel."

"That is an excellent idea," Stephen said through gritted teeth. "You should have no difficulty hailing a hackney coach in Oxford Street."

"No!" Cecily stamped her foot. She would not submit to another of his peremptory commands. Not now and not ever again; the truth had, indeed, made her free. "There will be no hackney coach and no hotel. Dennis is my guest, and he will stay here."

She peered over Stephen's shoulder and beheld Evans standing just behind him. The butler's eyes were glazed with shock, and the cups and saucers, the condiments, the teapot itself were fairly dancing round the tray he carried. Cecily stepped past Stephen and snatched the tray from Evans's hands before he could drop it on the foyer floor.

"Pray see to it, Evans," she instructed crisply. "Show Mr. Drummond to the vacant bedchamber and be sure he's provided with every amenity."

Cecily marched to the sofa table, and by the time she'd set the tray upon it and straightened again, Dennis and the butler had disappeared.

"Would you care for a cup of tea, Stephen?" she inquired politely. "I fancy it is still warm enough to drink."

"No, I would not care for a cup of tea," he snapped. "What the devil are you at, Cecily? I didn't wish to create a scene in front of Evans. A *further* scene, I should have said."

"No, I daresay you didn't." She whirled away from the table, strode back across the room, and looked directly into his slitted yellow eyes. "You operate much better in secrecy, don't you? You vastly prefer to conduct your negotiations when no witnesses are present. Without witnesses, you can . . . Well, you can actually *invent* a conversation, can you not?"

"I haven't the faintest notion what you're talking about."

"It's too late, Stephen," she reiterated dully. Her anger had given way to a bitter sense of betrayal. "Dennis told me exactly what you did in Sheffield: you threatened to ruin him if he wed me. With Uncle Frederick's assistance, of course. You threatened to shut the doors of the King and Dragon and then destroy his other businesses. I suppose I should grant you some credit for giving him five hundred pounds in compensation. He was so frightened by then that he probably would have given me up for nothing."

"And you believe his story."

Stephen had once more summoned up his thespian skills; his tone was a perfect blend of incredulity and disgust.

And it was that—his remarkable talent for deception—which rekindled Cecily's wrath.

"Yes, I believe it," she spat. "Why should I not believe it? You have lied and lied and lied to me—"

"So what is your intention now?" Stephen interjected frostily. "Now that you've established Drummond cozily beneath our roof. Do you think to initiate a grand *affaire*?"

"Would it signify if I did?" she retorted. "You've made it abundantly clear that *you* don't want me."

She hadn't planned to say it, and—however deep and fresh her wounds—she didn't mean it. But before she could retract her words, Stephen's long fingers snaked around her elbow.

"It signifies immensely." His voice was so low she could hardly hear him. "Whatever our differences, you are my wife, and I will not be cuckolded. Not by anyone, anywhere; and especially not by Dennis Drummond in my own house. Do you understand me, Cecily?"

"Release me at once," she said levelly.

To her surprise—and his as well, she thought—he abruptly dropped her arm.

"And don't ever try to intimidate me again." Her voice, like his, had sunk to a whisper. "You made your bed, Stephen, and you will have to lie in it. Or not lie in it, as the case may be." She could not quell a sardonic chuckle. "You will simply have to wonder about my relationship with Dennis. You cannot wonder too overtly, of course, for we must project the image of a blissfully happy marriage. At least until Lucy's engagement is announced."

"Engagement?" he gasped. "Lucy?"

"Yes, we are having a small dinner party this evening in honor of Lucy's betrothal to Lord Ashford. I collect that his lordship wasn't unduly overset by the reports of your adventure with Mrs. Tidwell, but I don't know the reaction of his father and aunt. We must therefore conduct ourselves with the utmost propriety till we see which way the wind is blowing. And now, if you'll excuse me, I shall check to be certain Dennis is comfortable."

She stepped past him again, ignoring his black scowl, and she was halfway to the staircase when the doorbell pealed. As miserably as her day had thus far progressed, she would not have been in the least surprised to discover that the devil himself was seeking entrance, and she turned warily around. But when Stephen flung the door open, Uncle Frederick walked across the threshold.

Well, he was floating more nearly than walking, Cecily amended, and his appearance was so ludicrous that in other circumstances, she would have howled with laughter. He was soaked to the skin—his evening ensemble plastered to his rotund body, his orange hair trailing limply in his eyes—but despite his obvious discomfort, his mouth was frozen in a foolish, glassy grin.

"Cecily." He spoke like a man in a daze. "Stephen. I've come to retrieve my clothes and take them back to Esther's."

"Yes, you do that," Cecily snapped. "And remind her of the dinner party this evening. It will begin at half past seven, but you might wish to arrive a bit early. Perhaps you and your partner in crime can hatch a new scheme before the soup is even served."

She spun back round and flounced up the stairs, leaving Sir Frederick to drip all over himself and his partner in crime as well.

❧ 13 ❧

Aunt Esther subscribed to a theory that physical illness often resulted from mental distress, and Cecily was prepared to own that she might well have brought her headache on herself. But whatever the cause of her condition, her temples throbbed with increasing severity as the day progressed, and at seven o'clock she decided she was quite unfit to attend the dinner party. Lucy would be disappointed, of course, but Cecily's absence would not affect the betrothal announcement . . .

Yes, it might, she amended wearily, the thought generating a new stab of agony. She did not, in fact, know Lord Rotherham and Lady Crandon's reaction to the rumors about Stephen, and her failure to appear at table would surely be viewed as an indication that the story was true. Furthermore, without her to monitor his behavior, Stephen might treat Dennis with such shocking rudeness as to create a further scandal. Indeed—she shuddered at the prospect—he might dramatically order Dennis out of his home.

So there was nothing for it but to go to the party after all, and by half past seven, Cecily had somehow managed to struggle into her white crepe dress and stumble down the staircase. She feared that her smile was as fixed and vague as the one Uncle Frederick still wore, but if it was, her guests were polite enough to pretend not to notice.

In the event, the dinner party proceeded far better than Cecily could have dreamed. The most awkward moment occurred at the very outset, when Dennis—clad in another elegant new ensemble—strode into the dining room.

"Drummond?" Sir Frederick's astonishment was such that his glassy grin wavered a bit. "What the deuce are *you* doing here?"

This was the one complication Cecily had neglected to anticipate, and her mind was so befuddled with pain that she could not immediately conjure up a response. But even as she cast about for some remotely credible explanation, Dennis flashed a pleasant smile.

"I had business to attend in town, and—foolishly—I did not think to book a hotel room in advance. The son of an innkeeper should know better, should he not? At any rate, when I discovered myself without accommodation, I recollected Lord and Lady Trowbridge, and they kindly offered me a bedchamber."

Cecily stole a glance at Stephen, wondering his reaction to this imaginative tale, but except for an almost indiscernible clenching of his jaws, his face remained wonderfully impassive.

Uncle Frederick nodded—clearly so distracted he was prepared to believe anything—and after that, the party continued without a hitch. By a great stroke of fortune, the *on-dit* Lady Crandon had heard concerned Stephen's involvement with a General and Mrs. Teasdale; and, luckier yet, she was actually acquainted with a couple of this name.

"And General Teasdale did not die in battle. In point of fact, he has not yet died at all; he is happily retired on an estate in Shropshire. His father was the Earl of Heathfield, you know."

Lest there be any doubt of the general's lineage, Lady Crandon related the entire history of the Teasdale family. Her booming voice, which Cecily had heretofore remarked only with idle amazement, now served to drive hot bolts of torment through her skull; but she was so grateful for the innocuous drift of the conversation that she gritted her teeth and tried to nod or shake her head at all the appropriate points in the countess's narrative.

"And it is quite inconceivable that Grace Teasdale would be discovered in a compromising situation." At length—at *great* length—Lady Crandon returned to her original story. "Whatever the quality of her character, the poor woman is prodigious homely. Teasdale would never have wed her had *her* father not been the Marquis of Swanwick."

Her ladyship's second genealogical treatise carried them well into the entrée. Though Cecily had eaten nothing for nearly four and twenty hours, she had no appetite at all; but in an effort to ease her headache, she shut her ears to the countess's interminable discourse and concentrated on cutting her food into the smallest possible pieces. When she had completed this project, she looked up and found Aunt Esther's pale eyes upon her, her mouth pursed with disapproval. Judging it quite possible that Lady Osborne would shortly order her, in front of everyone, to "clean her plate," Cecily succeeded in choking down a few bites of mutton and two full stalks of asparagus.

"I consequently granted the rumors no credence whatever," Lady Crandon concluded with a great sniff. "Your honor quite apart, Lord Trowbridge, I was confident you possessed sufficient *taste* not to attempt a seduction of Grace Teasdale."

Her ladyship lapsed into silence at last, and Lord Ashford—apparently calculating that this might be his first, last, and only opportunity to speak—leaped to his feet and declared that it gave him great joy to announce that Miss Lucy Chandler had consented to be his wife.

"War?" Lord Rotherham bellowed. "Napoleon has escaped again?"

"Wife!" Lady Crandon shrieked. "*Wife*, Charles! Philip has just said that he is to marry Miss Chandler!"

"Well, this time I shall not stand idly by!" The marquis slammed his fist on the table. "I may be five and seventy years of age, but I am still a man! Man enough to run that wretched little Corsican through—"

"There is no war, Papa!" Lord Ashford shouted.

The debate raged on. The footmen cleared the entrées, served cheesecake and champagne, and still the debate raged on. Cecily supposed she should be grateful for this diversion as well: the universal eagerness to set Lord Rotherham straight had superseded any doubts about his son's precipitate engagement to Lucy Chandler. But as their voices grew louder and louder, her headache grew worse and worse until—by the time the footmen brought the coffee—she was feeling distinctly queasy.

It was Stephen who ultimately resolved the impasse. Cecily saw him whispering to Evans and assumed he was communicating some suggestion about after-dinner spirits— the more so when the butler scurried out of the dining room. But when Evans returned, he was carrying a sheet of paper and a pencil, and Stephen quickly scrawled a note and passed it down the table to the marquis.

"Engagement?" Lord Rotherham roared. "Why did someone not say so? It is long since time you settled yourself down, Philip." He crumpled Stephen's note, jumped to his own feet, and hoisted his wineglass. "Permit me to propose a toast to my son and his lovely bride."

The marquis beamed up and down the table, and Cecily perceived that he didn't know who the "lovely bride" was. His happy eyes did not linger on Aunt Esther—who was obviously too old to be his imminent daughter-in-law— but he extended equally fond and fatherly gazes to Lucy, Lady Shawcross, and Cecily herself.

However, no one else seemed to notice his lordship's latest attack of confusion, and after his toast was duly drunk, Stephen rose and offered his own salute to his sister and her fiancé. This second toast served to drain the champagne glasses, and at that juncture, Lady Shawcross voiced her hope that Lady Trowbridge might consent to escort the company to the music room and play the piano for them.

"I'm afraid I do not play the piano," Cecily murmured.

"No?" Her ladyship's violet eyes widened with surprise. "Well, I am far from being an accomplished musician, but I could perhaps pick out a tune or two."

The group enthusiastically agreed to this proposal and, Lady Shawcross leading the way, trooped out of the dining room and up the staircase. By accident rather than design, Cecily brought up the rear of the cavalcade, and when they reached the music room, she realized that her ladyship had unwittingly provided her a perfect opportunity to escape. Her absence would not be remarked until the end of the impromptu concert, and by then, the guests might well conclude that their hostess had been compelled to slip away and attend some urgent household duty. As the others jostled for seats, Cecily crept on along the first-floor corridor and, once she was safely out of sight, raced up the stairs to the second story and down the hall to her bedchamber.

Cecily's mad dash for freedom had exacerbated her headache, if such a thing was possible, and she collapsed full-length on the counterpane and clutched her temples. She must try to sleep, she thought, though she wasn't certain that would be possible either; and at length, she drew herself gingerly up to a sitting position. She normally did not trouble Eliza to help her undress, but she honestly doubted she could manage the task unassisted, and she reached up and weakly tugged the bellpull beside the bed. Her condition must have distorted her sense of time, she soon surmised, for it seemed only a very few seconds had elapsed before she heard a knock on the corridor door.

"Come in," she croaked.

The door squeaked open, but it was not Eliza who peered across the threshold. It was, instead, Aunt Esther, and when she stepped into the room, Cecily saw Uncle Frederick just behind her.

"You see, Frederick," Lady Osborne hissed, "I told you you could not delay a moment longer. The poor child is literally *ill* with distress." She drew her obviously reluctant husband over the doorsill, closed the door behind them, led Sir Frederick to the bed, and dropped his hand. "Your uncle has a confession, Cecily."

"A confession?" Cecily could not repress a bitter laugh, and the harsh sound of it brought a fresh onslaught of pain. "It's a trifle too late for confession, Aunt Esther. I puzzled out yesterday what Uncle Frederick and Stephen had been at." Was it only yesterday? she marveled. "I overheard them dividing up my fortune."

There was a moment of silence during which Sir Frederick stared down at his shoes and Lady Osborne stared pointedly at Sir Frederick.

"Tell her, Frederick," Aunt Esther snapped at last.

Uncle Frederick emitted a little whimper and sank beside Cecily on the bed. "You did not hear us dividing your money," he said heavily, "because there was no money to divide. The truth of the matter is that I lost your inheritance. I lost every farthing; not a single groat is left."

"If it is any comfort," Aunt Esther put in, "he lost a good deal of his own fortune at the same time." Her tone made it clear that *she* did not find this of any comfort at all.

"Lost it?" Cecily echoed incredulously. She entertained a ludicrous notion that he had carelessly mislaid twenty thousand pounds. Stuffed great wads of bank notes in an old pillowcase, perhaps, and learned to his later horror that one of the chambermaids had tossed it out. "Lost it how?"

"Not all at once," Sir Frederick said defensively, as though a gradual disappearance of twenty thousand pounds was infinitely preferable to a sudden one. "There were a number of investments—"

"*Foolish* investments," Lady Osborne interposed with a sniff.

"Some of it was invested on the Continent and lost as a consequence of the war." Uncle Frederick ignored his wife's interjection and went on. "Some in the Custom House fire three years since. Some . . . But it is a long and depressing list, Cecily, and the details no longer signify. I most recently invested your last six thousand pounds and six thousand of my own in a sugar enterprise. A Liverpool firm that holds several plantations in the Indies. But the company suffered a series of misfortunes, and when I traveled to Liverpool to review the situation for myself . . ." He stopped and shook his head.

That is it then. Cecily heard Stephen's words as clearly as if he'd been standing in the room. *The whole twelve thousand pounds.*

"The whole twelve thousand pounds was *lost*," she gasped aloud.

"I regret to say it was." Sir Frederick shook his head again.

"And Stephen knew it probably would be," Cecily said. It had not turned out as they planned; it had turned out as they *feared*. "Knew before you went to Liverpool."

"Of course he knew." Aunt Esther leaped back into the conversation. "He and Frederick arranged your come-out specifically because . . . Tell her, Frederick. Tell her that portion of the story."

Uncle Frederick visibly squirmed, then heaved a deep sigh. "I was never in a rush to bring you out because I calculated that any man would be delighted to wed a girl with a fortune of twenty thousand pounds."

"But there wasn't twenty thousand pounds," Cecily protested. "You'd already lost a considerable part of my legacy by the time I turned eighteen."

"So I had," Sir Frederick agreed, "but I continued to delude myself on that head. Continued to persuade myself that with one brilliant investment, I could earn it all back. And even if I could not, you still had a dowry of *six* thousand pounds. Not a sum to be disdained. It was not until I realized I stood to lose the last six thousand that I . . . I . . ."

"You succumbed to total panic," Lady Osborne supplied.

"I perceived that I could delay your debut no longer." Uncle Frederick once more elected to ignore Aunt Esther's words. "It is often possible for a penniless woman of good family to make a suitable match when she is young and handsome, but her prospects deteriorate rapidly as she ages."

Having barely turned one and twenty, Cecily could hardly view herself as "aged," but she bit back a sharp retort.

"So in desperation, Frederick wrote to Stephen," Aunt Esther said. "And dear Stephen . . . Tell her, Frederick. Tell her what Stephen did."

"Stephen concurred that it was imperative to bring you out at once, and in light of my . . . ah . . . financial embarrassment, he offered to pay for your debut. To pay for your clothes and Esther's clothes and the ball itself."

"But that wasn't all," Lady Osborne said. "You are leaving out the most important part."

"I had not *reached* the most important part, Esther," Sir Frederick snapped. "Pray permit me to finish." He returned his attention to Cecily. "When Stephen got to Derbyshire, he additionally offered to provide you a dowry and lend me any funds I might require to see me through my . . . er . . . temporary difficulties."

And, Cecily reflected, Stephen had made these offers after sending a substantial check to Lady Shawcross. An act, she was now persuaded, prompted by nothing more than the motive he had claimed: a desire—a *duty*—to see her ladyship properly settled. It was scarcely a wonder he'd instructed Cecily to "order sensibly" when she went to the mantua-maker. Hardly surprising that he and Uncle Frederick felt the situation had ultimately been resolved "far better" than they might have anticipated. By marrying his cousin himself, before she could conceive a *tendre* for another man, Stephen had at least been spared the necessity of furnishing a dowry.

"Why didn't he tell me?" she said bleakly.

"Stephen did not tell you because Frederick had sworn him to secrecy," Aunt Esther replied. "And Frederick did not know of your suspicions until this afternoon. Following your remark about 'partners in crime,' he questioned Stephen and learned of your belief that the two of them had stolen your inheritance. When Frederick subsequently advised me of the situation, I insisted he confess the truth at once. And now you have"—her pale eyes shifted to her husband—"you may go on, Frederick. I wish to speak with Cecily alone."

Sir Frederick drew a great sigh of relief, sprang off the bed, and hurried to the door. Cecily could not quell an impression that there was something else they should discuss, something of critical importance; but her brain was fairly whirling with the shock of his revelation, and she could not remember what it was. He stepped into the corridor and shut the door behind him, and Lady Osborne took his place on the bed.

"Dennis Drummond." Aunt Esther said the name so abruptly that Cecily's mouth fell open. "Frederick also informed me that only two days prior to your marriage, you alluded to the possibility of wedding Dennis Drummond. I assured him your remark stemmed from a cockleheaded fascination with an utterly unsuitable *parti*. I should now like *your* assurance that *my* assurance was valid."

"Of course it was!"

Cecily spoke with absolute sincerity; she had recognized long since that she had no real affection for Dennis. But Aunt Esther's words belatedly prompted her to wonder what had really transpired in Sheffield. Stephen's motives had been honorable—she was now convinced of that—but it was not beyond him to go to questionable lengths in order to avoid any hint of scandal. Stephen himself had admitted to an obsession with propriety; he might well have threatened Dennis, bribed Dennis, to give her up and keep his silence. And if he had not, if *Dennis* had lied, why had Dennis come to London?

"Then why is Drummond here?" Lady Osborne might have been reading her mind.

"He . . . he . . ." Would the fabrications never end? Cecily thought dismally. "As he stated, he had business to attend in town." Aunt Esther's eyes flickered with doubt. "And I daresay he's always eager to escape his parents." Cecily stumbled on. "As you well know, his father is a fearful tyrant, and his mother is a rumpot—"

"A rumpot? Peggy Drummond?" Lady Osborne vigorously shook her head. "If the woman possesses but one admirable quality—as, I am sorry to say, she does—it is her sobriety. Peggy Drummond's father died of drink, and she has never touched a drop of spirits in the whole of her life. And if Drummond told you otherwise, I can only surmise he was attempting to win your sympathy.''

As he had always tried to win her sympathy, Cecily suddenly perceived. Now she thought on it, she could recollect a dozen occasions when Dennis had glibly justified his ruthless business practices—blaming his father or the sad state of the local economy, even blaming fate. Blaming everyone and everything but himself. And if he had lied then, lied all those times, he had surely lied about what happened in Sheffield. *Then why had he come to London?*

"You must send Drummond away, Cecily.'' Despite the bluntness of her words, Aunt Esther's voice had turned gentle, and she reached out and took one of Cecily's hands in both of hers. "I am persuaded of your innocence, but you cannot expect Stephen to share my confidence. You and he have quarrelled most bitterly—or so I collect—and Drummond's presence can only serve as salt in an open wound. Send him away,'' she reiterated, "and then you can concentrate on salvaging your marriage.''

"If it is not too late,'' Cecily whispered.

"It is never too late,'' Lady Osborne said firmly. "I have learned that in the past four and twenty hours—that it is never too late to make amends. Not if two people truly love one another.''

But what if they did not? Cecily wanted to ask. What if the two people had been forced into wedlock against their wills? One impelled by honor, the other a victim of her own sapskulled foolishness—

There was a tap on the corridor door, and Aunt Esther released Cecily's hand and crossed the room to admit Eliza.

"You rang, ma'am?'' the abigail said.

"Yes.'' Cecily stood and noted with relief that her headache had eased a bit. "Yes, I wish to retire, Eliza.''

"An excellent idea.'' Lady Osborne nodded. "Get a good night's rest, dear, for tomorrow . . . Well, you know what you must do tomorrow.''

She stepped into the hall, and just as she closed the door, Cecily recalled the critical matter she had failed to discuss with Uncle Frederick. She had forgotten to inquire

whether he might inadvertently have launched the rumors
about Stephen and Mrs. Tidwell, and if she was, indeed,
to salvage her marriage, she must discover who had been
responsible. Must, at least, persuade Stephen that she had
not betrayed his confidence.

But she was too tired to summon Sir Frederick back
tonight, she decided, as Eliza began removing her dress.
So tired that she was literally swaying on her feet. She
would go to South Audley Street early in the morning . . .

Eliza turned down the bed, and Cecily crawled beneath
the bedclothes and fell asleep the instant her head touched
the pillow.

❧ 14 ❧

Cecily slowly opened her eyes and—when this endeavor
failed to bring the expected stab of pain—cautiously sat up
in bed. To her immense relief, her headache was gone,
and she sprang to her feet, rushed to the window, and
yanked the draperies apart. The weather would not prevent
a walk to Aunt Esther's this morning, she saw: the sky was
a cloudless blue, and the sun so bright that she was compelled to squint a bit against its brilliant light.

Cecily dropped the curtains and dashed to the wardrobe,
but even as she withdrew her russet walking costume, she
perceived the futility of hurry. If she arrived in South
Audley Street before Uncle Frederick was awake and insisted
that the terrible Mrs. Fawcett knock him up, their conversation was likely to prove most unsatisfactory indeed. Sir
Frederick hated nothing more than being driven prema-
turely from his bed, and even when he woke at his own
convenience, his thoughts were excessively muddled until
he had consumed his customary three cups of coffee.

No, it was pointless to go to Aunt Esther's much before

noon, and it wouldn't do to disturb Dennis at an early hour either. Their confrontation could only be unpleasant in the best of circumstances; it would be quite unbearable if Dennis was sleepy and peevish when it started.

Furthermore, Cecily realized, fastening her lutestring spencer, she was hungry. Not merely hungry, she amended: she was famished, ravenous, almost dizzy from the lack of food. So, she decided, she would have a leisurely, hearty breakfast, and while she ate, she would determine exactly what to do next. Whether to walk first to South Audley Street and confer with Uncle Frederick or—as Aunt Esther had put it—to send Dennis away.

The breakfast parlor was deserted when Cecily reached it, but there was a veritable feast laid upon the miniature sideboard, and she helped herself to generous portions of everything. An enormous serving of scrambled eggs, four rashers of bacon, a kidney, a bowl of porridge, two muffins, a cup of coffee. She bore this treasure to the table, her stomach audibly rumbling with anticipation, and, as there was no one to witness her disgraceful conduct, attacked her plate like a starving wolf. Within the space of five minutes, she calculated, she had devoured all the porridge and half the rest, and at that juncture, she heard a rustle behind her.

"Good morning, Lady Trowbridge."

Cecily instinctively stiffened at the sound of Lady Shawcross's voice, but she soon recollected that her ladyship no longer posed a threat. "Good morning, Lady Shawcross," she said cheerfully.

Cecily was pleased to observe that her ladyship scowled a bit as she strode across the room to the sideboard. She poured herself a cup of coffee, put a single muffin on her plate, and took the chair immediately across from Cecily's. Cecily was additionally delighted to note that her lavender morning dress was precisely the *wrong* shade of purple and did not become her ladyship at all.

"How I wish I could eat as you do!" Lady Shawcross gazed at Cecily's plate and heaved a great sigh. "But if I attempted to consume so much food, I fear I should grow dreadfully fat."

Her ladyship's tone made it apparent that she also feared—

nay, *hoped*—that Cecily's dietary practices would render her dreadfully fat as well.

"Well," Cecily said kindly, "I daresay that as I grow older, I shall experience a similar problem."

Lady Shawcross, having fastidiously torn her muffin in two, now dropped both halves on her plate, showering herself and the tablecloth with crumbs. "You were missed at the conclusion of the party last night." Her voice was gratifyingly shrill. "Everyone was remarking your mysterious disappearance."

But Cecily would not be baited, not today, not with victory so close at hand. "I'm sorry if my disappearance seemed mysterious." She paused and deliberately ate, deliberately savored, her third piece of bacon. "The fact is I was suffering a small headache, and I didn't wish to make an issue of it."

"I trust you're recovered this morning?" her ladyship snapped.

"Quite recovered, thank you."

Lady Shawcross scowled again, and Cecily finished her kidney.

"I do fancy the party was a success," her ladyship continued at last. "I can scarcely believe that mousy little Lucy has finally got herself a husband."

Cecily bit her lip and buttered her second muffin.

"I suppose her engagement is but one more example of the blindness of love," Lady Shawcross said. "I have repeatedly observed that a woman—however homely she may be—will eventually stumble upon a man as unattractive as she."

This was too much, and Cecily parted her lips to say so. Lucy, the new Lucy, was nothing short of breathtaking; and Lord Ashford, in his way, was as attractive as any man Cecily had ever encountered. But she recognized, just before she spoke, that Lady Shawcross wanted her to object, was goading her to object, and she sank her teeth into her muffin.

"Though I must own myself surprised that Lord Ashford and his family attached so little importance to the rumors about Stephen," her ladyship went on. "Well, as I indicated, love is blind, and Lady Crandon fortunately heard the wrong name. And Rotherham—old fool that he is—hasn't heard or understood anything these past ten years.''

''Umm,'' Cecily muttered around the final bite of her muffin. She patted her mouth with her napkin, laid the napkin on the tablecloth, maneuvered her chair back from the table, and started to rise.

''Indeed, I was surprised *you* were not more overset.'' Lady Shawcross spoke very quickly, evidently perceiving that her prey was at the point of slipping away. ''When Stephen told you of his contretemps with Mrs. Tidwell.''

''When Stephen told me, I had no idea the story would become a great *on-dit* . . .'' Cecily belatedly registered her ladyship's words, and she sank back in her chair. ''How did you know Stephen told me?'' she hissed.

''I . . . I . . .'' The violet eyes darted about, as if they were seeking an answer in the corners of the room. ''I didn't *know*, of course. I merely surmised—''

''No, it was no surmise.'' Cecily saw it all now, saw it so clearly that she wondered how she could possibly have suspected Lucy, suspected Uncle Frederick. ''You were on the listen when Stephen told me. You lurked at the door of Aunt Esther's parlor until . . .''

But she would not tarnish that magical moment by discussing it with Lady Shawcross.

''Until you were certain he was through,'' she concluded. ''Then you burst into the room and spirited him off, and the next night you began whispering the story round Almack's.''

''And dear Stephen collected that you'd betrayed him.'' Her ladyship, abandoning all pretext of innocence, sketched a chilly, triumphant smile.

''But why?'' Cecily was genuinely confused. ''Why should you wish to sow discord between us? Surely you know Stephen well enough to realize that he'd never seek to dissolve his marriage. His marriage to me or anyone else. Regardless of the provocation, he wouldn't put his wife aside.''

''Would not put his wife *legally* aside,'' Lady Shawcross corrected. ''But one need not necessarily have a husband in order to have a man. As long as you and Stephen are at odds, he will buy me a new gown from time to time and

see that I'm invited to the best assemblies and serve as my
escort when we attend them. And—who knows?—I might
eventually entice him into my bed as well."

Her ladyship's frankness set Cecily's cheeks to blazing,
and before she could turn away, Lady Shawcross emitted a
derisive snort.

"Don't affect to be horrified. Not when you have just
imported your own lover from the country."

Cecily's mouth fell open, and her ladyship sniffed again.

"Perhaps everyone else believed Mr. Drummond's explanation of his visit, but I am invariably inclined to
suspicion when a young man suddenly appears in a young
woman's home. I consequently took the opportunity to
speak with Drummond after the musicale, and I am sorry
to say that he was rather indiscreet."

How indiscreet? Cecily wondered fearfully, struggling
to keep her face blank.

"He referred to you by your Christian name—it was
'Cecily' this and 'Cecily' that—and it soon grew apparent
that the two of you had been *very good friends* prior to
your marriage. I cannot say much for your taste, by the
by, but I shall charitably assume there is a dreadful dearth
of men in Derbyshire."

At least Dennis hadn't mentioned their elopement, Cecily
thought, and she now strove to hide her relief. "You must
realize," she said, "that I shall tell Stephen you initiated
the rumors at Almack's—"

"And *you* must realize," Lady Shawcross interrupted
coolly, "that I shall deny this discussion ever took place.
It will be most interesting to see whom he believes, will it
not? I can't suppose he is overly confident of your hon-
esty. Not with Drummond skulking about."

Cecily detected a tap of footfalls in the dining room, and
as she spun her head around, Lady Shawcross leaped to
her feet.

"Mr. Drummond!" she said warmly. "Lady Trowbridge and I were just speaking of you. I was telling her
how very much I enjoyed our conversation last evening.
But if you will excuse me, I am sure the two of you would
prefer to chat alone."

Her ladyship hurried round the table, passing Dennis en

route, and the latter stalked to the sideboard. By Cecily's estimation, it was not yet half past ten, and she could not conceive what had inspired Dennis to rise so early.

"Damned sunlight," he growled, as though in answer to her unspoken query. He began filling his plate, irritably clattering the serving utensils against the bowls and platters. "It streams across my pillow the instant the sun rises; I've been awake above an hour."

Cecily elected not to point out that, in fact, the sun had risen many hours before. With a final clang, Dennis added a kidney to his plate, marched to the table, and took the place beside the one Lady Shawcross had occupied.

"I should like to be moved to a room at the other end of the house," he said through a mouthful of scrambled eggs. "One with a west window instead of an east."

Cecily hesitated, reminding herself that it wouldn't do to approach Dennis when he was grouchy. But he was always more or less grouchy, she soon recollected; he behaved politely or kindly only when he wished to create a favorable impression. There would never be a "good" time for their conversation, and he had provided her a perfect opening.

"I'm afraid that won't be possible, Dennis," she said. "Indeed, I fear it won't be possible for you to stay here any longer. I . . ."

She paused again. She had started to say that she now knew what had transpired in Sheffield, knew he had lied to her. But whatever his deficiencies, Dennis Drummond was not stupid. He would swiftly read between the lines; there was no need for a direct and hostile accusation.

"I have come to realize that your visit poses certain . . . certain problems," she continued, "and I must regretfully ask you to leave." Despite the circumstances, her words sounded dreadfully harsh, and she decided to cast a small bone to courtesy. "While you pack, I shall send one of my servants to engage a room in a suitable hotel—"

"No," Dennis interposed heavily, "no, I shan't remain in London. I shall go immediately back to Buxton."

Cecily hadn't dared to dream he would be so accommodating, and she repressed an absurd little prickle of guilt. "That would be best, of course," she murmured.

"Yes." Dennis swallowed a great bite of kidney and swabbed his mouth with his napkin. "Yes, I shall go back as soon as I have the money to pay my fare." He tossed his napkin on the table and leaned back in his chair. "That is *my* problem, Cecily: I find myself embarrassingly short of funds."

"You have spent . . ."

She gulped back the rest of her gratuitous question; of course he had spent the whole five hundred pounds. He was wearing still another magnificent new ensemble, and she had no doubt he had left half a dozen more behind, hanging in his wardrobe. And he had lately expressed a keen desire to own a high-sprung curricle like Sir Robert Norcott's, with two matched black horses to draw it. His father was too penurious to pay for such an equipage, Dennis had complained . . .

But there was no point in issuing an accusation on this head either; it was well worth the expenditure of a few pounds to be rid of him. "Very well," Cecily said levelly. "I shall pay your fare to Buxton. How much do you require?"

"Umm." Dennis delicately sipped his coffee. "I fancy a hundred pounds will suffice."

"A hundred pounds!" Cecily gasped. "A hundred pounds would see you across the sea and back several times over."

"I daresay it would," Dennis agreed. "Did I wish to go across the sea. But I wish only to return to Derbyshire and mend my broken heart as best I can." He drew a dramatic sigh. "Lord Trowbridge's compensation seemed adequate at the time—when we discussed the matter in Sheffield— but after I learned the two of you had wed . . ." He sighed again and spread his hands.

"I don't have a hundred pounds," Cecily said flatly.

"How very unfortunate." Dennis shook his sandy head. "Without the requisite funds, I shall naturally be compelled to remain in London. And as long as I am here, there is always the danger that I shall inadvertently mention our elopement."

"Please, Dennis. I would pay you if I could—"

"Indeed, I might chance to mention it at the opera

tonight." He flew relentlessly on. "Lady Shawcross found herself in possession of an extra ticket and generously offered it to me. Her late husband's sister was too ill to travel up from Hampshire for the Season. Or is it his cousin?" He furrowed his brow in thought. "No, I believe it is his second cousin—somehow related through his grandmother."

"I shall try to find the money," Cecily whispered.

"Try?" Dennis echoed coldly. "There will be no *trying* about it, Cecily. Your husband is a wealthy man; he'd readily wager a hundred pounds on the turn of a single card. You've only to fabricate a reasonable excuse—new gowns, new bonnets, new shoes—and ask him for the money."

A reasonable excuse? Cecily doubted Stephen would give her a few shillings for a box of chocolates, much less a hundred pounds for dresses and hats. But she wouldn't reveal her marital difficulties to Dennis, and she essayed a noncommittal nod.

"It will take some time, of course," she said. "Time to . . . to talk Stephen round."

"I shall give you till five o'clock." Dennis rose and brushed a few wayward crumbs from the lapels of his handsome amber frock coat. "As I have never visited London before, I should like to see a bit of the city before I leave. *If* I leave," he amended ominously. "If you have the money by five, I shall hire a chaise to take me back to Buxton, and if not, I shall dress for the opera. And in the latter case—as I have indicated—I might carelessly drop some hint of our elopement."

He executed a remarkably accomplished bow, strode around the table, and disappeared from Cecily's view. She was not persuaded he was really gone until she heard the distant opening and closing of the front door, and she remained frozen in her chair a full minute after that, waiting to be sure the door would not creak open again. When it did not, she sprang to her feet and raced through the dining room, up the stairs, and down the hall to her bedchamber.

Cecily kept her money in the reticule she had carried from Osborne Hall, and she now withdrew it from the top

drawer of the chest and dumped its contents on the counterpane. She had hoped to discover more than the three-
and-ten she remembered, but, in fact, there was somewhat
less: two pounds and sixteen shillings. She entertained a
brief suspicion that one of the servants had robbed her of
fourteen shillings, but she then recalled that during her
various shopping excursions, she had paid in cash for a
lace handkerchief and two new novels. Not that it
signified, she owned. She was so far from possessing a
hundred pounds that fourteen missing shillings mattered
not a whit.

Cecily collapsed on the bed, her head once more beginning to ache. She had perceived from the start that she
couldn't ask Stephen for the money, and her thoughts
turned to Uncle Frederick. But upon reflection, she doubted
he had a hundred pounds to spare. Doubted he had *any*
funds to spare; he had alluded just last night to the possibility of borrowing from Stephen. And even if he did
chance to have a few pounds at hand, he would demand to
know why she needed it. She would be compelled to tell
him of her elopement, and he . . .

The scene was too awful to contemplate, and Cecily
clenched her hands, distantly noting that her palms had
grown damp. She could not go to Stephen, could not go to
Sir Frederick, and there was no one else except Lucy.
Lucy! Cecily's relief was so enormous as to render her
literally dizzy. Lucy might well have a hundred pounds in
cash, and if she did not, she could readily procure the
money from one of her accounts. Or from Lord Ashford;
that would be simpler still. Yes, between them, Lucy and
the earl could surely produce a hundred pounds, and—best
yet—they would not ask Cecily to explain her request for a
loan. Nor would they press her for repayment. Sooner or
later, Stephen would trust her enough to provide some sort
of household allowance, and she could gradually reim-
burse Lucy and Lord Ashford.

Cecily jumped off the bed and rushed back along the
corridor to Lucy's bedchamber. The door was closed, and
when her frantic knocking failed to elicit any response, she
surmised that Lucy and the earl must be driving in the
park. Which did not necessarily pose a problem, she re-

flected optimistically. To the contrary, if she awaited their
return downstairs, she would be assured of speaking to
them together, before Lord Ashford had an opportunity to
leave. She whirled around and—as so often seemed to
happen—found herself face-to-face with Evans.

"Miss Lucy isn't here," the butler said helpfully. "She
has gone out with Lord Ashford."

"So . . . so I collected," Cecily stammered. She reminded herself that though he had a magnificent talent for
appearing at exactly the wrong moment, he could not
actually read minds, and she summoned up her brightest
smile. "Indeed, I had just decided to wait for them in the
library."

"Well, I fear you will have a long wait, ma'am. They
will not be back until six."

"Six!" Cecily sagged against the door.

"Yes, they drove down to Greenwich so Lord Ashford
could present Miss Lucy to some relatives of his. Two
maiden aunts, I believe she said. Or was it maiden cousins? Two elderly ladies, at any rate."

"And you are sure they will not return till six?" Cecily
said weakly.

"Oh, yes, Miss Lucy was very clear in that regard. She
mentioned that they'd be quite hard pressed to dress for the
opera in time, but this was the only day they could go to
Greenwich. His lordship's relatives are leaving tomorrow
for Margate or Ramsgate or some such place."

"I see," Cecily murmured. An idea—a terrible idea—
had begun to nudge the back of her mind. "And . . . and
Lord Trowbridge?" she asked casually.

"No, ma'am, Mr. Stephen did not go with them. He is
at his club."

"I see," Cecily said again. "And when will *he* be
back?"

"Well, he didn't state an exact time, but based on
previous experience, I should guess he'll return about
six as well. When he has no plans for an evening dinner,
he . . ."

The butler embarked upon a long, complicated explanation, but Cecily registered only the fact that Stephen was
likely to be at White's all day, playing at macao. He

would not return till six, Lucy would not return till six . . . At length, she excused herself—cutting Evans off in mid-word, she feared—and made her way unsteadily back down the hall and into her bedchamber.

Cecily sank once more on the bed and stared at the door connecting to Stephen's room, her terrible idea creeping from the back of her brain to the front. She had shockingly scant knowledge of her husband's personal habits, but she supposed that all men shared certain common traits. And one of Sir Frederick's traits was a propensity to leave money scattered carelessly about. During her willful adolescence, Cecily had frequently been tempted to "borrow" a few of the bills invitingly strewn on his washstand or nightstand, but she had always stopped short, visualizing the horrifying consequences if she were caught.

But she would not have been caught, Cecily now perceived, for Uncle Frederick would never have known the exact value of the bank notes piled here and there around his bedchamber. Would never have missed two or five or ten pounds. And Stephen—fond as he was of gaming—would not miss a *hundred* pounds. As Dennis had pointed out, Stephen would wager a hundred pounds on the turn of a single card . . .

Cecily did not remember standing or walking to the connecting door, opening the door or stepping through it. She simply, suddenly, found herself in Stephen's bedchamber, with no recollection of how she'd come to be there. It was a handsome room, she observed absently. A man's room: the wooden furniture all dark mahogany, the counterpane, draperies, and upholstery done in a bold buff-and-burgundy stripe. Her eyes darted about, and she found what she was looking for on top of his chest of drawers.

What she was looking for but not as much as she'd hoped, she saw, swiftly counting Stephen's money. He had left a hundred fifty-nine pounds and a few odd coins; she would have to take nearly two-thirds of it to satisfy Dennis. She recounted the bills—laying ninety-eight pounds aside to supplement her pathetic two—and carefully distributed the rest across the top of the chest.

Surely Stephen wouldn't notice, she thought, critically

inspecting her artistic effort. And even if he did, he would readily understand why she'd acted as she had. Indeed, he would probably commend her for having so expeditiously got rid of Dennis.

Cecily hurried back to her own bedchamber, added Stephen's notes to hers, and counted out the whole hundred pounds all over again. Now she had the money, her only regret was that she must wait until five o'clock to eject Dennis permanently from her life.

❦ 15 ❧

As the day progressed, Cecily grew increasingly impatient to conclude her distasteful business with Dennis, and at half past four, she decided to wait for him in his room. It was quite likely he would return early, she reasoned: he'd be eager to collect his bribe or—conversely—to threaten her with new and dire consequences if she could not deliver it. If he approached the house on foot, she might well fail to see him from her bedchamber window, and she did not wish to waste a single instant. Indeed, she was tempted to dispatch a servant to Oxford Street to hail a hackney coach for Dennis's departure, but she felt sure he would demand her last few shillings to pay the driver for his waiting time. And a few minutes wouldn't signify, she thought optimistically. Even if Dennis did not appear till five, he would be well away by six.

Cecily scooped her hundred pounds off the counterpane and ventured cautiously down the hall. Dennis's door was closed, and after a cursory tap, Cecily slipped into the room and perched on the bed. Dennis had managed to wreak remarkable havoc in just above four and twenty hours, she noted, gazing disapprovingly about. The garments he had worn yesterday and last night were draped on the bedstead, the armchair, and the cheval mirror, and there was an unsightly pile of soiled shirts and underthings on the Brussels carpet. It would take him some time to pack, she reflected with dismay, but if necessary, she would help him.

Cecily detected the distant clatter of a carriage, and she instinctively leaped up and started toward the window. But she shortly recollected that Dennis's room was situated at the rear of the house rather than the front, and she sank back on the bed. Evidently Dennis had engaged a hackney coach to bring him back to Brook Street, but there was no point in rushing downstairs and instructing him to keep it. Even with her assistance, his packing would surely take upwards of half an hour.

Cecily laid her clutch of bank notes on the bed—notes now limp and damp from handling—and counted them again. Since she had performed this exercise at least a dozen times already, she would have been astonished to discover that there was any more or any less than a hundred pounds, but she judged it best to be certain. She did not doubt for a moment that *Dennis* would count the money and fly quite into the boughs should there chance to be ninety-nine pounds rather than a hundred.

But it was all there, there to the last pound note, and Cecily retrieved the stack of bills and began nervously riffling through it. She was starting to wonder what could be delaying Dennis when she heard the click of the doorknob. She sprang once more to her feet, rushed to the door, and threw it open.

"Stephen!" she gasped.

No, it could not be Stephen, she assured herself. She must be having a particularly realistic and awful nightmare. Evans had promised that Stephen would not be back until six. Well, he had not exactly *promised* . . . "Stephen?" she repeated weakly.

"Can you truly be so idiotish as to imagine that I wouldn't perceive at once what you're at? Wouldn't look for you here before I looked anywhere else?"

He glanced over her shoulder, pursed his lips with disgust, transferred his eyes back to her. Eyes as harsh and yellow as the morning sunlight.

"Well, I daresay you could be." He sardonically answered his own question. "Inasmuch as you were cockle-headed enough to assume I should somehow overlook your theft of ninety-eight pounds."

"Theft!" Cecily shook her head in frantic protest. "You don't understand at all, Stephen. I thought—"

"I know quite well what you thought," he hissed. "You thought I'd never miss ninety-eight pounds. Thought I'd surmise I'd lost it gaming. Did it not occur to you that I wouldn't leave my gaming money behind when I went to White's? I had reserved a hundred fifty-nine pounds, four shillings, and sixpence to settle Evans's accounts with the butcher and the greengrocer and the wine merchant."

"But you don't understand," Cecily insisted. "I—"

"Oh, I understand," he interposed savagely. "What *you* must understand is that your and Drummond's little game has come to an abrupt end. You will not steal my money pound by pound and divide it between you." He reached forward, snatched the sheaf of bills from her hand, and stuffed it in his coat pocket. "And now, if you will excuse me, I've matters of importance to attend."

"Please, Stephen. Please listen to me . . ."

But he was gone. He had spun around and disappeared, and Cecily was staring at—talking to—the blank wall across the corridor from Dennis's door.

Well, so be it, she thought furiously. As usual, Stephen had drawn all the wrong conclusions, granted her no opportunity to explain; and she wouldn't go groveling to him again. Let him grovel for a change. When Dennis left, he would see that he had erred and sheepishly beg her forgiveness.

But Dennis wouldn't leave, Cecily suddenly realized. She gazed at her empty hand in belated, horrified comprehension. Without the money, the money Stephen had taken, Dennis would not leave. He would remain in London and execute his threat to reveal their elopement . . .

Cecily pounded down the hall, past Lucy's bedchamber, past her own, and stopped at Stephen's door. It was ajar, and before pausing to consider his reaction, she pushed it on open and stepped into the room. A trunk lay on his bed, its lid upraised, and Stephen was viciously jerking clothes from one of the drawers in his chest.

"What . . . what are you doing?" Cecily whispered.

He started and whirled toward the door. "I should think it would be rather obvious what I am doing," he snapped. "I am packing."

"But where . . ."

Cecily detected a movement from the corner of her eye, and as her voice trailed off, Evans loomed up beside her.

"You rang, sir?" the butler panted.

"Yes. Please desire Jordan to have the traveling carriage hitched and make himself ready for a journey. And then send Parker up to help me with my packing."

"Yes, sir."

Evans raced away, and Cecily moistened her lips.

"Where . . . where are you going?" She could not seem to speak in anything but staccato jerks.

"I am first going to pay a brief call on my man of business." Stephen dumped a great armload of clothing on the bed and turned to face her. "I am going to instruct Fletcher not to give you a single shilling of my money without my express permission. I trust I need not add that such permission will not be forthcoming. You can crawl to him—crawl to me—on your hands and knees, and you will not receive a groat."

"Please, Stephen, you don't understand—"

"I should very much like to put you in the street." His tone was conversational, almost casual, as though he were discussing the weather. "However, if I were to close the house"—he gestured vaguely round the walls of his bedchamber—"I should severely inconvenience Lucy and Priscilla. So you and Drummond will have a roof over your heads and food in your bellies at least until the end of the Season. After that, you will have to conduct your *affaire* elsewhere."

"Please listen to me, Stephen. There is no—"

"Nowhere else you can go?" he interjected harshly. "Well, do not tease yourself about it. I frankly doubt Drummond will stay even until the conclusion of the Season. Unless I badly miss my guess, he'll soon tire of having no cash in his purse and set out in search of greener pastures.''

He strode back to the chest and began emptying another drawer, and Cecily ground her fingernails into her palms. He was clearly not prepared to entertain her verbal arguments—much less believe them—and she desperately snatched at a different straw.

''And after you have visited your man of business?'' she asked. ''Where will you go then?''

''Then I shall go to Oaklands, my property in Hampshire.'' He stalked once more to the bed and deposited a second heap of garments beside the first.

''I should like to go with you,'' Cecily said levelly. Surely this, if nothing else, would persuade him that she didn't care a whit for Dennis.

''Go with me?'' Stephen laughed. ''And how long would it be before Drummond appeared on our doorstep?'' He affected a deep frown of calculation. ''Actually, since I intend to stop en route, I count it quite likely he would be waiting for us when we arrived. No, Cecily, you will not go with me.''

Cecily's anger had long since given way to shock, and her shock was now beginning to turn to panic. She would have to try to talk him round after all, and as she had fearfully little time in which to do so, she paused to sort out her thoughts. She must first tell him of Dennis's threat, she decided; that should soothe him sufficiently to listen to an account of Lady Shawcross's machinations. She cleared her throat, but even as she parted her lips to speak, Parker— the young footman who also served as Stephen's valet— rushed past her and skidded to a halt in the middle of the room.

''You wished my assistance, sir?''

''Yes, I want everything packed in my trunk. Since I'm in a bit of a hurry, I shall finish clearing out the chest while you see to the items in the wardrobe.''

Parker nodded, proceeded to the mahogany wardrobe, plucked out Stephen's moss-green frock coat, brought it to the bed, carefully folded it, carefully placed it in the trunk. Meanwhile, Stephen was busily removing the contents of the center drawer of his chest, and Cecily could not quell an unsettling notion that she had been rendered invisible. At length, she cleared her throat again, and Stephen glanced up, his puzzled expression indicating that, indeed, he had quite forgotten her presence.

"There are matters we have yet to discuss, Stephen." She looked pointedly at Parker, who was bustling back and forth between the wardrobe and the bed. "If you could spare me a moment more—"

"No, I fancy that won't be necessary," he interrupted pleasantly. "As I have indicated, my man of business will be authorized to act in my stead. Before I quit town, Fletcher will be *well* aware of my precise wishes."

He transferred his attention back to the chest, withdrew two last neckcloths from the drawer, and carried the fruits of his labor to the bed. He murmured an instruction to Parker—something about being certain to fold the pantaloons along the seams—and Cecily perceived that he truly did not intend to grant her a further private word.

She might have stayed nonetheless, stayed till the proverbial eleventh hour, had she not chanced to observe the curious gaze Parker cast her before he bounded back to the wardrobe. She'd been ready to swallow a good deal of pride in order to make her peace with Stephen, but she would not permit him to humiliate her in front of a servant not a day older than Cecily herself. So with a cool nod, which neither of them noticed, she backed into the corridor, stole to her own bedchamber, and stationed herself at the window.

Stephen's traveling carriage was already drawn up in front of the house, Jordan lounging on the box, and within a few minutes, Evans marched into view. The butler—evidently fearing his master might starve in the wilderness between London and Hampshire—was carrying a picnic hamper, which he shoved through the open door of the coach. He had just withdrawn his arms when Parker and Stephen staggered across the footpath, bearing the latter's trunk between them. Apparently, Cecily reflected grimly, Stephen was in such a hurry that he'd declined to ring for a second footman to carry his luggage.

With Evans's assistance, Stephen and Parker hoisted the trunk into the carriage as well, and Stephen clambered in behind it, raised the steps, and closed the door. The coach rolled away, but Cecily continued to peer down Brook Street, her eyes fastened to the spot where it had disappeared.

"Cecily?"

As was her habit, Lucy opened the door at the same moment she spoke, and Cecily's eyes flickered toward it. She had lost all track of time, but if it was six, she estimated she had been standing at the window for upwards of a quarter of an hour.

"You are here then." Lucy closed the door and crossed the room to Cecily's side. "I must have been mistaken. As Philip and I were driving along Oxford Street, I thought I saw Stephen's traveling carriage proceeding in the opposite direction. The coachman looked astonishingly like Jordan."

"It *was* Jordan," Cecily said dully. "It *was* Stephen's carriage. He has gone to Hampshire."

"Hampshire?" Lucy's brows knit with concern. "Is there a problem at Oaklands?"

Cecily was sorely tempted to seize upon this explanation, to spare herself the humiliating necessity of revealing the actual circumstances of Stephen's departure. But Lucy would inevitably puzzle out the truth—when days or weeks passed with no communication from Stephen—and Cecily had learned all too well the bitter consequences of deceit.

"No, there is no problem at Oaklands," she whispered. "The problem is here in London. I am the problem, Lucy. Stephen has left me."

"Left you?" Lucy gasped. "But that can't be. Stephen is mad for you."

"Mad for me." Cecily had intended to laugh, and she was utterly at a loss to comprehend why she burst into tears instead. "Oh, Lucy . . ."

She had not realized until that instant how dangerously near her defenses were to crumbling, and with the first tear, they simply washed away. She could not bear it any longer, could not keep it bottled inside a second more, and the words spilled forth like water over a broken dam. Spilled forth in bits and pieces punctuated by great gulping sobs, but at length, she choked out the whole story—from

the moment Stephen had discovered her elopement and
been compelled to offer for her himself till the moment he
had climbed into his traveling carriage and left for
Hampshire.

"And now," she concluded, with a final undignified
sniff, "I shall never see him again."

"Don't be idiotish," Lucy said crisply. "The solution is
very simple, Cecily: you must go after him."

"Go after him?" Cecily echoed incredulously.

"You won't have to travel all the way to Oaklands."
Lucy had obviously misinterpreted the nature of her objection. "Stephen told you himself that he plans to stop en
route, and as he doesn't care to travel at night, I should
guess he'll stop two or three hours along the road. On the
route he normally takes, that can only put him at Leatherhead, and in Leatherhead, he always patronizes the Green
Boar inn. Yes, I can almost promise you will find him at
the Green Boar, and that is only twenty miles away."

"But what of Dennis?" Cecily protested. "If I leave, he
will surely mention our elopement at the opera."

"The way Aunt Priscilla mentioned Stephen's encounter
with Mrs. Tidwell?" Lucy emitted a disdainful snort.
"You observed what happened to that *on-dit*, and I assure
you Dennis's will suffer the same fate. It will be a great
sensation for one night, producing all manner of outlandish
rumors; and within four and twenty hours, everyone will
decide the rumors are *so* outlandish they cannot conceivably be true."

"But . . . but . . . ." It sounded too easy; Lucy had too
quickly offered hope in place of Cecily's abysmal despair.

"Perhaps I failed to divine your emotions correctly."
Lucy's tone had turned a trifle cool. "You do love Stephen, do you not?"

Cecily started to say that she had already explained the
circumstances of their marriage, but before she could for-
mulate the words, the truth hit her with such stunning
force that she sagged against the windowsill. Of course she
loved him. The coals of her girlhood *tendre* had flamed
into a woman's passion, and she'd been too skitter-brained
to see it. She loved him, and she would chase him to

Leatherhead, chase him to Hampshire, chase him round the world if she had to.

"A very wise friend of mine once said that you must listen to your own heart." Lucy flashed her dimpled smile, but it was noticeably unsteady at the edges. "And follow where it leads you."

"And your friend's very wise friend repeated that advice at just the right time."

Cecily's throat was a bit clogged, but she was so galvanized by joy, by energy, that she couldn't remain weepy for long. She drew herself up and dashed across the room, issuing instructions over her shoulder.

"If you will order out the barouche, Lucy, I shall pack a few things. Desire the grooms to hurry; I shall be ready when the carriage is. *Before* the carriage is," she corrected happily, tugging her trunk from beneath the bed.

"Yes, I shall do so at once . . ." Lucy's voice expired in a little moan. "But you can't take the barouche. I hadn't considered that. With Jordan gone, there is no one to drive it."

"Then I shall go to Leatherhead on horseback." In which case, the trunk would not be needed, and Cecily spun away from the bed. "Instruct one of the grooms to ready a saddle horse while I change my clothes."

"But you can't go on horseback either," Lucy wailed.

"Indeed I can," Cecily said indignantly. "I learned to ride not much after I learned to walk."

"I daresay you did, but you can't ride twenty miles alone. Not on deserted country roads, the last part of it in the dark."

"Umm." Cecily could not but own that Lucy had a valid point, and she nodded. "Then have *two* mounts saddled," she said. "Neither with a sidesaddle. And appoint the most accomplished horseman among the grooms to accompany me."

Lucy bobbed her own head—albeit with considerable reluctance—and as soon as the door had clicked shut behind her, Cecily raced to the wardrobe and withdrew her . . . her . . . Stephen had called her riding costume a "thing," she remembered, and virtually commanded her to leave it in Sheffield. Perhaps she would solicit his opinion again at the end of the night.

But many hours remained till the end of the night, she reminded herself, and many miles lay between Brook Street and Leatherhead. She removed her walking dress—her fingers trembling with nervousness and haste—tugged on her riding costume, and rushed into the hall, where she literally collided with Dennis.

"Cecily!" he said peevishly. "Where the devil have you been?"

She could not determine whether he'd been lurking in the corridor for some time or had just that moment marched from his bedchamber to hers. Whatever the case, he plucked a gold watch—another new acquisition, Cecily believed—from his waistcoat pocket and studied its face with a dark frown.

"I trust you are aware," he snapped, "that the time we agreed upon has long since come and gone. It is nearly a quarter to seven."

He thrust the watch in her face, so close to her eyes that she couldn't possibly read the hands, then jammed it back in his pocket.

"Fifteen minutes before seven," he reiterated, "and you were to have the money at five. I am a patient man, Cecily, but my patience is exhausted."

"How very unfortunate." Cecily deliberately chose the phrase he had used that morning. "I fear your patience will be sorely tried indeed when I tell you that I still don't have the money."

"When will you have it then?" he demanded.

"I shall never have it," she hissed. "I won't give you a hundred pounds today, tomorrow, next week, or fifty years hence. And lest you decide your patience isn't exhausted after all, permit me to add that you are to be out of my house within the hour. I mean precisely what I say, Dennis: I shall grant you one hour to pack your things and be gone."

"But I am due at the opera in an hour! And I warned you what would happen if I went."

"Then I shall desire a servant to pack for you," Cecily said soothingly. "Go on to the opera and spread whatever *on-dits* you wish. When you return, your luggage will be on the footpath. Well," she amended, "it will be on the footpath if no one has stolen it. I'm sure you understand that I can't spare even a footboy to guard your valise for three or four hours."

"But . . . but . . ." Dennis's face had turned a most alarming shade of scarlet, and he tugged at his neckcloth till it gave way with an audible rip. "I wasn't lying to you, Cecily," he croaked on at last, his complexion returning to its normal pasty color. "About my lack of funds, I mean. I haven't enough cash to pay my fare back to Buxton."

"Then I fancy you will have to walk," she said. "The mode of your transportation doesn't signify to me; not as long as you're gone in an hour."

"Walk!" His voice was shrill, as high and grating as that of an hysterical woman.

"What the *deuce* is amiss?"

Cecily had forgotten that Lady Shawcross's bedchamber lay directly across the hall from her own. Her ladyship had yanked her door open and was peering irritably into the corridor.

"Ah, it is you, Mr. Drummond," she said forgivingly. "You're dressed for the opera and impatient to leave, no doubt . . ." Her violet eyes traveled from his face to his neckcloth, which was neatly torn in half, and her smile wavered a bit. "Well, not *quite* dressed. But by the time you're ready, I shall be ready to go as well."

"What an excellent suggestion!" Cecily said. "Why did I not think of it before? You see, Dennis, fate really does intervene when we least expect it. Lady Shawcross is leaving tonight as well, and the two of you can surely combine your funds and agree upon a mutually convenient destination."

What destination this might be she would have been hard pressed to say, for Hampshire and Derbyshire were situated in opposite directions out of London. But as she had calculated, her ladyship was far too surprised to question the details of Cecily's statement.

"Leaving?" she repeated instead. "Whatever gave you the notion I was leaving?"

"There's no notion about it," Cecily said. "I am *ordering*

you to leave. I gave Dennis an hour to be out of the house, but as you'll be traveling with him, I shall grant the both of you till eight. Please be sure you're gone by then. I should hate the situation to become . . . unpleasant.''

"*Ordering me to leave*!" Lady Shawcross screeched. "We shall see what Stephen has to say about that."

She flounced into the hall, and Cecily regretfully shook her head.

"Stephen is not here, Lady Shawcross. We have decided to spend the night elsewhere—a delayed honeymoon, shall we call it? I expect we'll be back tomorrow morning. Should you still be here when we arrive, I shall be forced to summon a constable and have you arrested for trespass."

Cecily had no idea whether such an action was possible, but her ladyship clearly believed it was: she staggered to a halt, and her delicate little mouth dropped open with shock. Cecily nodded at her, nodded at Dennis, and, without another word, hurried on along the corridor and down the staircase. As she proceeded across the vestibule, she could hear their voices two floors above, raised in furious argument as to how they were to finance their journey and precisely where they would go.

Lucy was standing on the footpath, nervously clutching the reins of one of the saddled horses waiting in the street. A groom was holding the other horse, and when Cecily reached the footpath, Lucy introduced him as Coker. He had an open, freckled face and was, Cecily judged, not a bit above sixteen.

"Like I told Miss Chandler, your ladyship, I've been ridin' all me life." Coker spoke as if he had read Cecily's thoughts. "And since I've been to the Green Boar with his lordship several times, I know the way."

"Excellent," Cecily said. "Let us be off then."

"This here is his lordship's own horse." Coker indicated the great black stallion he was holding. "Sultan. A right feisty bas—Uh, pardon me, your ladyship. But this one here"—he patted the rump of the other horse—"is a nice, calm little gelding. Nothing to be afraid of."

"Fine," Cecily snapped. "I'll ride Sultan, and you ride the nice little gelding and try to keep up with me."

She mounted the black stallion, and as a much-subdued Coker adjusted the stirrups to her short legs, Lucy gazed up at her.

"I . . . I say," Lucy stammered. "Your . . . ah . . . riding habit is most unusual."

"Is it not?" Cecily agreed cheerfully. "But it will get me to Leatherhead and back."

Coker completed his adjustment, then lengthened the gelding's stirrups and swung himself into the saddle. He glanced at Cecily, and when she bobbed her head, they simultaneously clucked their mounts to a start.

"Good-bye, Cecily," Lucy called, waving from the footpath. "And . . . and good luck."

Cecily's throat tightened again, but this was no time for tears. She smiled at Lucy, bent low over the stallion's neck, slammed her heels into his ribs, and they tore down Brook Street and careened around the corner into Park Lane.

Cecily did not believe she had felt so happy, so wonderfully free, ever before in her life. At first, she attributed her joy to the mere fact that she was riding again—riding a horse far larger, much stronger, and infinitely bolder than Moonbeam. She had no doubt that if she asked him, Sultan would leap over the line of carriages ahead of them one by one or die in the attempt.

But as she and Sultan, Coker and the gelding raced out of London and through the quiet suburban towns on its fringes, Cecily realized that her euphoria far transcended that of a devoted equestrienne privileged to ride a particularly splendid horse. She had left no problems behind her; she was confident that Dennis and Lady Shawcross would be gone when she returned to London. But what of the difficulties ahead? She had persuaded herself that—because she loved Stephen—she could wave a magic wand over their marriage and put everything aright. Persuaded or deluded? she now wondered. Perhaps Stephen's bitterness ran too deep to permit of any healing.

So she was only assured of these few golden hours between London and Leatherhead. A few hours suspended in time and space, on the back of a magnificent black horse, a warm summer wind rushing through her hair. She consequently did not object when Coker wheezed that the gelding could not, in fact, keep up, and they must slow their pace. No, far from objecting, she was prepared to trot through the twilight forever.

"Forever" ended shortly after twilight itself: it had been dark approximately half an hour when they reached Leatherhead and began clopping through its silent streets. As Coker had promised, he knew his way to the Green Boar, and as Lucy had promised, Stephen was there—his carriage clearly visible at the front of the innyard. Cecily and Coker drew rein at the entrance, and she clambered stiffly down from the saddle. She had never before ridden so far at one time, and she massaged her aching arms and legs.

"Shall I come in with you, ma'am?" Coker asked. "Miss Chandler said as how I was to watch after you."

"No, that won't be necessary," Cecily murmured. "See to the horses and then get a room for yourself. I shall advise you of our plans when I know them."

"Yes, your ladyship."

He nimbly dismounted the gelding, led both horses toward the stable; and Cecily slipped through the door of the inn and tentatively approached the desk. It occurred to her that Stephen must have encountered just such a situation at the White Lion in Sheffield, and she wished she knew exactly what he had said. How did one demand to be told the room in which So-and-So was staying?

"Yes?"

The man behind the desk peered lazily up from his newspaper, but he did not lower the paper an inch, and he remained comfortably sprawled in his chair, his long, plump legs crossed at the ankles. Cecily perceived at once that she was speaking with the landlord himself: none of his employees would dare to greet a prospective guest with such discourtesy.

"I am Lady Trowbridge," she said briskly. "My husband advised you I'd be joining him." She extended her hand as if in expectation of a key.

"Lady Trowbridge." The innkeeper studied her riding costume and wearily shook his head. "I have never understood how you . . . ah . . . *ladies* invariably manage to ferret out the identities of the gentlemen kind enough to honor me with their patronage. Nor why you persist in inventing the most absurd excuses in hopes of gaining access to their bedchambers. Particularly inasmuch as I have emphasized time and time again that my establishment is a respectable one."

"You think . . . you think . . ." But it was abundantly apparent what he thought, and Cecily's cheeks blazed with mortification.

"This time you have quite wasted your efforts." The innkeeper sounded almost kind. "Lord Trowbridge was exhausted when he arrived, and he declined even to have dinner before he retired. I assure you he will not require your services tonight."

"And I assure *you* that I am Lady Trowbridge," Cecily said, glimpsing a ray of hope in his words. "But let us not quibble any further; we can readily waken Stephen and insist he identify me. If you are right, he'll be immensely grateful for your vigilance. If you are wrong . . ." She allowed her voice to trail ominously off.

"Now I think on it, I do seem to recall that Viscount Trowbridge mentioned his wife would be coming." The landlord dropped his paper on the floor, leaped from his chair with astonishing alacrity, and plucked a key from the board behind the desk. "Number one-oh-two, ma'am, at the head of the stairs on the first floor."

As he had indicated, the room was just at the top of the staircase, and it took Cecily fearfully little time to reach it. She inserted the key in the lock, and the door surrendered so quickly that she almost tumbled across the threshold. Almost; not quite. At the last instant, she recovered herself, crept inside, softly closed the door behind her, and gazed at the bed.

Stephen was, indeed, asleep: lying on his back, the bedclothes drawn up to his waist, his arms folded loosely across his bare chest. Cecily belatedly wished she'd brought a nightdress with her; she could have packed some sort of saddlebag. But she had not, and—after stepping out of her shoes—she unfastened her riding costume, stepped out of it as well, and kicked it across the floor.

And then, clad only in her corset and drawers, she stole on across the room and climbed into the bed.

❧ 16 ❧

Cecily propped herself on one elbow and stared at her sleeping husband. The bright day had become a bright night, and in the moonlight streaming through the window, she could clearly see his features and his chestnut hair, hair now tousled and tumbling round his face. Well, she couldn't see him altogether clearly, she amended: she couldn't make out the tiny lines at the corners of his eyes or the threads of silver in his hair. With these small signs of his age invisible, he looked precisely like the young man she had met so many years before, and she experienced such a rush of love that she could scarcely breathe. She thought she would be quite content to remain here through eternity, lying at his side and merely watching him.

Stephen sighed and flung one arm across the bed, as if to warn her that time could not be made to stand still; and with a shaky sigh of her own, Cecily lowered her head and laid her mouth on his. His lips parted, ardently returned her kiss, but just as his arms began to steal around her ribs, he started and jerked his head away.

"Cecily?" he croaked. "Is it you?"

"Who else could it be?" she whispered. "A man as proper as you would never permit any woman but his own wife in his bed. Though I do remember once promising not to attack you in the middle of the night."

He struggled to a sitting position, forcing Cecily to sit up as well, and shoved a pillow between his back and the headboard. "What time is it?" he asked.

Though this was not exactly a romantic overture, neither was it a hostile one, Cecily reflected optimistically. "I'm not certain," she said. "About ten, I should guess."

"Ten." He shook his head. "Drummond abandoned you even sooner than I expected. I had supposed your liaison would at least survive the night."

Cecily's optimism abruptly evaporated, but there was nothing for it but to forge ahead. Not unless she was prepared to give him up, and that she would never do.

"Dennis did not *abandon* me," she said. "I ordered him out of the house."

Stephen's eyes narrowed, glittered with suspicion, but at length, he granted her a slight nod. "Go on," he said tersely.

Go on? she thought wildly. She had created such a dreadful bumblebath that she hardly knew where to begin.

"I . . . I know what really happened in Sheffield," she stammered at last. Surely that was the logical place to start. "Uncle Frederick confessed last night that he'd lost my inheritance, and I realized then that you hadn't wed me for my money. But you must see, Stephen—you *must*— why I drew the conclusion I did."

"Umm," he growled.

"After that"—she was gaining a bit of confidence—"I was sure Dennis had demanded a bribe to give me up and hold his tongue about our elopement. Just as you'd said he did. So this morning I asked him to leave."

"This morning?" Stephen repeated sharply.

"That is what the hundred pounds was for: Dennis demanded *another* bribe to go. If I didn't give it to him, he threatened to stay in London and reveal the story of our elopement. I had only two pounds of my own, and I couldn't get the rest from anyone. Not from anyone but you, and that is why I . . . I stole your ninety-eight pounds."

"Did it never occur to you to come to me?" Stephen said. "To tell me what Drummond was at?"

"No, it never did," she admitted. "You didn't trust me, Stephen. I can't say I blame you for that, but the fact is you wouldn't have given me ninety-eight pounds to pay Dennis."

"Of course I wouldn't have given it to you!" he roared. "I would have thrown Drummond bodily into the street and taken keen delight in doing so."

"But what of my elopement?" she protested. "I was trying to protect you from the consequences of scandal—"

"I've learned a good deal about scandal over the past few days, Cecily." He flashed a crooked grin; she could see the gleam of his teeth in the moonlight. "I teased myself about Mrs. Tidwell for nearly ten years. And within four and twenty hours after the rumors of our encounter emerged, Lady Crandon was assuring me they couldn't possibly be true. No, I'll not be a slave to propriety again." He paused a moment. "Which is not to say," he added severely, "that I forgive you for having initiated the original *on-dit*."

"But I didn't!" Cecily said. "That is the other thing I wished to tell you. It was Lady Shawcross who started the rumors at Almack's."

She related the tale—her words spilling all over one another in her eagerness to resolve this last problem—and Stephen sat silent and motionless in the moonlight.

"I ordered her to leave as well," she concluded at last. "I hope you don't mind. I told her and Dennis both to be gone by eight o'clock and advised them that if they were still at the house tomorrow morning, I should summon a constable and have them arrested for trespass."

"Arrested for trespass?" Stephen laughed—a great explosion of genuine mirth. "That would be a prodigious difficult case to prove, Cecily, but I cannot but commend your ingenuity."

He lapsed into silence again, but now he was watching her, regarding her with the same disconcerting interest he had displayed that first night at Osborne Hall. They had surmounted every obstacle but one, she thought, and it was the highest and broadest of all.

"I love you, Stephen," she said levelly. "I've loved you since I was a child, loved you almost half my life. So if you care for me at all—"

"Care for you?" He reached forward and pulled her into his arms. "Dear God, Cecily . . ."

His mouth found hers, unleashing that terrible, wonderful ache; and as she melted against him, he lowered her to the bed and stretched out beside her. He tore the bedclothes impatiently away, and Cecily instinctively stiffened

when she realized that—divested of the covering sheet and
blanket—he was wearing nothing.

"Don't be frightened," he whispered. "I shan't hurt
you, sweetheart; I'd never hurt you."

He kissed her mouth again and then her neck and then
her shoulders, his hands gently stroking her body all the
while, until no trace of fear remained, and there was only
pleasure. At length, he removed her clothes, his fingers so
tender, so careful, that it was like another caress. He
pulled her against him, and she gasped at this new
sensation—at the feel of his bare skin meeting hers, the
whole lengths of their bodies touching. His hands and lips
began to move again, creating sensations she had never
imagined, and she writhed beneath him, her own fingers
twisted in his hair.

"Please," she begged at last. "Please."

She did not know what she was asking till he took her,
and then she understood it all. She gave herself totally up
to his possession, followed him farther and farther into
ecstasy, until they tumbled off the edge of the world, and
she lay shuddering in his arms.

He held her for a time, her head resting on his shoulder,
his breath stirring the hair at her temple. Then he rolled
himself up on his side, ran one finger lightly down her
nose, and grinned down at her.

"Was that so terrible?" he whispered.

"Umm," she murmured languidly. She suddenly registered his expression. "You're smiling!" she said in
wonderment.

"Why should I not be smiling?" His grin broadened.
"I'm in love with the handsomest woman in England, and
I have *finally* lured her into my bed."

"Love?" Cecily repeated, scarcely daring to believe her
ears. "You . . . you love me?"

"Ahem." He coughed, and though it was impossible to
be sure, Cecily thought he colored a bit. "As you've been
honest with me, I fancy I should be honest with you. I am
consequently obliged to own that I wed you under somewhat . . . er . . . false pretenses."

"False pretenses!" she said indignantly.

"You may recollect my telling you that Lucy's opinion

contained a degree of truth. In point of fact, Lucy was *entirely* right: when I saw you again at Osborne Hall, I fell over head and ears in love. No, perhaps that isn't quite accurate. I'd always loved you, loved the girl you used to be; and, in retrospect, I think I must have entertained half a notion of waiting for you. Waiting till you grew up. At any rate, when I encountered you that evening, I found all the charm of the girl I remembered wrapped in an excessively enticing new package.''

His eyes swept over her, and Cecily's cheeks blazed. "Stephen!" she chided. But she could not repress a giggle.

"So I immediately began casting about for ways to keep you to myself,'' he continued. "Though it pains me to confess it, I even pondered the possibility of reneging on my promise to finance your come-out and furnish you a dowry. I calculated that as soon as you'd made your debut, every eligible young dandy in London would start to court you, and you would, indeed, be engaged before the Season was half over.''

"Then my elopement was—"

"Your elopement was a *godsend*,'' he interposed, his teeth gleaming in another grin. "It provided me the perfect excuse to insist you marry me at once.''

"You're a very devious man, Stephen,'' Cecily said sternly. But she was smiling back at him; she couldn't seem to stop smiling.

"I feared Aunt Esther had surmised the truth as well.'' He went blithely on, quite ignoring her accusation. "When you returned from your first visit to her house and told me she'd supplied an explanation of our marriage. However, you shortly revealed that she thought I'd wed you for your money.''

No, that wasn't what Aunt Esther had thought, Cecily reflected, recalling their conversation. Aunt Esther had surmised the truth after all, had guessed that Stephen was reluctant to expose her to the eager young bucks in town. But there was nothing to be gained by correcting him. Not now, when every obstacle lay behind them and only happiness ahead.

"Umm,'' she murmured again. "Be that as it may, I don't wish to talk about the matter any longer.''

"My dear love." He clicked his tongue against his teeth. "Much as I hate to disappoint you, I must advise you that I shall require an interval of rest before I can engage in another such strenuous performance."

"Stephen!"

She tried very hard to sound horrified, but a great chuckle welled up from her throat, a laugh of pure joy. He lay back down on the bed and pulled the covers over them, and she buried her face once more in his shoulder.

"How did you get here, by the by?" he asked sleepily. "Did one of the grooms drive you in the barouche?"

Cecily distantly wondered why she and Lucy had failed to consider this alternative. "No," she mumbled, her lips brushing his skin. "No, I rode Sultan."

"Umm." He drew a deep, contented breath, then jerked back up to look at her. "You *rode*?" he echoed. "There is not a sidesaddle at Brook Street."

"No? Well, I wouldn't know. I requested not to have a sidesaddle."

"Am I to collect that you wore that . . . that *thing*?" He sat all the way up and peered around the room, as if he expected to find her riding costume dancing mockingly about. "That hideous garment I *specifically* instructed you to leave in Sheffield?"

"Oh, hush, Stephen. You should be glad I didn't leave it. It served its purpose, did it not?"

"Perhaps so," he agreed grudgingly, reclining once more on the bed. "But you must not misinterpret my remarks about propriety, Cecily. However liberal I may have become, I won't have you parading about in such disgraceful attire. You're to leave your riding costume here, and this time I shall brook no objection."

"Very well." She sighed and threw one arm across his chest. "If you feel that strongly about it, I shall return to London in my underwear."

"Excellent." He drew her close again, thrust her abruptly away. "Your underwear!" he repeated.

"I brought nothing else," she said apologetically. "Nothing but my riding dress."

"Then you will have to wear it back to town," he conceded. "Upon our arrival, I shall destroy it."

"No, you will not destroy it, Stephen. I'll need my riding costume again."

"Need it?" he barked. "Need it for what?"

"I'll need it when I bring Moonbeam to Oaklands; I believe she and Sultan might become very good friends. And I shall certainly need it the next time you attempt to escape me and I have to chase you down again."

"You have a valid point." His arms once more tightened round her. "Since you seem determined to defy me, I judge it quite likely that I might try to engineer another escape as soon as tomorrow morning."

"It will do you no good," she said. "If you're not here when I wake, I'll set out after you and track you to the ends of the earth."

He laughed, then crushed her against his ribs. "I'd never leave you, Cecily," he whispered fiercely. "You do know that, don't you? Know I was only jesting? We'll discuss your riding costume tomorrow."

Tomorrow, Cecily thought. Tomorrow and tomorrow and tomorrow; ten thousand shining tomorrows lay ahead of them. She touched Stephen's face, nestled into the strong, warm arms around her, and smiled at the moonlight.

The sensuous adventure that began with

SKYE O'MALLEY

continues in . . .

**He is Skye O'Malley's younger brother, the handsomest
rogue in Queen Elizabeth's court . . . She is a beautiful
stranger . . .** When Conn O'Malley's roving eye
beholds Aidan St. Michael, they plunge into an erotic
adventure of unquenchable desire and exquisite passion that binds them body and soul in a true union of
the heart. But when a cruel betrayal makes Conn a
prisoner in the Tower, and his cherished Aidan a harem
slave to a rapacious sultan, Aidan must use all her skill
in ecstasy's dark arts to free herself—and to be reunited
forever with the only man she can ever love. . . .

**A breathtaking, hot-blooded saga
of tantalizing passion and ravishing desire**

Coming in July from Signet!